Uxori delectissimae

I, autodidact: Aye! Aye!
M S F Johnston

Published by Ceramicon 2022
Malvern, Worcestershire,
United Kingdom.

Printed and bound by
Aspect Design
89 Newtown Road, Malvern,
Worcs. WR14 1PD
United Kingdom
Tel: 01684 561567
E-mail: allan@aspect-design.net
Website: www.aspect-design.net

Cover Design Copyright © 2022 Ceramicon

ISBN 978-1-7397221-0-4

I, autodidact:
Aye! Aye!

Voice off: 'Do not think the past another country; return, yours cannot be their story when the living are blind and the dead still see.'

Curtain up

Prologue

We are on Mount Parnassus, home to the nine muses
of poetry, (epic, lyric, sacred and love), history,
comedy, tragedy, dance and astronomy.

The summit of the mountain towers a mile and a half above the
Gulf of Corinth and up there, these timeless entities sometimes
adopt human form and this they have done. Fetching, lissom,
ineffably becoming and draped diaphanously, that form is forever
female.

Taking time-out from Terpsichore's regular beach volleyball
session (she, muse of dance, believes this the best way to keep
everyone limber), the muses are gazing at hand-held clay tablets.
All that is except Urania, the muse of astronomy, who is scanning
the heavens. Polyhymnia, sacred poetry's muse, breaks the silence.

Polyhymnia: 'You know…, and I've just got to say this, I'm
actually bored… jus sayin.'

Calliope, muse of epic poetry, answers without lifting her eyes:
'I know what you mean. I like the volleyball and posing like
this but…, me too, if you know what I mean?'

Polyhymnia: 'It wasn't always so dull. We all used to hold hands
and dance in a circle – there was something for everyone….'

Calliope – still gazing: 'Yeah, back in the day we used to do it
all together, back when the mortals could talk to animals. We
were a team….'

Polyhymnia: 'That's right, we're all broken up now. Clio's got history coming out of her ears, Erato's love poetry is everywhere, they can't avoid Euterpe's music every time they go shopping, Thalia's comedy is never off, Melpomene's tragedy is streaming all the time and they do the Terpsichore dance every Saturday night. Our stuff not so much anymore.'

Calliope: 'What about you Urania? Do you feel left out too? They used to watch the sky every night. It's all they did if they weren't singing, dancing or eating.'

Urania does not respond. Chirpy Thalia, the comedienne, chips in.

Thalia: 'Do you want to play volleyball some more then?'

Melpomene, the tragedienne: 'It's not about the volleyball Thalia! They want something to do, a project, with us all together like in the old days…, if I read you right Calliope?'

Calliope: 'Yeah, I'd like it to be like in the old days. You, Clio (historienne) and Thalia had a lot of fun with that thing you did the other day.' Calliope is referring to the prequel.

Euterpe, musicienne: 'I was in on it too.'

Terpsichore, danceuse: 'And I was!'

Calliope: 'See what I mean? Can't we do something all together, like we used to do, before we got pigeon-holed?'

Urania steps down from her viewing platform. This happens very rarely. The rest put aside their tablets and give her their full attention.

Urania: 'Muses! I have just the idea! Let me fill you in. There's something for everyone!'

1

Finished, Damian Email turned to the last pages of 'Girl in the Gaslight', looking for any appendices, but this wasn't that type of book and, after going back to the start to read the acknowledgements, which ran to three pages – that's how many people it takes to make a book these days he thought, about 70, he set it down on the cast-iron garden table next to him.

Everybody had got their just desserts in the end, except the dead one, and the two-burst read had been satisfyingly transgressive as Clare didn't approve of him getting his mitts, as she called them, on her new books before she'd had the chance herself. Her addiction to psychological crime thrillers was endearing but she always had a lot on the go, and rarely the time to read them – she was more of a doer. He was crafty, and careful not to leave any clues such as turned-down pages, drink stains, dirty finger marks, anything which might denounce his secret vice, despite having permissive access to the plentiful family library which offered enough to satisfy any urge, excepting that for the illicit.

His book-binge had to stop some time and it was always a pleasure to become aware, in the late afternoon, at this time of year, of how the day was faltering and would soon crumple into deepening gloom. Then would come the inevitable; darkness. Time quickened at dusk. Day yearned to be overwhelmed by night. The here-and-now was slipping away with each heartbeat, always a little bit darker, a little bit darker.

The trancelike stillness mesmerised. Natural laws of the universe were conspiring with the material world to cause a dewy loss of warmth in the air which glued him bookless to his seat as the evening came on. How long could he stay where he was, imagining the cosmic forces holding it all together, feeling the transience? Time's schedule was relentless. At a given moment in the countdown his huddled form sat outside in the blackness would look officially weird when viewed from the kitchen window, but that time wasn't yet, although it had to be soon.

Damian and Clare had shared their first six months together in gaiety and joy with frequent late-slumberings and trips out to castles, cathedrals and museums, sometimes as far as London. And they'd tried new things: she'd introduced him to walled gardens and he'd shown her his favourite glaciated landscapes one memorable weekend in the Lake District. Looking through the guidebooks they'd bought on their excursions was one of their private 'things', and Damian smiled at the scudding recollections as they passed by – yes, that was their special time, mid-morning, just before a restorative brunch, looking through the guidebooks together. She didn't seem to notice his particularities and he admired hers, especially her expertise in varied historical craft disciplines: stained-glass, ceramics, silk-work and leather-tanning being just the ones she charged for. What energy she had – a radiant charisma of attractiveness and competency clad in double-denim and cheesecloth!

Damian could see her now. His favoured reading-spot at the end of the sloping garden looked down into the half-glass gallery which wrapped this side of the house. Clare was moving around in the kitchen, disappearing for a moment, then there she was again in the big studio window, then gone, now back in the kitchen.

He enjoyed looking through windows when lights had been left on at night. It wasn't to pry; it was more to relish the aesthetics. Wasn't it always wonderful how lighting seen from outside gave rooms a delightful orangey glow making them appear warm and more welcoming as the light fell away at day's end? There was sometimes the temptation to knock on a stranger's door just to let them know how attractive their interior illumination was. The thought of doing it was appealing, but he'd never done it. Surely that's what it was to be human? To want to do something, but not to do it; primitive soulful glee brought to heel by bourgeois social conditioning, and thank God for that.

Maybe it was culturally specific – in some parts of Holland it was held to be anti-social if you drew your curtains. Maybe you had something to hide? He began wondering if animals had similar notions, then put the thought to one side as it obviously needed some research doing and could be left for another time. A momentary blankness of intellect offered his lurking subconscious the chance to eject a troubling qualm which struggled towards his mind like a downed pilot escaping a sinking fighter plane and fighting his way to the light through five watery shades of blue. Only six months before he'd been living in his bedsitting room and quite happily minding his own business, but now, a windy gust ruffling the newspaper next to him, the memory of that time came back and discomforted. Had he been quite himself then?

The night he'd first met Clare had been the happiest of his

life. Thrown onto the small stage in the upstairs cabaret venue, his diatribe against Henry IV had brought the house down and he'd been baptised with beer and sundry other drinks, lauded to the rafters, and made man of the moment. What a night! Clare was there with her sister, the famous and media-friendly historian Lorna Dune, and he'd chatted out the rest of the event with the two of them. The next day he'd been inducted into the openly secret Autodidactiiae history association by his study mentor, Mr Harry-Dan Dolmetscher, and he'd properly got together with Clare shortly after.

Damian had ridden the wave of his success and done his diatribe at other places, but his celebrity had preceded him and it had never been quite the same, or quite as good, as that first time; audiences knew what to expect, and he knew what to expect. It wasn't like coming from nowhere and wowing a cold room like he'd done the first time. He'd stopped doing them now, and refused all invitations, because he'd sometimes been asked by an over-curious member of the audience, in the chit-chatting melée at the end of a gig, where he got his material from? What sources had he used?

He couldn't say Wikipedia as his credibility would be entirely compromised and they'd feel short-changed, and he certainly couldn't tell them about the other thing with the tombs. He'd come to dread meeting such people and that had put him off. Talking to the dead had seemed so reasonable, necessary, and very much the right thing to do at the time. It'd got the job done, but Damian had been having misgivings about his use of first-person testimonies from interviews with tomb effigies. These now broke surface. Gasping dark thoughts were swimming for their lives on black oily water – had he really been speaking with the dead? Was he guilty of…, guilty of…, of necromancy?

The word was not an ugly one. Its sound suggested the taking of two bites out of a crisp apple, but he, Damian Email, a necromancer? There was an ugliness about that for sure, about being called a necromancer. What would Clare think, having a necromancer for a boyfriend? It wasn't her style, he didn't think. If it was true, and he had been really communing with spirits from the other side, then what other gifts might he possess? And what did it mean for physics in general?

If it wasn't true, and he wasn't a necromancer, then he must have had a psychotic episode over several days, and that was the more likely, and more troubling, explanation. Not just 'more likely explanation', the supernatural was called 'the supernatural' for a pretty damn good reason. He probably hadn't learnt anything from them that he hadn't already known before. It was much, much more likely to have been psychotic rather than psychic. Still, meeting dead primary sources hadn't been at all unpleasant, apart from that one time with Henry IV, and the process had proven itself very useful by giving him a closer connection to the past and the people in it. Their input had energised his diatribe and made it compelling. He was grateful to them.

Those conversations had helped in other ways too. They'd been a therapy. He'd been diagnosed as 'blocked'. Harry-Dan Dolmetscher had told him so himself, and Damian had got himself unblocked using his own bootstraps. Anyway, he'd liked talking with them. It had felt special, intimate. They'd had nothing to hide, except Henry IV, who'd been hiding everything. Was that the giveaway? That he'd had to adopt the persona of a police inspector to confront the usurping king? Did that prove it was all in his head and that it had been purely imaginative, and nutty, all along? His thoughts were rambling and he tried refocussing.

Could he become a better historian by ignoring the tomb effigies? Leave behind all the hampering impedimenta of his old ways: Wikipedia, the chicken, mayonnaise and tarragon sandwiches, the inauthentic Italian beer from Burton-on Trent, the Excel spreadsheets, the talking to tomb effigies, all of it, and take it to the next level? Move on? Was he capable of looking people in the eye when they asked him where he got his material from and replying 'Yes, I think you'll find it's all in the appendices, email me if you want any clarifications'? Would his love affair with Clare stand the strain of this new-look Damian? There was one way to find out. Thought to deed Damian!

The book, newspaper, cup, glass, smoking paraphernalia and other bits and pieces were swept from the table and gathered into an unwieldy high-risk bundle which would save him making two trips. Leaves were being blown across the front of the house looking like spotting on an old film, and it was getting colder. Damian made his way down the path to the house, smugly satisfied that he was a few minutes ahead of the moment when he would have made himself look odd. The garden floodlight was triggered as he was halfway to the door. It was a nuisance when it did that, too bright and glaring, but also useful as there were a couple of steps and a trailing hosepipe to navigate.

2

'Could you see me?' Clare stood distracted in the middle of the kitchen and Damian liked to add dramatic flourishes when making an entrance.

'Where?'

'In the garden.'

'I didn't look. Have you seen my book?'

Clare looking for things and him finding them was one of their standing jokes. Her glasses, her phone, her car keys, were always somewhere else and Damian was the recognised expert in getting them back for her. He'd established such primacy in recovering anything she lost that he could use his self-consciously indulgent and irritating 'Have you looked for it?' gambit every time. The most vexing reply to the seeker of something was: 'I haven't got it,' but this time he already had it so, sensing the chance for a play-fight without pillows, he tried the other one.

'Where did you see it last?'

'I think that would be in your hand!' and she snatched the keystone of his bundle away with a brusque yank. 'You said you wouldn't! You always get them dirty or bend the pages. We've got plenty of others. Why do you do it when you know I don't like it?' Damian wanted to say 'Because..., because..., I love you so much' as he was picking up the broken cup and glass. She would laugh, throw her arms round his neck, go up on tip-toe to kiss him whilst kicking a leg back in abandon with a mock-angry 'You...! You…!' and melt into him just after putting another kiss on the end of his nose, but that wasn't happening. This time he was scrabbling around on the ground, and she was cheesed right off.

'I've been looking all over!'

'Sorry. Sorry about that. I thought you were busy tanning some leather for the cathedral commission and…, and I was very careful with it.'

'I finished all the leather yesterday. It's just the stained-glass window to do and I'm starting that tomorrow. I told you.'

'I'm sorry.' Conflict resolution required him to evidence contrition more explicitly. 'I won't do it again'.

'You'd better not!' Clare was annoyed and with justification. He did it time and time again, but the issue was too trivial to continue with and she, having been pretend-diagnosed with Positive Mental Attitude by kindly nurse Irene when in hospital having her tonsils out when she was 7, and thenceforth ever conscious of the importance of moving on when milk was spilt, like now, took charge of events with a mollifying 'We've got loads of them, help yourself, just keep your mitts off mine!'

There was no point Damian playing dead, he knew that. It was only a minor domestic tiff and didn't warrant it. He'd have to move things forward another way and his 'I certainly will,' with a Stan Laurel face and hair twiddle, did the job. Show you mean it. Make an offering. Make a sacrifice.

'Uh…, shall I get started on tea?'

'Yes please. I want to read my book!' Damian wished that she'd added 'you naughty man,' to show that all was fine. There was silence however. But she might have been thinking it.

'I think I'll do chicken with tarragon if we've got all the makings.'

'How long will it take?'

'Half an hour.'

'Sounds like a plan, I'll be in the lounge.'

'Ok.'

Putting the dish together was going to be intense as it was all done on the hob and stuff needed getting, chopping, browning, and supervising. Damian was glad to be distracted from the disturbing questions he'd raised with himself concerning his psychological health, and they receded entirely as he opened the fridge and scanned the shelves for what he needed. It was all there. Chicken yes! Tarragon yes! This was a good sign. They were harbingers of…., of…, harbingers always harbinged doom. It was always doom with them. No, this was a different kind of harbinger. A harbinger of…, the over-lit interior was mutely patient, a harbinger of the…, the beginning of the…, the fight back!

Epiphanic revelation! You could vary the ingredients. Dry tarragon or fresh tarragon. A dash of wine or lemon. With or without cream. There must be loads of recipes. Should he make a sacred vow right then and there? A vow to dine on only chicken and tarragon henceforward, either made on the hob or in the oven, the rolls and sandwiches of hitherto now obsolete, until he had finished whatever it was that he had to do to make himself fully…, fully…, well, whole. Not all actions needed a sacred vow to underwrite them, surely? Damian vowed to be guided more by moral imperatives and leave out the vows for now.

It took longer than expected as it had to cook under a lid for a while, so Damian turned it down low otherwise it might burn, and laid the table for their regular quiet-night-in. Why had he read her book? He knew she liked to be the first and he was the same with books. Maybe it was out of love – to find out about her and understand her better, or maybe it was forbidden fruit, or both. Damian was about to say, 'or neither', caught himself in time, and cursed the thoughtlessness that could fan the most insignificant smoulderings into hissing infernos, as had so often happened over the years. 'Danger! Danger! High Voltage!' He would have to be more careful, more considerate.

When the time came, he called through 'It's on the table!' Clare, bookless, came into the kitchen's dining area and sat down with an everyday smile. Status quo ante had returned, and they dined without rancour.

'Thanks, that was very tasty. Where did you get the recipe from?'

'I've been sitting on it for a while. I don't know if I told you, but I used to like chicken, mayonnaise, and tarragon rolls when I lived at Epsilon Precinct. There was a special beer which....'

'You still live there!'

'Yes I know, technically, but I mostly live here – I mean before you.'

'Before me?'

'You know, when I was living there before I met you. I never did anything complicated with chicken and tarragon, just sandwiches and rolls. I'd almost forgotten about it, but it's come back, and I want to take it to the next level. Find new ways with it.'

'Suits me. I love chicken and I love tarragon. I could eat it all day. And this is great wine!'

'Yes,' Damian affected a French accent, 'it is from the 'Dolomiti', how you say, 'the Dolomites', in Eeetaleee.'

'Why are you speaking French, it should be Italian, or even German?' Clare had been on a climbing holiday there with her parents when she was 16 and knew all about the linguistic distributions occasioned by the fall-out of World War One. Her father had had a particular interest in the Via Ferrata military mountain road and wanted his daughter to experience it first-hand, but she hadn't enjoyed it.

'Yes pretty lady...,' that was enough role-playing for the time being – he wasn't sure if he was acting a waiter or a seducer and his 'Like another glass?' came unaccented. Damian was telling himself off for not getting to the point because he knew he was playing for time. He would have to unburden himself sooner or later but was worried that he might somehow, unwittingly, offend her. You never knew what the consequences could be when you tried to explain something, and the more so when you didn't quite know what that thing was, or what it meant. 'Clare..., Clare..., would you like some cheese?'

'Sure, hit me with some of your Gloucestershire double cheese woud'ja Joe...,' she said with a put-on Los Angeles diner film-noir voice, pretending to chew gum, drawling 'and I'd go heavy on the chutney if you know what's good for ya!' in a standoffish come-hithery way, but her well-meant repartee only made Damian wince inside.

There had been chutney before as well. Chutney! Chutney! Damned chutney! Was that all he was capable of? Fraud, deceit, imposterising and making ruddy chutney? Chutney all the way down. Down to a primeval vat of pullulating ..., pullulating..., pullulating bloody chutney! Stinking vinegary, fruity, spicy chutney! His throat tightened. His forehead went clammy. Acidic anxiety dissolved a hole in a poison capsule somewhere between his heart, lungs and liver and its toxifying contaminants were leaking out into his adrenal system to bind themselves indissolubly with his haemoglobin in an infection of polluting globules, which Clare could see in his eyes.

'What is it Damian?'

'You know that history stuff I was doing when we met?'

'Yeah, Henry IV and all that?'

'Yeah, that stuff.' Damian needed to get it off his chest. All of it: the talking to tomb effigies, him being an unwilling necromancer – all of it, but it wouldn't come. 'I've got to go back.'

'Never go back honey.' She reached across the table, took his hand and held it.

'I gotta…, I gotta go back! I gotta go back and fix Henry IV for good this time,' he replied, seizing the rope she'd thrown him and getting into character again.

'Honey, a man's gotta do what a man's gotta do'. Clare used the well-worn cinematic trope, which nevertheless, and notoriously, had no specific film reference, to crystallise with cliché her feelings for Damian in this moment.

'You know it, dollface!'

3

'What's the matter with your diatribe Damian? I really enjoyed it. You made it come alive. I never enjoyed history at school. It was too dry and boring. I'm more of a hands-on person. I got into it later, with the leather tanning. Lorna and I did a couple of 'Living History' summers in a medieval village museum. What they used for tanning I can't tell you – so pongy! But great laughs, such great people. Why does Henry IV bother you so much anyway?'

'I don't really know. I just seem pulled into him. I don't know why I was pulled into doing the diatribe on him, but I don't think I did a proper job on it. It should have been better, bigger, like maybe I missed something…, something massive. So massive I missed it, like an elephant in the room.'

'How could you miss something if it's as massive as you say? What is it you've missed?'

Damian was fumbling for the answer. It was massive and he'd missed it. The universe was massive and made of dark matter holding it all together to make everything work, except you couldn't see it, and it was undetectable. Something like 97% of what was there wasn't. If scientists had got it right, then that was massive…, and invisible.

What had he missed that was invisible and massive? 1399, foppish and useless Richard II is usurped by butch Henry IV, stealer of crowns. Richard and Henry. Richard and Henry. 97%. Massive. Undetectable. Invisible. Ideas were abstract and invisible, but words gave them form, gave them mass.

Words were detectable. But actions spoke even louder than words. It was actions that gave ideas form and mass. Could a scientific instrument which could detect particles of dark historical matter be constructed right here in the kitchen?

'Hold that thought..., I'll just get....,' – to the fridge, back to the table – 'these beauties,' and he opened a plastic tray of cherry tomatoes, 'and we'll need....,' he returned to the fridge, picked out a selection of vegetables, 'some of these methinks,' which he put in a heap next to the tomatoes, sat down again and moved the plates aside to clear a space between them. 'Right! More wine?' and her nodded assent brought them both a generous double top-up. He wanted a smoke outside to defer the gratification, as he sensed that this could be 'it', but he couldn't be sure that the unseized moment would come around a second time, and so began his experiment with unwonted discipline.

'Let's look at the big picture...,' he said, placing a red pepper in front of him, '... and establish first principles. This is William the Conqueror, okay?'

'Ok.'

'Okay.' He put two tomatoes in front of the pepper, in line astern, to make a short two-tomato trail pointing towards Clare. 'And these are the next kings of England, one after another – but both his sons in fact, William II and then Henry I, okay?'

'Ok.'

'This one...,' indicating the tomato nearest her, 'hasn't got any male children so his daughter will be queen, but there are..., umm..., shenanigans and...,' he would sidestep Matilda, Stephen and The Anarchy as irrelevant, 'she can't, so there's a hiccup, but in the end her son can be king anyway, okay?'

'Oh kaaaay…'

'Let your yes be yes and your no be no!'

'Ok,' she replied, masking her uncertainty. Damian, sensitive, was reassured.

'Okay, there's tomato number three for Matilda and Stephen, and we'll put a mushroom next to it to show there's a bit of dispute,' Damian had caught himself wanting to gloss over some events which were slightly unhelpful to his developing thesis and found his use of the mushroom marker evidence of integrity.

'So now we have tomato number 4, the grandson of tomato number two…,' and he placed it in line with the others, 'being Henry II.' He paused to let it all sink in, pleased to see his tomatoes pushing their way across the table towards Clare, and to replenish their glasses again, before continuing:

'And here's his son, tomato number 5, Richard the Lionheart. But he dies. No children. Owns half of France.'

'Wow!'

'Yes wow! And here comes tomato number six – actually number four's other son – which is Bad King John, who loses a lot of it.'

'Ahhh!'

'Yes ahhh! And then we have John's son, tomato number seven, Henry III.' Damian had a fleeting vision and watched himself doing his demonstration on an internet video. That could be one way of making the kids sit up and take notice – history wasn't just 'all dead people, innit?' – it could come alive! He could call it something like 'History Bingo.'

'Number eight. A son. It's Edward I! Number nine: tomato,

son, Edward II – he was kicked out by…, it doesn't matter because his son came next anyway. Number ten: Edward III, tomato – but his son the Black Prince dies too early – and we have his grandson, and that's Richard II!'

'Thank you Damian, it all seems so clear to me now.' Sarcasm didn't have to be dark, it could also be funny, and they carried on giggling together as Damian tried to answer Clare's questions, not all of which were serious ones. Between them lay 350 years of English history as represented by a line of red tomatoes, one with a mushroom next to it, stretching across the table from Damian's red pepper and almost reaching Clare's wine glass, which she'd already had to move once to make way for the advancing English monarchs.

4

'Ok, I can see it all. There's an unbroken line of sacred royal redness going all the way through, including the mushroom bit.' Only a 'Eureka!' or a 'Howzat!' could have been adequate to an occasion that Damian's teacher-training school would have given him full marks for. Learning had taken place and Clare's unprompted feedback had made evidence for it explicit. 'Careless of Henry the First though, having a girl for daughter.' Damian ignored the seemingly innocent comment as he knew what it meant: medieval patriarchal norms had piqued her. The development of a potentially distracting side argument was to be avoided. He wouldn't even try to explain them.

'Now watch this!' His eyes twinkled with knowing glee as he picked up the cucumber and laid it just in front of Clare to make a green dam against the aligned savoury fruit. Selecting a wrinkled potato, greening in parts, eyes sprouting and with a bad blackened bit, he placed it beyond the cucumber to leave it teetering on the edge of the table, almost about to roll off it and into her lap. 'And that my friend…, that's Henry IV!'

'You really do have it in for him, don't you,' she said, laughing and taking a slurp of Dolomiti wine.

'It could have been anything,' he replied, almost winking. 'It was the nearest,' he lied.

'Well, what was he if he's a potato on my side of the cucumber?' She'd heard Damian's diatribe several times but hadn't expected to be tested on it.

'He's a usurper.'

'I knew that.' Damian had to fine-tune some of the dials on his machine. Some of the readings were out of whack. 'He was a grandson of a king, but not like Richard II who was the son of the king's first-born son. Do you get it? Henry was just the son of Richard's uncle, not of a king.'

'Isn't that still sort of okay?'

'Did anybody else take the crown who wasn't next in line?'

'Stephen?'

'It was debateable. He thought he was and there was Matilda hanging around who thought she was as well, and it went back to her son in the end in any case.'

'Granted. Edward II was deposed. And killed.'

'Also granted, but after him came his son.'

'Was Henry IV next in line anyway?'

'No, there was someone else.'

'A girl?'

'No.'

'Jeez!' Sons, sons, sons. It was all patriarchy! Patriarchy all the way down! All men! 'I think that's about all I can take Damian, it's pretty overwhelming.'

'Hang on in there dollface, stick with it, you're doin' great, just fine. What about we take a break and have us some Eskimo pie and kawfee?' Damian needed to slow down the pace of instruction, so he prepared small bowls of ice cream for dessert, which they enjoyed, cleared away the dirty dishes from the table, made themselves some coffee, had a quick smoke, and got back to it. The hiatus had not affected the running of the detector machine and Damian could see the real story coalescing out of the detail.

'Alright? Ready?' She was revived and interested again. 'So

we have lineage, an unbroken succession of rightful heirs, going back to 1066. Everyone plays the game and knows the rules. Nobody isn't the rightful heir. Even with the mushroom, it's either Matilda or Stephen, they both have a claim based on next in line, whether that's through the male line, or the female line. But then there's a cucumber, and the rules are broken. An exceptional man makes new rules. It's a disruption.'

Words which ought to have meant a lot could disappoint and sound banal, like 'disruption' and he didn't want to spoil it all by ranting. He'd try again. 'There was a rending of the royal-line continuum,' which was suitably portentous but didn't work either. What about chasms opening, or canyons yawning, or fissures? None were adequate to the task. Wordlessly, he went to two drawers. In one he rummaged and selected a tea towel and from the other he found some scissors which he used to cut a short nick in the middle of the top edge, keeping his back to her to disguise what he was doing. Turning round quickly, he advanced towards Clare whilst holding it up with both hands, stretching it out into a banner, exclaiming: 'This is what Henry IV did!' and ripped it apart with a strength that surprised him to leave half a tea towel hanging from each raised fist, his eyes shining. 'Now how easy do you think that would be to put back together again, eh?'

Clare experienced the violent end of her father's souvenir *Via Ferrate delle Dolomiti Centrale* tea towel with sentimental detachment; it was an undignified retirement from the active and public world of the kitchen, though faded and threadbare it had been for a long time, and the memento's final years would be spent in the darkened domain of the scullery's shoe-cleaning box. There was a sadness in its demise for sure, but there was also an understanding. She was a practical person on purpose. All things must change. All things must pass.

'I see what you mean. What was whole is now not whole, and can never be put back together again, like Humpty Dumpty.'

'Yes, that's it! That's it! Just like Humpty Dumpty! It could never be put back together again!' His dark-matter device was on overload – spools of computer tape were spinning, stopping and rewinding, computer punch cards were cascading, teleprinters were hacking out streams of folding reports and tickertape was shooting out in papery streams of data all over the floor. Damian saw it all. Henry IV had done something that could never be repaired, reversed, mended or put back together again.

Henry IV wasn't Humpty Dumpty. The sacred thread of legitimacy, the monarchy, his crown was Humpty-Dumpty, and his descendants would be left to face the music and pick up the pieces. Henry IV was exceptional. Henry IV had changed history all by himself. The disruptor. The agent of destiny. You couldn't fail to be impressed by the usurper's affrontery. Damian wanted to say, 'What a guy!' and didn't understand why Clare said, 'Don't worry about it, let's go through to the lounge' when he said, 'What a bastard!' out loud.

Company boffins would process the computations and take the info round to his private research office in his own historical institute; a post-modern steel, glass and white-stone beacon atop a sunny, breezy ridge in…, in Spain, and in the meantime, he would open a dossier to receive the seismic readings when they came. Clare was already up and moving towards the door, and he rose to follow her.

5

Clare's house belonged to both her and her elder sister Lorna, as beneficiaries of her father's will, and she'd been happy to come back there when things hadn't worked out stateside with her husband Tyler Hogsflesh, the well-known Harvard academic. It was the ideal location for her activities. Built in a red-brick domestic style as a small nineteenth-century printing works, it offered a well-lit workroom and other accommodation on a larger-than-average scale.

Lorna wasn't there. She was living the life of a media-friendly historian with her partner and their children in Manchester. Clare had never wanted any, and she hadn't met Damian's grown-up daughter Louise – married, and making her way in Providence, Rhode Island, something in the music business. The Dunny girls had gone their separate ways, Lorna even changing her name to Dune, but they were quite close in age, looked forward to their infrequent catch-ups, and remained very much the daughters of their father's house.

Clare hadn't been able to be with him at the end. Released from hospital to a care-home, he'd slipped away in his armchair on the afternoon of the first day. The nurse had mistaken his deeper sleep for an afternoon nap and he'd been able to take his last doze in perfect peace. Her mother had passed away in similar circumstances twenty years ago. Mr and Mrs Dunny were everywhere in this their home, each part of it an enduring showcase for their collected artefacts and changing taste over the years.

The last tide of interior design to wash through No 8 had been a late 80's cottagey style which had chintzed up the front room and latticed the doors of interior cabinets and exterior windows alike. The corn-coloured kitchen cupboards touted their mismatched collections of crockery behind glass covered in oblique parallels of criss-cross tracery which watched over work surfaces of creamy tiles. Complementary vegetal motifs and green detailing decorated the ceramics and a sprinkling of dated fruity designs added visual interest and made the overall effect more cosy, but would provide reason enough for a future rip-out should ownership of the house change hands.

New fashions had left their vestigial 'nows' throughout Number 8. Pogroms against the unmodern had banished entire movements, but tolerated exemplars had been allowed to stay on, sometimes forever, their adherence to the old ways notwithstanding. Prominent amongst the dissidents were two clunky post-war occasional tables with thick legs, some forward-looking 50's furniture, Danish-styled 60's bric-a-brac in burnished steel and oiled wood, maybe wedding presents and some Hey-Wow-70's retro-collectables at the back of little-used storage spaces. Others skulked clinging to life in the nether regions: the scullery, garage and death-row outhouse.

Clare and Lorna had tidied away or otherwise disposed of her father's personal things respectfully, but there remained much to remind the two of them of him, and they liked it like that. Damian plopped himself down beside her on the sofa. She put her arm around him and snuggled in closer.

'Thanks for the demonstration, it was very interesting. Where's the controller?'

'The...?'

'The remote-control.'

Damian scanned for possible locations. After computing the various likelihoods, he found it, after two rummaging false starts, under a cushion, in a preposterously short time by Clare's standards, and seemingly without effort, just by wriggling.

'Thanks Damo. There's a documentary on about using beeswax, shall we watch it, or shall I record it?'

'Uhhh......' Damian was still dealing with the cucumber's significance, was confused and couldn't decide. He didn't mind finding out more about beeswax as he'd always wanted to maybe get a signet ring made and use it to close some of his letters with it, important ones. It could be the start of something. You never knew. His mind was open. But the documentary could also be recorded and they could do something else. Clare had intuited his predicament with the cucumber's import and given him a choice because thoughtfulness and kindness enrobed her as blubber did a seal. Damian's diffidence compelled Fate to rethink its scheme and his hesitation, not for the first time, opened him a door, which Clare flung wide open.

'Remember I told you my dad was working on something historical? Why don't you go and look through his stuff to see if it's your thing?' Clare didn't mind the idea of Damian rekindling his work on Henry IV but he had done it all before already surely and maybe he needed something else to broaden his outlook. She'd watch the beeswax show on her own. Damian's running commentaries were often quite funny but she had a professional interest and watching this programme would be more like work to her. She'd record it as well in case she thought he'd missed something.

'What was it?'

'Well, he was working on stuff about World War One which made him angry, and he spent years on it..., we had to go with him round battlefields.' The rent tea towel imaginated itself in her mind's-eye. She closed it. 'We even went climbing in the Dolomites to see what soldiers had to put up with.'

'What kind of stuff?'

'There's a book he used, and his notes, in the library. He couldn't let it go.'

'What was it about?'

'He was so worked up about it for a time, then he left it and went more into crosswords from then on. He wanted a super-tribunal to sit in judgement of the United Nations, find them guilty of starting the war, order each country to apologise to each other and set up a peace and reconciliation enquiry to get closure.'

'Wow,' thought Damian, 'that was a big one!' and he was certainly very interested in finding out more about that. A profound sympathy distilled within for the man whose photograph sat down holding a baby: in the garden with Mrs Dunny: bent over a desk writing, was trapped behind glass in the silver, plain black, and fancy embroidered frames which were adorning the mantlepiece in front of him. Clare could tell him about the beeswax later, and if he needed a ring making then she could probably do him one.

'Sure, I'd love to take a look. Where's his stuff again?'

'It's in the cabinet in the library, and there are shelves of his books too.'

'I've seen his war books.' Damian had already been dipping in for a while. 'Thanks for that. I'll have a look. You don't mind? Enjoy your show. I'll catch up with you later.'

6

The family library had originally been a manager's office. It gave directly into the present kitchen, formerly the clerks' dayroom, which led in turn to the printing presses' former factory area, currently serving Clare as her work studio. A scruffy leather sofa, it's back to the library's redundant fireplace, faced the door; a rumpled overseer superintending a room now busy with books.

Damian Email, playing the detective, noticed dull scratches on the parquet floor which betrayed the sittee's frequent use as a stepladder to the higher shelves. Behind it, neatly filling the space surrendered by the abandoned hearth, was a compact 1930s escritoire with drop-down writing desk, and a wicker-work wastepaper basket stood at its side. To get to the desk you'd have to go round behind the back of the sofa and it looked to be a tight squeeze. Probably they edged round it to get to the desk and then pushed it backwards with a nudge of their backsides and used the back of it as a sort of perching seat. Damian thought that looked uncomfortable, so he knelt on the sofa and got to the desk over the top, which had been, in fact, their standard mode of access.

The writing flap was in the down position, but its interior was obscured by an untidy pile of Clare's 'Girl this – Girl that' crime melodramas, a plastic bag of odds and ends and sheaves of junk mail. Damian picked out 'Gun Girl', 'Girl and Tonic', and the other 'Girl' books one-by-one and laid them carefully on a cushion in the corner – he'd read them all – and put the bag and the redundant post on top to get a clear view of what was inside.

There were two books; one was old, worn out and hanging together by scanty threads: 'Is war now impossible?', an 1899 English abridgement of J.S. Bloch's 1898 work, and the other was a reprint of the same book from 1991 and evidently well-used but in much better condition, along with tubby document wallets which filled the rest of the available space. Damian used extreme care to put the older book back before it came apart in his hands, replaced the couple of folders he'd taken out, after a quick inspection of their contents, and dropped back into a conventional sitting position to see what he was dealing with.

He flicked his way through the younger and more robust version to get an overview of what it was about, which didn't take long; it was a scientific treatise concerned with the practicalities of war-making and was stiffened with tabular arrays of numbers explaining the effects of firepower, diagrams of comparative expenditures, maps of objectives, distances and drawings of human and animal bones which showed the ballistic trauma of bullet-impacts over differing ranges.

It put together a closely argued prediction of how the next European war would be fought. Data-led and dry, it was horrific. Damian spent the next two hours reading its long preface which took the form of a conversation between the author and W.T. Stead, famous campaigning journalist and, as he was later to discover, Titanic victim, and then went onto Bloch's own frontispiece for this condensed translation of his original 1898 epic six-volume plea for peace. A queasy numbness grew in him as he read and began to understand what it meant.

Clare indicated her intentions by shouting through from the stairs; she was going to go up and he called back that he wouldn't be long. He might have believed what he said but it proved a lie, though well-meaning, and another 3 hours of reading and document-rifling passed before he felt that he should stop and go to bed, but not till after he had gone outside to commune with his shaman. He hadn't been able to do that at all in Epsilon Precinct as his bedsit had only the one door, at the front, and loitering outside it would have looked odd, but here there was a back door sheltered under a glass-covered arcade, so he could stand outside it with a cup of tea, or whatever, smoke, look up, and commune.

A march-past of silvered conscripts speckled the floodlit swathe of night to the tympanic drumroll of a rainy downpour. Damian added a musical overlay, a repeated and insistent instrumental bass thudding which beat out the call to advance.

Duh-duh-duh duh   Duh-duh-duh duh   Duh-duh-duh duh

Then came an ominous approaching horror:

Duhhhh ——, Duh!   Duh!
Duhhhh ——, Dah!   Dah! – Mars, the god of War.

The first glass of whisky topped with water began to slow his turbulent thoughts and the second shouted at them to halt, so he could think. J. S Bloch had predicted World War One and had tried to stop it before it happened. 15 years before it happened. Bloch had even presented his findings to the distinguished senior officers of the British navy and the army in a 1901 lecture at their Royal United Services Club in Pall Mall. No one had worked harder for peace than Bloch. He died in

1902, so didn't have long to get his message across, but he did his best to convince Europe's military elite of what was going to happen; a war in Europe would inevitably destroy the states who waged it, which must make it, by any rational calculation, something impossible to countenance.

Bloch had predicted the catastrophe in detail: the extinguishing of professional armies after their exposure to modern firepower, the replacement of their destroyed regiments with an endless call on civilians to fill the empty ranks at the deadlocked front, and then the final collapse of societies compressed by an unending attrition without mercy. It was too much. A third glass. A cigarette. Smoke billowed upwards in belching guffs, wrapping the falling droplets in swathing serpents of choking cordite and gas.

They had known all along how the war would be fought and what its cost would be. Bloch had been right. The people he begged to listen to him had not believed what he told them was going to come. Or maybe they had believed what he'd told them. Maybe they had always known. Maybe they had drawn different conclusions from his evidence, or had known all along. Had planned for it. Maybe war was not rationally impossible. Could it maybe be fought and won with…, with propaganda? The population that was willing to make the greatest sacrifice would win. Weaker nations, less resolute nations, less worthy nations, would crack, would throw their cards in and fold. The war could be won, but not rationally. It could be won irrationally, with sentimentality, with legends of heroic self-sacrifice. Such patriotic abstractions could prop up wavering populations and tottering regimes: King – Kaiser – Country – Vaterland – Patrie – romantic national virtue trumped petty

31

individual morality every time, literally. Propaganda would be the new wonder-weapon.

Had Bloch, in surely the greatest and most grotesque example of the unintended consequence in all history, actually even encouraged the generals to think their way through the problem of having to rely on scrawny civilians for victory? Mr Dunny was right. There was guilt there. A guilty sweet cloying stench of the twentieth century's original shaming sin. The original sin of the nations of Europe when they turned their countries into soldier farms. And then had come the fall into another circle of hell 20 years afterwards, in round two of the inferno. Damian looked for his shaman.

Had his own country been amongst the worst? It hadn't even had a tradition of conscription like the others. One day it's cap-waving volunteers, the next it's universal conscription, and you went whether you wanted to or not, and they didn't even let you off if you said, 'I don't want to kill anyone', unless you really dug your heels in, and if you did that, they put you in prison. The state now owned you, but it hadn't before. You had to fight for liberty, but you weren't free. Things you weren't allowed to do, didn't want to do, were illegal, now you had to do them, or be shot. Peace. War. Surely it wasn't Yin and Yang? Surely one was right, and one was wrong? Damian looked up, where was his shaman?

Bloch had predicted the future, tried to change history, and failed. Damian remembered how he had danced with nuns in a circle to try and stop the invasion of Iraq and been accused of not backing Britain by someone who claimed to have been in the 'military', though precisely what was unspecified, as if a military status conferred authority, and implying that he,

Damian, a nun in each hand, dancing for peace, was guilty of sedition. Had it been an agent provocateur? Damian, like Bloch, had also failed to stop a war, but what could he do about it now?

What could he do? Mr Dunny had tried to change history, the verdict of history, and his folders were filled with essays, letters to newspapers, book outlines and engagements with historians who said that the British were lions led by donkeys, or that the officers weren't that bad, especially when they got the hang of it towards the end, but he had failed too. There would be no super-tribunal to bring the United Nations to justice, no convictions, no apportioning of blame for World War One. There was Mr Dunny's Bloch stuff, but Damian wanted his own stuff. He needed guidance, help. He'd better call Dolmetscher.

His shaman had been watching him from above the falling rain, from beyond the floodlight's glare, and now was the time – fire-thrown shadows gouged the spangling calcite on the cave walls, animal calls echoed through the chambered caverns, bare feet pounded the ground with thrumming insistency, and Damian was drawn in to the dance.

7

Damian was up late the next day but down earlier than Clare who slept on, giving him enough time to get the breakfast together before she appeared downstairs, betowelled and fetchingly barefoot, for a quick cup of tea and a bite to eat. Last night's succession of whisky with whisky chasers had precipitated out as a peppery emulsion which coated the inside of his eyes, cheeks and forehead. Damian found the hangover oddly preferable to the regular morning mind-fug, as long as it didn't linger, and Clare didn't notice.

His breakfast-making routine helped to keep a lid on a seething pot of distorted and unsettling images: star-shells silhouetting broken tree-scapes littered with watery pits, jagged and splintered cannonry half-buried in the ground, their inert gunners leaking dusty red worms, their faces to the earth. He'd cut his face shaving, just above the corner of his lip, and had been using his tongue to clean off the wound's leaking blood, hoping it would soon coagulate. Its metallic taste was unpleasant and filled his mouth. Damian got a glass of water, rinsed, spat, drank, then made a small cup of black instant coffee to wash it away outside with a cigarette.

There was Bloch's futile warning, which deserved some recognition from posterity for its prescience surely? And there was Mr Dunny's futile demand for an inquisition. He would take all that to Dolmetscher. He would know what to do with it. And there was..., there was..., what else had there been? A marker pen had redacted his memory in unsteady lines of thick black ink.

He'd pictured his mentor taking the documents from him with a 'You don't have to worry about that. Leave it all to me, thanks,' and then he'd woken up. No, there'd been something else, just before…, another dreamy fragment…, something else. Shoulder-tapped from behind, he whirled round, and the recollection was in front of him. Yes! When he'd been outside. He'd imagined making a mix-tape of his top sounds, all his best high-energy rabble-rousers, burn them to a cd and call it 'War Cry!' He'd nearly forgotten. Lucky he hadn't. It wouldn't sidetrack him; it might even help him move forward – a war cry vibe for the new improved diatribe. Damian tossed off the coffee and got back to getting on with it.

When Clare stepped into the kitchen, he was already serving out the French toast, sprinkled with tarragon, streaky smoked-bacon rashers and chipolata sausages, her part in the eating of which she was only too happy to play, and it didn't last long.

'That was great, thanks. Have you been up long?'

'Not really, sleep well?'

'Yes, really well, although it took me a while to nod off as I kept having ideas about beeswax. It's actually pretty versatile…, I thought I knew a lot about it…, great to see an expert who can show you something new…, it was a really interesting documentary. I've saved it for you if you want to watch it.'

'Thanks, a spot more coffee?'

'Please… Thanks…, how did you get on with dad's stuff?'

'Good…, good…, I had a really good look…, very interesting…, I'm going to take it to Dolmetscher and see what he thinks.' Damian knew that Mr Dunny had been an engineer who had been able to parlay several technological breakthroughs into profitable patents across diverse industries, and his wife had been first a botanical engraver, then his personal assistant, but how had he got into the business of correcting history? Toast and coffee, munched-slurped too quickly, obscured his question, and he had to repeat it.

'What made your dad get into it? It's a bit outside his normal line of work. I thought he was more into machinery.'

'It was mum who got him going. She got a call from the government asking if she would like to go to Belgium. They found her uncle's body and they were going to bury him with full military honours. Mum and dad went to that and when they came back, he went on Wikipedia to find out why the war went on so long with nobody trying to make peace, and he wouldn't stop.'

'Ah-huh.'

'There's newspaper articles about it in the library, did you see them?'

'Maybe..., there was some stuff..., there was a lot to look at. I'll have another look.'

Clare went back upstairs to get dressed and Damian returned to the writing cabinet. It didn't take long to find the relevant page of folded newsprint, as he was looking for it. A small monochrome full-face picture of a young man wearing a forage cap. Lance-corporal Brown of the Argyle and Sutherland Highlanders had been shot and bayoneted to death on the 26th of September 1915, his 20th birthday, near Loos in Belgium, and a road-widening scheme had found his remains 86 years later.

There was also a half-page colour photograph. His body had been properly excavated using trowels, brushes, buckets, sieves, and his skeleton lay exposed proud of the clay in an undignified contortion surrounded by his rusted equipment: boots, helmet, clips of ammunition, rifle and water canteen. Damian wanted to shudder, glad that he'd never become an archaeologist; he'd once thought it the ideal profession for him, but a documentary on the excavation of a cemetery blocking a railway extension in central London had put him right off.

There'd been bodies at least six deep: coffins, inscriptions, mementos. They'd had to be respectfully removed and put somewhere else. Was being an archaeologist like being in the army? Did you have to do what you were told, or could you raise a conscientious objection? Could you say you were too sensitive and be given another job, maybe just digging up stones? Maybe stone-digging was the archaeological equivalent of a penal battalion. He would have needed a lot of therapy to get over that cemetery, if he ever did. Post excavation trauma disorder. Somebody had to do it, but it wouldn't ever be him.

Lance-corporal Brown was positively identified by one of the artefacts found by his body: a Post Office pen. His cap badge and other insignia indicated his unit and its regimental history, and the location of his body cross-referenced to those missing in action gave a list of candidates. The pen gave a postman. All they had to do was find out who had been in the Post Office, and who had gone missing, and if there was just the one, it had to be him. A lucky break. When Damian found Clare in the kitchen again, he tried to show her the newspaper clipping.

'No thanks, don't show it to me. I think it's horrible. I can't stand that picture. It makes him look like a dinosaur – I mean fossilised, you know, coming out of the earth.'

'Like an archaeopteryx?'

'A..., a....' Then Clare remembered what an archaeopteryx was. 'Yes, just like an archaeopteryx. That's a good way of putting it. So you know what I mean?'

'Yes,' he answered, and he really did. Damian's mother had had a great-uncle who'd gone missing in that war. He'd left the Outer Hebrides to make a new life in Montana and joined the National Guard over there. They were the first ones sent over by the Americans in 1917. He'd disappeared. His only memorial was his name chiselled into a stone with thousands of others. After the war, somebody from Montana came over to the Isle of Lewis and gave his mother some money – his share of a lumber yard. She'd lost another son with the British Army, and one other son had lost his leg with the Canadians. Damian's brother was named after the great-uncle's twin brother and Damian had met him.

Clare was getting her head together for Day One of the cathedral commission and it was going to take a lot of thought, a lot of work, and time. She didn't mind starting late. She liked working late. She liked to work into the night when everyone else was asleep, when time ticked by more slowly.

'Should I go back to my old bedsit for a couple of days to let you get on with it? I can get it sorted with Dolmetscher and let you get on.' Damian envisaged a convivial meeting with Dolmetscher and some me-time in his old bed-sit. Get his scooter back. Go for a ride.'

'No way!' Mock indignation laminated her retort. 'No way you are! You're going to stay right here. We can work on it together and if you get bored, well too bad – or there's the library here. Or do some gardening or something. Dolmetscher can come here. You're staying right here with me.' Clare was coming over quite proprietorial. Previously Damian would have found that repellent, he knew, but here and now he could see himself making a fire, tidying the garden, reading a book, making cosy suppers and light lunches. Probably she wouldn't mind if he had to go out and see Dolmetscher. A daytrip? A long half-day at least.

'Just checking.'

8

Damian became temporary warehouse manager in charge of the Goods Inward department by helping Clare sort out all the materials for her cathedral commission into stacks, piles, and heaps of merchandise which had been cluttering up half the workroom and was now all arranged neatly at one end. Sheets of glass bound in bubble-wrap and packing tape were carefully laid out by thickness, colour, and texture. Custom-made brackets and mouldings filled steel storage shelves, and every box, carton and container had been set out neatly, ready to be used when its time came, their descriptions and labels clearly visible, any trip-hazards marked in yellow and black tape.

Clare checked off contents against inventories and made sure that smaller items were decanted into bins, trays and lockers. Warmed by their exertions, they sat at the extra-large metal-topped worktable drinking tea and surveying their labours with a simple pride.

'It looks great all sorted like that.'

'Doesn't it just. Great job.'

'Great job you too.' Damian took a biscuit.

'How long's it going to take to do?'

'Pffffffhwuh…, that's a tough one…, until it's done. There's a lot of stages to go through but basically its 'conception', then 'realisation' answered Clare, using index fingers in each hand to add inverted commas. Damian broke the biscuit and put half in his mouth; he would have used 'execution' instead of 'realisation' and French-accented both key words, but Clare's 'realisation' as in 'making something real' was actually better, although his other preferred word: 'concretisation' came close, he thought, if you didn't mind being misunderstood. He was about to ask why the leather-tanning had to come first, and what part it played in the stained-glass window-making process, but the moment had passed, and he never got around to asking again.

'I'm full of ideas and I need to get on and start story-boarding them and that's going to take a while in itself.' A mouthful of tea came in on the tide to rinse the sludgy crumbs from his teeth and wash it down his gullet:

'What are you going to do? What's the brief?'

'There is a brief in general terms, and there are specifics: a certain number of panels, different sizes, blah blah...,' she pulled a ring-binder manual to her from where it was on the table and flicked it open, 'it's all in here.'

'Looks complicated!'

'It's not that bad, I've done it loads of times and know what to look out for. I was caught out once and that's not happening again, no siree Bob! Right now, it's about getting the ideas for it sorted out in my head.'

'What's it going to be about then?'

'I'm doing the St Dunstan part, but the whole thing is about St Edmund.' Damian had known that the commission was for Bury St Edmunds cathedral and was unprepared for the interloping appearance of the lesser-known holy man.

'What's St Dunstan got to do with it?'

'It's a great story, you'd love it. It's very detailed and it lends itself to glass. There are lots of motifs and references to pick out, maybe some jokes.'

'Jokes?'

'We always put some in.' Damian saw stony backsides bared by cheeky carvings high atop columns, faces pulled, bishop's mitres on capering baboons.

'Like how?'

'Well..., top of my head..., umm..., Saint Dunstan..., well 'dun' means light-brown, and 'stan', maybe a 'stone'..., maybe I could put that in, or there's 'dunce', a dunce with a tan, or..., or a rebus.'

'A bus?'

'A picture for a name. When I was in America, I once put a little piglet in something I did. I've dropped that name. I'm not Mrs Hogsflesh anymore. Now I'm Miss Dunny again, so maybe..., I don't know..., maybe a light-brown knee?' Damian held back. Practical people were sometimes wont to be too prosaic. He tried to help Clare out.

'Did anything happen in his life that was funny?'

'Well, he did get thrown into a cesspit once...,' Damian saw the potential at once and was poised to offer his input, but Clare's '... by his enemies' stayed his hand, and '... which gave him blood-poisoning,' shrank the humorous design formed in his mind's-eye first to a dot, then to nothing. 'I don't start with the 'funnies', they're for later, when there's space to fill at the end.' Damian could help in other ways.

'Ok – St Dunstan..., give me the elevator pitch.'

'What?'

'We're in a lift. You tell me about St Dunstan before the doors open. I'm a bigwig. You're a wannabe. Off you go.'

'We going up or going down?' Clare's regular need for more context whenever he was telling a story was expected and charming.

'Minx! Ok…, now! St Dunstan! Going up!'

'St Dunstan, yada yada yadda – Archbishop of Canterbury – yadda yadda – coronation ceremony – yadda yadda – armiger yadda yadda – Abbo of Fleury – yadda yadda – the devil. Fast enough for ya?'

'Neat work sweetcheeks. Detail me: coronation ceremony?'

'He invented it.'

'Devil?'

'He bested it.'

'Not bad, you've done this before. You've got the job. What was that 'darmiger' bit?'

Clare explained that it was 'armiger'. It was the man who told St Dunstan about St Edmund, who then told it to Abbo of Fleury, who put it in a book. Armiger wasn't his name. It meant 'armed man' or 'sword-bearer. A title for a trusted servant.

'I've been doing my homework.'

'You have. You certainly have.' A movement in the clouds admitted a low beam of sunshine that lit her from behind and Damian had to move his stool to get his eyes out of the light.

'St Dunstan is in the commission because he got the story of St Edmund first-hand from the armiger: a man who had actually met St Edmund. The armiger was the king's man, but I've forgotten which king.'

First-hand? It seemed very much second-hand to Damian; Abbo met the man who met the man who met St Edmund. It was always like that in history. Unreliable sources. It was, in fact, third hand: Armiger-Dunstan-Abbo, but this wasn't his show, so he didn't press the point. She looked so attractive there in her natural environment, haloed at home in her own studio, everything laid out for her ready to start getting on with things, animated by her passion for creation. Her denimy dress-style could sometimes look dated when they were out and about, but here, sunshine stippling the work top as it passed through the trees, in the place where she was going to do what she loved, her outfit was perfect…, and would be perfect in other places…, acoustic guitar singalong…, scent of patchouli from summer skin …, a fire on a beach…, he was becoming distracted.

'You finished for the day?'

'You have just got to be kidding me! This won't do itself you know. I'm going to throw a few moods into my sketchbook and start knocking it into shape. You've got stuff to do as well, yes?'

'You're quite right.'

Damian regretted leaving Clare in the workroom. He would've liked to have got more involved, but it was her thing, and he took the hint. He did the kitchen and mooched to the library after filling the dishwasher. Clare was going to be pretty much stuck into it for the duration. He needed a space where he could wait it out. A bolthole. No, more like an 'Operational H.Q'. He had stuff to do as well. He needed a workroom of his own, and he needed a plan of action. Clare had it all mapped out. He needed to map it out. Action this day! Call Dolmetscher!

He didn't have a number, never had had. Email then. He got his laptop, opened up the 'Gaunt' folder containing all his diatribe notes, and was about to create a subfolder when he realised that wouldn't do. That was the stodgy old standard operating procedure of the past. He retraced his steps. What was needed was a master-dossier. One folder to bind them all. He made a new one, put the old Gaunt folder into it, which he renamed 'Old Gaunt', and added a new one, which he called 'New Gaunt'.Voilà! Behold the new Damian! Now create a digital document for the draft email to Dolmetscher. No, no need for a draft, cut the gordian knot, just do a simple undrafted email.

Damian prided himself on the clarity of expression he employed when composing emails. Nothing to do with his name, he reasoned, just good old-fashioned expertise gained when they'd drummed into him how to write a précis or a summary as two discrete skills in school, though they'd never taught him the difference between 'discreet' and 'discrete', and he'd never quite got the hang of them, though he knew what they meant. Language had to be spare and uncompromising; meanings distilled and reduced to bald glyphs in laconic sequences. No waffle. The subject…, hmm…, the subject…? Damian tapped out:

A .. s .. e .. c .. c .. o .. n .. d w .. i .. n .. d.

The contents? That came more easily, almost at once:

I .. s b .. l .. o .. w .. i .. n .. g.

A pause. A little too opaque…, should he add 'hard'? No, but it was a fine line between clarity and obscurity, it needed a pinch of…, just one more word:

M .. e .. e .. t .. ?

and signed it: r .. e .. g .. r .. a .. d .. s   d .. a .. m .. i .. a .. n,
and sent it.

9

Bisecting the half-open roll-shuttered goods entrance, mug in one hand, roll-up cigarette in the other, was the condensed and burly figure of Harry-Dan Dolmetscher, smoking, drinking muddy tea and counting his blessings.

His local history association never seemed to stay anywhere long enough for him to put down roots. Its benefactors could always find somewhere for it, for him, but the cut-price or donated spaces were continually being given new modern purposes and they'd need the premises back, and he'd have to move on, so here he was, homed in a light-industrial unit on the outskirts, miles from his former city-centre set up, which had been a most congenial one.

Not a very appropriate location, but leastways it could house his cherished capsule-collection of vintage office furniture, which had been a comfort. There'd been no need to split it up. Yes, it was a millstone, but he and it had grown together. They'd even begun to resemble one another – he also favoured a heavy dark-toned palette in his clothes and silver accents were there as well if you looked for them: buttons, rings, something he wore at his neck, and his venerable leather waistcoat was very much redolent of the plushly-padded swivelling boss chair he prized above all. He held his stomach in for a couple of moments, thinking about going on a short crash-diet, then gently let it out again.

Maybe he might become lonely and too introspective here. It was too far from the welcome distractions of downtown, and there wouldn't be many unexpected walk-ins to chat to about historical matters, and perhaps too cold as well, as he was unsure as to how the uninsulated steel-framed building would respond to the heating measures he'd put in place as the year wore out. Maybe he'd need one of those hot-air blowers like jet-engines? Misgivings about the situation put aside however, there was always plenty to look at from the cargo-bay door as people popped in and out of the other units, on foot, from vans, out of lorries, going about their business. And there'd been a telephone call.

So Damian Email was back in the market for history after a bit of a quiet spell. It was about time. Damian had been an interesting character to work with; slow on the uptake, sometimes downright obtuse, but he'd really let rip at the end and his diatribe was still being talked about in house-party wash-up sessions. He'd certainly made an impact and fully deserved his induction into the Autodidactiiae. And Damian had made contact. Whatever was coming, colder days, solitude maybe, something was stirring, and it wasn't springtime.

But there was no need to rush, get all excited and frantic, that wasn't his way. That's why he had this job. It would be, if it were to be, an exercise in self-control, of keeping off, not an explosion of angsty self-expression, paint flying around, empty bottles strewn everywhere. No, his rough leathery hands would lovingly find the soul of the wood, find what it wanted to be, with steely chisels chasing out paper-thin curls, shavings spiralling from the spinning lathe, and he, mentor-craftsman, would set it free, whatever it was. Liberate…, not make.

The telephone call would be actioned soon. It was the only contact he ever had with the society's benefactors. There was otherwise no other supervision, and he appreciated their light-touch management style. A call would come prompting him to do something, or look into something, in this case an email, and the rest was up to him. They knew his ways. He preferred to initiate contact by post and follow up with a meeting. It had to be personal, physical.

Ok, sometimes there might be some email tennis. He could play that game but didn't really like it. It was so one dimensional, so much could be lost in misunderstandings. They knew that. He'd been doing the job for long enough, knew its ins and outs; face-to-face was best and letters just set the agenda. Putting a letter together could be fun, emails were dull. It could wait. His workload was low but there was still always too much history going on to let him live in the past. Dolmetscher would use his break to gift himself a few moments to reminisce, to catch up with his own life's story, to enquire with detachment as to how he had become him.

There must have been many, many days but where had they all gone? History took the repeated daily detail and discarded it, to leave only stand-out highlights. It was astounding. His past-self was a character in a T.V show with a disorganised story-arc. Or a caricature in a cartoon. Where was the development, the continuity? You drilled back down, excavated your life and could only capture a part of it. It was just the skin of the cooling milk which clung to the sieve, the rest stayed in the pan. Most of it slipped through. Maybe that was the point?

What story could you be tempted to make with your own story? With the bits you sieved out? Could you be tempted to bend the truth maybe? Bend it into a story. Maybe lie? His life-history came over as chaotic and chancy. Had it been directed by his own will? Was he responsible for it, or had it been shaped more by the people he'd met? One encounter had been especially significant certainly.

Social sciences had been good to him, giving rolling student years of changing specialisms, majors, credits, student bed-sits and squats all over Europe, but it was clear now that he'd never properly enjoyed his studies; the extensiveness of his extra-curricular activities was evidence of academic satisfaction denied, surely? Why else had he indulged himself with po-faced arty side projects, which were now somewhat embarrassing?

There had been the summer in Paris when he and Jean-Marc had made it their job to get themselves in the background of tourist snapshots with the intention of providing an interesting detail when the photo was looked at in years to come. More than casual photo-bombers, they'd been living art installations creating secret future confrontations with people they didn't know, who would be forever 100% unaware of who they were and what they'd been doing. Oh the purity!

There were the far-out and cacophonous jazz happenings of Plasmoid Blood Bowl in Brussels. It had been fun for a while. For a while? It was probably just a week. Maybe just one night. And there was even, shame to think of it now, the period, towards the end, when he would put on clown make-up in the daytime and then take it off for his nightly stand-up-comedy gigs in a humourlessly pathetic attempt to find meaning for his 'Man with Two Faces' stage persona. Jeez, he'd gone deep that time.

10

He'd been lucky to come back from The Man with Two Faces.
Lucky he'd met Alberto, Alberto Varvaro, at the Naples Comedy
Festival, by gate-crashing the sponsors' late-night after-party,
working the room, scoffing and drinking too much, and finally
cornering someone too polite to get away. He'd been lucky
that he'd forgotten to put on his clown make-up after coming
off stage, and he'd been lucky that Alberto had listened carefully
to what he said through his outpouring of drunkenly tearful
incoherence.

'Cheer up kid, why are you wasting your time trying to be
The Man with Two faces. You've got something, sure, but that's
not it. Why don't you come and work for me?' wasn't exactly
what Alberto had said, the recollection was bound in fetters
of alcohol which he couldn't undo, but it had been something
like that. He'd woken late the next day, ashamed; it had felt
like a mental breakdown, but Alberto must have listened to his
rambling anguish, and heard him, because he spent the next six
years working for him and they were the happiest of his life.

It had been tough to start with. His Italian was rudimentary
and dealing with the surly librarians had been tiresome; he'd
fill out the request slips, hand them to the functionaries,
hang around, sometimes for hours. There was never any chit
chat with them, they spoke only to each other in a particular
trade-murmur which was inaudible to outsiders, until the time
when a junior servitor would come back with the requested
materials. Some of the stuff wasn't normally allowed off the

premises but Alberto's reputation was enough to release them to him, and then it was back across to the office. That was maybe why he clung so much to his furniture, to remind him of Alberto's office, and those days.

Alberto had always seemed to be about 70 years old and looked like a shoe-mender in an old-style narrow-fronted workshop set between a television-repair shop and another little store specialising in imported pumps and gaskets. No picture showed him other than how he always looked; a comfortable Irish-tweed jacket over a faded green V-necked pullover, dull tie, short thinning hair cupping his large oval head in silvery grey, a leather satchel always there. Only a few months later and Alberto's love and respect for philology had been fully passed on to the young Harry-Dan. Alberto Varvaro would forever represent the best, the very essence, the absolute quintessence, of all learning: a paragon of academic chivalry.

Alberto had opened the acolyte's eyes. Philology was the bedrock of the social sciences, maybe of all sciences: the study of words and their histories. This was what he had been put here on Earth for, to learn from Varvaro, the last master, the last philologist. Dolmetscher thought of Alberto nearly every day and, still thinking of him, he threw his tea slops into the gutter at the entrance, flicked his dog end away into the buddleia-filled bit of waste ground at the corner of the building, and returned to business.

The try-hard brevity of Damian's email was so typical of the man, but its message was a timely life-sign from someone Dolmetscher held high hopes for, and he was glad to get it. The diatribe had been a good entry-level piece of work and granted its author the right to apply for progression into the higher levels of the Autodidactiiae fraternity-sorority, as and when opportunities arose. Had such a moment presented itself? Was this maybe it, or a sign of it? What to write back?

Dolmetscher had been to the Dunny house many times, supervising the Bloch dossier, but Mr Dunny's convictions had taken worrying and pedantic turns. He'd gone too far, too quickly. It had burnt him out and it might prove dangerous for Damian too. Bloch wasn't for Damian. Alberto was for Damian, but not yet – it was still too early. Damian had to find his own way first. But Bloch needed sorting out, somehow. There was plenty at the Dunnys' for Damian to get his teeth into whatever it was he was on about, which ought to keep him going for the present, and in the meantime he could work through the Bloch problem, find a solution.

Harry-Dan answered Damian's 'A second wind' message with first 'Library', then, concerned that Damian would, in his literal way, misunderstand his intent, and go to the one in town, he prefixed it with 'Go to Clare's...', and then, on the point of signing-off and sending, he stayed his hand just in time.

'Whoa! Whoa there big fella! Whoa! Engage your brain! It's Damian you're dealing with!' He suffixed '...in the house' to the instruction and rapped the send key. There could be no misunderstanding.

11

Checking the computer every 20 minutes, it was late afternoon by the time a little yelp from the laptop signalled the receipt of an email and it was not before time. Damian had spent the best part of the day running his sauntering gaze up and down the padded keyboards of books in the library, but his excitement had waned as the shelves' dusty contents became overfamiliar, and he'd settled into a drudging routine of taking out, flicking through, putting back, and checking his emails.

'Go to Clare's library in the house.' It was a very specific instruction, and he was already there, in it. It must mean the Bloch stuff, but that wasn't the second wind he had in mind. It was uninspiring. A second yelp announced another communication which read, 'not Bloch' in capitals. So, Harry-Dan knew about Bloch, and the library, of course he did, he was Harry-Dan, and an eventual meet-up, hopefully with all the trimmings, seemed the nearer.

'What sources did you use?' is what they'd asked him in the meet-and-greets after the diatribe had wowed them. He'd have to find some sources, proper acceptable sources, for his second wind. Probably there were some here in the library, 'Thanks a lot Dolmetscher, already on it.'

But Damian's balloon wouldn't fill. Air was escaping from somewhere and Damian couldn't get himself motivated: finding ruddy sources, reading the ruddy indexes, cross-referencing ruddy page numbers, making illegible notes, forgetting where he'd read stuff and generally getting in a tangle. What a fag!

Maybe it was too late? It was nearly teatime. He could put it off and come at it again, refreshed. He'd do it, but not today. This was only a reconnaissance patrol, not an advance-to-contact with a firefight at the end, so it was probably ok to put it off. Start tomorrow for sure.

Examining the family's loosely organised fiction and non-fiction, he had happened on a showcase of hits from the 'golden age' of crime-writing: Christie, Sayers, Chesterton and the rest. Within it was a sub-section representing the works of Josephine Tey in depth – somebody must have been a fan. Tey's 'The Daughter of Time' was an early find and he dipped into it on the sofa whenever his energies sagged, and he'd nearly finished it by the time the evening meal was put into the oven. The title was familiar to him. He'd come across it when researching his diatribe. It wasn't relevant to his questions about the Richard II – Henry IV affair, it was about Richard III, and that was 70 years after, but the book used an interesting concept. It was fiction about facts, but not historical fiction or costume drama; it was set in the 'now', well the early '50's, and he was glad to find it.

Clare was well into her work and couldn't spare much time for a shared meal. She was in, ate with some talk of what she'd been doing, and then was off, and back out to her work again. There'd only been enough time to ask who the copy of 'The Daughter of Time' belonged to and show her the inscription in the flyleaf. It had been her mother's book. Josephine Tey had signed it for her when she'd come to visit her old school, Anstey's, where Clare's mother had lived, her parents being teachers there. The 'E.M' in the dedication – 'Dear Barbara, remember: Truth is the daughter of time, not of authority!

Yours E.M.' – stood for the authors real name, Elizabeth Mackintosh. Josephine Tey was her pen name.

Damian washed up and went back to the library to polish off the last of the novel. An entire generation of future historians, so Wikipedia said, had been enthused to learn about history after enjoying Inspector Grant's tussle with long-dead Sir Thomas More in Tey's book. A curious genre-busting crossover, it had once been voted the best crime novel of all time by the Crime Writers' Association, but it wasn't really a crime novel at all.

Tey's detective is laid up in hospital with a broken leg, which has to get better, which is going to take time, so he's stuck in bed with nothing to do. Naturally he'd rather be out there in a different story and solving cases, but he's not and he's frustrated, and he's bored, very bored. After exhausting the possibilities offered by staring at the cracks in the ceiling, his restless mind alights on a picture of Richard III hanging on the wall, and his copper's instinct tells him something's amiss. The face in the portrait looks more congenial than Richard III's reputation would allow. Surely this can't be the face of the murderer of the princes in the tower? It's a cold case for sure but he gets stuck into it and discovers fraud, false testimony, distortions and cover-ups.

This crime novel wasn't conventional. It wasn't really a story. It was more like a history book. No, it was more like the story of an investigating magistrate's sifting of the evidence used to make a story, or the case for a prosecution. It was a story about the story they told about Richard III, which they called history. It was a neat job done well. No index. No bibliography. No footnotes. No appendices. No self-serving introduction setting out the stall for brother academics to inspect the wares on offer, and nod approvingly at this 'new' contribution to their field, no acknowledgements of help received to please the friends and appease the critics. 'The Daughter of Time' stood up all by itself and challenged the reader to go and do likewise.

Historical writing had laid down its muddy sediments in layers of authority which had hardened to rock over the years. Time flowed like a river, cutting through and exposing the stone strata on the canyon walls. Authorities, sources, flatterers, liars, apologists, sources, academics, interpreters, priests of dogmatic orthodoxy, sources. Damian didn't want sources, he wanted voices..., like the effigy voices..., voices you could believe in, feel, hear. Damian wanted to listen to them.

Authentic voices in a library? Words in amber, sounds in print? Damian cherry-picked a start-up pile of candidates and others that took his fancy. Revitalised, he scoured the room: there was a Penguin Classics edition of the chronicles of Froissart..., and there was..., there! Another compendium of filleted chronicles, but no more, that was it. Ok..., extend the scope..., a book on Henry IV, why not? One on medieval parliaments..., could be useful. And there were others, but his gatherings didn't look like they would pack much of a punch.

It was a rather paltry dog-eared set of..., well ok, if they wanted sources, he'd give them sources – but he'd be careful. It might be an unimpressive start, but Damian could feel that something was finding itself, that this was the beginning of the final take-down, and that Henry IV would not be getting back up again after this one. Ever.

12

Clare re-joined Damian in her chintzily comfortable sitting-room whilst he was in the middle of watching a documentary on Sir Walter Scott – historical fiction's Dr Frankenstein to Horace Walpole's Igor, his new sources strewn nonchalantly on top of the daily detritus littering the glass-topped coffee table in front of him.

'Fancy a drink?' he asked, hopefully.

'No thanks,' she replied, 'it's a bit late for me. What time is it?'

'Just gone 10.30. That was a long one.'

'That's how it goes when you start to get stuck in. I've got a couple of drawings in the bag and sketched out some ideas, some quite good I hope, and it's all cued up for tomorrow.' Clare didn't understand Damian's 'It's all up on the key,' rejoinder. She wasn't familiar with car salesman lingo for 'ready to go', and he had to explain it, but she was tired, and it didn't get her going. Damian envied her her day and wanted to share his.

'I've got some ideas as well, for a new diatribe.'

'Dad's Bloch stuff and the United Nations?'

'Uh…, uh…., that might fit in…, somehow…, I'm going to start back with Richard II and Henry IV, and go from there.'

A concerned frown wrinkled her forehead. Clare never covered the same ground twice, and going round in circles, being caught in an eddy, could push you into the river's slack and stagnant parts, from whence there was no escape. She glimpsed her father's face below the water, under the surface's collected scum, looking back at her.

'Why go back? You could start something new.' Damian wasn't able to voice his worries about sources; the well-meaning disinterested enquiries from fans had, over time, become barbed wounding jibes in his memory and the sickly-sweet stench of necromancy was polluting his mind with its carrion smell of decaying corpses hidden by roadside vegetation. To leave it all behind he had to go on and go back.

'I think I missed something…,' was all he could think of saying, and he changed the subject by picking up the book on Froissart, about to ramble on about his half-baked ideas but Clare whisked it from his hand and was now waving it at him aglow with delight.

'Oh you! You've found my book. My name's inside…, look! Dad gave it to me as a prize for coming top in the reading group – I was eight – I read it so many times. Knights! Battles! All that. I loved it. Is that what you're going to do, get into Froissart?'

'Yes…, maybe…, I'm having a look anyway,' and they began to riff 'Froissart' with each other using the syllables to make jazzy improvisations.

'Ffuh…'

'Ffuh!'

'Fffwuh…'

'Fffwuh!'

'Fffwwuhcch…'

'Fffwuhchuh!' But Clare was too proud of her French pronunciation not to want to make sure that Damian made accurate vocalisations.

'I'll teach you, you ninny, you need to get his name right. It's 'Ph' as in 'Phew.''

'Phew, what a scorcher?'

'That's right, I knew you could do it.'

'Thank you nurse.'

'This is the hard part. After 'Ph…','

'As in…?'

'Shut up. After 'Ph', you think there is a 'wah' sound, but there isn't. Not yet.'

'What is it then?'

'It's more like the sound an expresso machine makes,' and they both competed to outdo each other with the most authentic 'chchchchcchh' expresso noise, until Clare decided it was time to move on. 'Now we can put it all together, go on!'

'Phhh….chchchcchh…. wah.'

'He's got it! I think he's got it!' Damian showed off his new skill with repeated 'phhh…chch…wah's, until Clare came back with the next part. 'Now it's 'sssss', as in sizzle, sigh, and so forth, do it now!'

'OK, Phhh…chch…wah…sssss, easy!'

'Let's get the last part to bed. Top tip. It isn't 'ahhh'. It's like a pirate Arrrh!, as in Arrrh Jim lad!, but, and it's a big but…,'

'How big is the but?'

'I'm only prepared to take this seriously if you are,' which made them laugh as it was usually Damian's line, 'the big but is that there is a secret sound at the end that's hard to describe.'

'Give me your best shot dollface, shoot!'

'Ok…, the 'rrr' in the sound isn't there. You're about to make it, but don't,' and she offered a helpful exemplification: 'kind of float the 'rrr' away and gently, very gently, coax a hint of chchchch espresso back in, and put it in at the end, as if it wasn't there.' Damian had a go, 'Fly little birdy. Fly! Fly!' and another:

'Phhh chch wah sss arrh?'

'Yes! Yes! Yes!'.

Froissart – Froissart – Froissart: they froissarted their way through all the ridiculous employments of the unexpectedly complex sound they could think of: pointing at things with a 'Froissart!', pulling faces with a 'Froissart!', and Damian was tempted to turn it into a proper pillow fight, with an exultant 'Froissart!' to come with every loving bash of the sofa cushions. He managed to dial down his new-found passion for the word to a tickle, then a cuddle, retaining the 'Froissart!' but using it more subtly, such good-natured playtimes being ever afterwards referred to by them as a 'Froissart', a 'Froissart!', or just 'Froissart?', depending on how they used it, and he'd remembered to get Clare to record the Sir Walter Scott documentary and wouldn't miss any of it, so it was a perfect Froissart.

13

Officially still summer but obviously now very much autumn, Damian puffed smoke out into the silky-pale morning light, long shadows contrasting with the glitzy garlands of sparkling gossamer lain across the grass, and watched daddy-long-legs cavorting in the watery sunshine.

The day may warm up, but now there was a naturally beguiling melancholy waiting to be broken by the first in a succession of noisy mechanical rending, grinding, drilling and screeching aural assaults offered free, gratis and without charge by neighbours, or their contractors, whose daily business was the provision of such gratuitous cacophony. The sound of the distant doorbell called him to the front door, via a side gate, and there was the ponytailed and paunchy shape of Harry-Dan Dolmetscher silhouetted against the sun coming through the trees. Shielding his squinting eyes with a salute, Damian saw the puffy face of his mentor who greeted his arrival with:

'Damo!'

'Mr Dolmetscher!' An affected formality masked Damian's surprise. 'What a surprise to see you here!' He went to shake hands and was met with a proffered elbow.

'Sorry, old habits…,' they shook hands. 'Yes, I would have called first, but I thought I'd drop in. Too early for you? I hope not.'

'Clare's not down yet…, it's great to see you.'

'And you…,' Harry-Dan had had a restless night, worried

that Damian might find the Bloch stuff and that he would be too late to stop it imprinting itself on him like a newly-hatched duckling seeing an unnatural mother for the first time, 'Thought I'd catch up with you..., talk about that second wind of yours.'

'Great...,' Damian was not at all put out and welcomed the chance of getting some pointers from his..., his friend? No..., master? The Autodidactiiae seemed too loosely affiliated to have such a rigid top-down hierarchy, and he'd never seen an organigram showing its reporting lines. No..., not master..., guide. It was guide..., his guide. 'Come in, come in.'

Damian shouted up to Clare and she would be down in a minute, which gave the two of them a half hour to catch up on their respective news and put together a scratch cooked breakfast before Clare appeared, and they ate it together. She had an easy way with Dolmetscher, betokening prior acquaintance.

'I didn't think you did house visits anymore,' she joshed. 'Aren't you too important?'

'Clare, you jest. Your family have always held a place high in my heart,' which introduced a melodious 10-minute interlude for Harry-Dan to find out all about how Lorna and her family were doing, and for Clare to talk about nearly all the things she'd been getting up to with Damian, which made Damian feel good, and her work. It was clear to Damian that Dolmetscher had been there before, was somewhat of a family friend, and had been close to Mr Dunny, and had worked with him, probably on some kind of regular basis. But Clare had to get on, made her excuses and told Harry-Dan to make sure he said goodbye before going, which left them alone in the kitchen. Dolmetscher got straight to the point.

'Damo, your second wind – where's it coming from?' Then, for clarity: 'What's it about?'

'I'm not exactly sure....' Same old Damian, there was still time. 'I need to..., to..., go back. I need to go back to...,' there might be a lot more time, 'umm…, back to Henry IV.' This was contrary to all pedagogic norms. Advance! Advance towards the sound of the guns! Go back? Go round in circles, chasing your tail? That could not stand!

'Back to Henry IV? But you've done that. You're in the Autodidactiiae now. You're fully inducted. Your license to practise can never be revoked…,' Harry-Dan here deciding to skate over the expulsion mechanism offered by the anti-pedantry clauses in the constitution, as enshrined in the society's very name. 'You should do something else.'

'Well, Clare has got some stuff of her dad's.' Dolmetscher felt his own blunder almost smother him. Damian had had a sniff of Bloch, but was he yet an addict? Could he wrest control back from the physical forces which were determined to doom the stricken bomber and send it plunging earthward? A direct intervention flew in the face of received wisdom but could it be justified? The sound of gunfire might actually be coming from the rear. Successful commanders should install tactical awareness in their subalterns, encourage them to exhibit flexible responses to changing circumstances.

'Actually, you know what, Henry IV will be fine. In fact, it's a good idea.' Having compromised his principles, albeit for the best of reasons, he may as well go the whole hog and sort it out with the C.O. after. Ask for forgiveness, not permission, 'I can help you. One word: Froissart.'

'Ph chch wah sss arrh, I think you mean.' This demonstration of linguistic mastery, coupled to a strangely knowing look on Damian's face, was nonplussing. 'I've got Froissart. Clare had it. I went to the library to look for stuff to start with, like you said.'

Dolmetscher felt the five acts of a tragic drama unfold in an atomic second – the inevitable train of fateful events instigated by himself. Greater powers overseeing, directing, enjoying the heart-breaking chain of tragic causality. Maybe what had to be, had to be. Your fate was your character. It was unavoidable. But it couldn't be…, not here…, not in this house…, again. If Damian could be put off, he'd have to put him off right now. Harry-Dan dug deep, then deeper, to find a ploy:

'That's good news, good to hear. What edition is it?' The answer offered hope. 'Penguin Classics edition! Pen…guin Class…ics! That's not Froissart! That's for children!' Faked indignation properly played could distract, but used now, in a state of righteous anxiety, he ran the risk of going too far and saying too much, which he did with:'… who don't like history,' which he regretted ever after, although Clare would never get to hear his cruel words repeated. 'What you need is Varvaro,' which Damian misheard as 'vavavoom'.

'Yeah I know. I felt a bit down, you know…, deflated…, after the diatribes…, but now I'm, you know…, back…, and I feel fine.' Dolmetscher couldn't let his mentee's emotional needs deflect him at this most crucial of junctures. He needed Damian to respond, even if he had to shove it down his throat.

'Alberto Varvaro. You speak French don't you?'

'Oui.'

'Medieval French a problem?'

'Non,' Damian was hopeful, but wholly inexperienced.

'Look, to save time, I'll do you a list. It – is – NOT, and I

repeat, NOT a reading list, ok? You understand?' Damian
didn't understand the other's touchiness. 'It is merely, and
only, a ..., well, we could have been chatting in a pub couldn't
we, and I might have just jotted down some..., headings..., or
something…, and left it behind, and you…, you pick it up…, to
give back to me later. Not a reading list. Clear?'

'OK back off big guy, write your pubby memo on this,'
he said, handing him a beer mat extracted from the small
collection occupying, on extended tenancy terms, the lower
reaches of his jacket pocket, souvenirs from his short-lived
diatribe tour, along with a pen from the kitchen drawer. The
whiff of skulduggery seemed discordant so early in the day but
Dolmetscher had his ways and who was he to contradict, let
alone judge him. Dolmetscher scribbled.

'Here, here are some..., some headings for you.'

'Thanks...,'

'Did you come across any of her dad's stuff?' Dolmetscher
had to know.

'Yes, there's a pile of it in the library.' Harry-Dan's personal
bubble of space-time spasmed. He was standing small and
8-years old in front of a stern father figure and about to be
beaten: 'I didn't think…' – 'Well that's just the trouble isn't it,
you didn't think!' He'd last seen it at the funeral reception.
It had been safely boxed away upstairs. It had been moved.
Sayonara scruples. In a low and controlled voice, H-D tried
hypnotising Damian into unquestioning obedience.

'Damo, have you got a bin-bag, preferably heavy-duty?'

'Yes, Clare's got loads.'

'Stay here will you?' Dolmetscher nipped through to the
studio and a muffled conversation could be heard. Then he was

back with a bag. 'It's ok with Clare, I mean she's ok with me taking it. I think you might not be able to read the beer mat. I wrote it too quickly. Give me another and I'll do it properly..., thanks. Give me a couple of minutes peace and quiet to concentrate, will you?' And he was straight out to the library. Damian expected the unusual from Dolmetscher, but this was strange.

Dolmetscher emerged, beer mat in one hand, bulging black plastic bag almost trailing the floor hanging from the other, his flustered face gleaming.

'I'm out of time. Got to go. Let's meet. I'll write.'

'Don't forget to...,'

'I've said goodbye. Here's the..., the beer mat.'

'Well..., thanks.'

'I'll see myself out.' He was going. 'See you when I see you.' He was going. 'I'll be in touch.' He was gone.

'Bye.'

14

The Dunny anti-war tirade was charismatically absent from the writing desk when Damian went to transcribe Dolmetscher's scrawl into his New-Gaunt digital info-dump, but Clare was not as concerned to hear about its disappearance as he had expected; Harry-Dan had asked to have a look at it but she hadn't thought he'd go off with it, oh well, it was probably for a reason. She was more put out to learn that he'd gone without so much as a parting word. A funny start to the day it had been for sure, but Clare was up earlier than usual, down working away, and he had things to do as well.

'Buy-Now', which he called 'Behemoth', would eventually own the planet in partnership with 'Lookyhere' under some umbrella-brand like 'BuyhereNow' in a future-world dystopian paradise. That was his prediction anyway. Consumer ethics put to one side, Damian resigned himself to a big splurge on sources from its warehouses. One high-impact spending barrage and he'd get all he needed in a day or two. Old-Damian would have got no further than amassing the pile of paid-for presents, that could come so quickly in a closed-loop of gifting and receiving, and not getting round to doing anything with them, but New-Damian had learnt to better distinguish between means and ends; the accumulation of stuff was only tactical, and strategic objectives remained to be set – what was he going to be doing?

Damian needed to connect with the inner-Damian that wanted so much to be a proper historian. On the sofa, beer mat

on his lap, hands resting on his knees, he inhaled, and he exhaled: 'I am an historian', and he inhaled, and he exhaled: 'I am an historian'. No, not 'an'. It choked. It was uncomfortable, like he was nearly biting his tongue. It had to be 'a'. 'I am a historian ....
I am a historian.' That was it.' The repeated mantra dissipated restless wave energy until the waters were calmed and he could see beyond to the historian waiting beneath.

What would he be doing? He must know that already, subconsciously. He knew as much as anyone, had been lauded and praised for what he'd done. Go back. Take a flaming torch to light the way, return through the caverns – flickering finger paintings on the cold walls – follow them through the dead cave air to…, to…, where it had started.

There'd been a vision; Richard II was dead, his corpse laid out on a gothic table, naked in the moonlight, and somebody else was watching over him, a female figure. The idea of getting first-hand eyewitness testimonies from tomb effigies had come from this, from her. That woman was the start of it. He'd given her names. First she was 'the lady in red' when she'd been spooky, then 'Romana Clay', when he felt more at ease with her, and finally she was Elizabeth Fitzalan, after he'd worked out what her real name was.

Elizabeth's was the only tomb effigy he hadn't talked to, and he was glad of that. That would have been a step too far, most certainly. There was no doubt or question about it. How might things have developed if the church housing Elizabeth's tomb hadn't been locked because of a local A.C.E Covid quarantine cordon sanitaire, and they'd met in the real world? It had been a very, very close-run thing and Clare was never going to know about it.

'I am a historian …, I am a historian.'

Richard II and Henry IV; he knew the whole story. Everybody did. What was going to be new about it? Perhaps he shouldn't have taken sides, should have been more objective. Ok, this time he would be more objective. Objectivity then! A king's first duty is to preserve his throne and Richard had not been able to do this. By that standard he was a definite loser. Ok, Richard II was a loser, fact! There was no need to argue any case here. No need to excuse, rehabilitate or start a campaign to bring him back to life. Maybe he wasn't the wimpy and foppish git of the histories, but it didn't matter because he was, nevertheless, one of the biggest royal losers of all time. Loser! Loser! Loser!

'I am a historian …, I am a historian.'

Objectivity! What about Henry? Henry IV had taken the throne in extraordinary circumstances. It was like Lord of the Rings. Henry IV was Frodo. Archbishop Arundel was Gandalf, or was he more like Sam Gamgee? Anyway, there's a small band of followers, like a fellowship. Henry leads them from exile in France on a mission to regain his heritage, gets some backing from the Riders of the Mark and Gondor, aka the Earls of Westmoreland and Northumberland, captures Richard without a battle but, with the subterfuge of a Gollum, throws the king into Mount Doom aka the Tower of London, gets the ring for himself, and gets himself crowned as the saviour of the kingdom and healer of the land. Or maybe Henry IV was a witch-king, a Nazgul. The whole Richard II versus Henry IV ding-dong was an unlikely story, but a true one, amazingly. Henry IV was one of the biggest royal winners of all time. You couldn't argue about that either. It was a massive win for Henry. Winner! Winner! Winner!

15

'I am a historian …, I am a historian.'

Was it all about sources, or could you apply deductive logic? Quantum physics was a different kind of reasoning. There weren't always facts in it. It was more abstract and speculative.

Richard II, big loser, ok. Henry IV, big winner, ok. History had made a story which justified how one deserved to lose and the other had to win – a story told by the winner. But the story was absurd. It was ridiculous. If the story was preposterously unbelievable, but true at the same time then…, what was the real story? Were there other facts, which were also true? If the accepted version was made of real lies, could there be an alternative factual story?

The actual story was too two-dimensional. One for a graphic novel maybe, or an implausible film. There had to be something missing. Something that existed in the real world of then, that had since faded from memory. Or been erased. Something that would make sense of the unbelievable, but true, story.

'I am a historian …, I am a historian.'

What would we look for if it happened now? The Richard II – Henry IV story is too…, too personal: one pitted against the other. The story is just about two men. That must be wrong. Richard is passive: things happen to him, and Henry is active and does all the doing. Henry was a narcissist. Elizabeth of Lancaster's tomb effigy had told him all about Henry's infant obsession with his father's Spanish crown, but what had made Henry go on to break so many taboos, sacred oaths and time-honoured conventions in order to get what he wanted, the crown? Henry was like a dramatic hero in a distorted Greek tragedy. One of his parents must have been an actual god, how else to explain the story? The implausible, preposterous, and unbelievable story.

'I am a historian ..., I am a historian.'

Nobody expected Henry. Nobody understood what they were dealing with. There was a crazy fault-line in the tectonic plate of English history. One man was not enough to crack open the crust of historical destiny by himself, whether he be god-like hero or narcissistic nut. But he had done. There had to be dark matter in the story's universe to explain how it had happened. Something not part of the accepted version. Something unsaid..., something the winners didn't want to talk about..., something which had to be hidden..., like in politics..., politicians are storytellers, they only tell their version..., it had to be something political. Something political and massive in the 97% dark matter of the story that could better explain what happened.

'I am a historian ..., I am a historian.'

There was Henry: his character and motivation and there was a political situation which could allow one to lose and the other to win. And there was..., what? The past itself? It was all in the past. Was that a problem? They were both dead kings, but their story must have had consequences for others, maybe still had, even for us now. Why was it important to get the story right? He'd call that 'So what?'

Henry .... Politics .... So what?

And what was he going to do with it, another diatribe? No, it had to be something else. A book? No way, it would be shredded by know-alls within seconds. What would it be? Call that 'What?'

Henry .... Politics .... So what? ....What?

'I am a historian ..., I am a historian.'

Damian's meditations had been fruitful. He couldn't wait to tell Clare of his cleverness and he would apprise her of it over their evening dinner, the preparation of which would be his special pleasure as he awaited the curtain opening on his new thing. He would keep it short and to the point to keep her attention, and a prop would be useful. Fruit or vegetables had their uses but this time he wanted something more formal, more serious, like a quotation.

One came to mind; something said in the parliament which deposed Richard II. Damian remembered putting it in a text box on a digital document somewhere but, ferreting for it for an hour and a half, he didn't find it. He did know the website it came from though, but the miserable chiselling weasels had put up a paywall now that the coronavirus moratorium was over. He was not going to pay on principle. It was an affront to democracy. Damian googled how to petition Parliament. Never no more could he idly sail his toy boat, her name: 'Enquiry', across the pond of medieval parliamentary records transcribed into modern English, without having to take his wallet with him.

Not finding the quotation flashbacked him to his recent bedsit days. There, neo-Buddhistic entities of his own devising: Doomak and Soomak, battled for supremacy in his smoky sanctum. Doomak had an everyday blighting yin presence; where were his glasses, his keys, his wallet? What was the password? Why had the milk leaked in the fridge? Soomak was yang: harbinger of harmony, bellwether of beatitude, and the more powerful, though she appeared rarely. The time he'd wasted on not finding the quotation galled, but it hadn't killed him. It had made him stronger.

No, nay, never…, no nay never no more, would he pay for the privilege, no nay never…, no more! A lone piper played a pibroch, the 'Lament for Mary MacLeod', across the lapping waves on an empty beach to the sun setting on the Atlantic horizon. Americans on oceanic boardwalks looked to the East for an answer but found none. Those bedsit days were gone. Damian was not the same man. Doomak could be overcome. His frustration would not engender anger. That was not the way of the historian, of the Autodidactiiae. Flow like water Damian.

There was a zip-up side pocket in his leather bag. In it was his Phial with the Philtre; a small silver capsule-like ornament – his official Autodidactiiae regalia – attached to a leather thong. Damian put it around his neck and secured the clasp at the back, tucking the dangling Phial under his collar, vowing to wear it every day until his work was done. In the future, when interviewed by Esteabheànn Blayke for the Irish 'Late-Night Talk!' chat show, when he was asked if he had an anti-establishment chip on his shoulder, Damian would answer 'No', perfectly honestly, and think of the bagpipes, the Phial, and this moment. And he inhaled, and he exhaled.

I am a historian   …   I am a historian   …   I am a historian.

16

Table talk over the main course let Clare download the progress she'd been making, and it was coming on well. The major themes were mapped out and the time was nearing when she would be twiddling with the details and furtling them around so they fitted together properly. Grappling with conceptual challenges had been tiring but Damian's gossipy attentiveness helped her replenish her energy reserves to the point where she'd fully recovered her playful self. She was happy to let her hair down and indulge Damian's boyish enthusiasm when the time came for her to hear about his thing, which was the intermission before dessert was served.

'Henry? But you've already done Henry!' Too playful and too provocative, she'd interrupted him too early, and Damian's obvious pride in laying his thoughts out in front of her was affronted. She was suddenly stiffly self-conscious. 'What is it about Henry?'

'His character, or his personality, something in it made him the special one.'

'I see. That'll be interesting…, for you to look into.'

'Yes. Next it's politics.' Damian was determined to show he had something convincing and gabbled to her about dark matter and quantum physics, none of which she understood, nodding and smiling. 'Then there's the 'So what?', which is key. I need to work that out, and lastly the 'What?' How will I present it? What form will it take, maybe a book this time? Not sure yet.' Clare hadn't been given much meat to get her teeth into. Damian needed to maintain momentum and headed for the fridge.

'Oooh, are you going to give me one of your fruity vegetable demonstrations?' What a look she was giving him, playing with her hair promisingly. 'Can we do something different this time? What about plums?'

'It's too late in the year, plums are over.'

'Walnuts?'

'Bit early.' Damian didn't want to use anything from the garden. He removed a tray of cocktail sausages and brandished it with a swaggering: 'We'll use these!'

'Froissart!'

'Froissart indeed!' His hand went back in. 'And a camembert! And some…, there!' and sat down again, putting the cheese where his plate had been, and a squeezy plastic bottle of hot Jamaican sauce next to it. Could he interest Clare in a critical period in late-medieval English politics without boring her to death? 'Ready for a lecture?'

'Aye aye captain!' Clare saluted and made a pirate face.'

'Today we are talking about politics. This is not the politics of the dark matter. This is the politics of the observable universe. Any questions so far?' She made a determined face, stuck out her bottom lip and shook her head. 'This camembert is Edward III. Clear?' She nodded. 'He has 5 sons,' and he set out 5 sausages, 'one…, two…, three…, four…, five,' making a dashed line in front of the cheese.

'Oooh can we call them little piggies?'

'Certainly. This little piggy…,' touching the first one on the right, 'is Edward the Black Prince,' and he anointed it with a little dollop of squeezed sauce. '50-year reign. Named after one of England's patron saints. No St George yet.'

'What's the sauce for?'

'There's going to be another row of sausages in front of this one. It's to tell them apart,' and he dolloped each of the little piggies with a splash of sauce as he introduced Richard II's uncles.

'Next to him is Lionel, dies too young.'

Splash.

'Then we have John of Gaunt, born in Ghent and the Black Prince's best-friend and comrade-in-arms. The Duke of Lancaster.'

Squirt.

'Then, here's Edmund, named after the other patron saint, the one you're doing – nice guy, but no charisma, the Duke of York…'

Splash.

'And then we come to Thomas,' Damian paused theatrically, waggled the sauce bottle and squirted the sausage, 'better known as the Duke of Gloucester. He's 14 years younger than Edmund. He's the important one.'

'Impotent?'

'No plenty of children, but none of them important. We're getting to the offspring now.' Clare was tempted to get Damian going by gobbling one of his royal sausages, but she was already full up, and there was Black Forest gateau to come, and soon she hoped.

'Here's the next generation,' and he placed a sausage at right-angles to the Black Prince. 'Sausage, no sauce. That's Richard II, his only child.'

'Oh.'

'Lionel has Phillipa, and her children will be next in line to the throne, if Richard cops it with no kids. Sausage.'

'I see.'

'John of Gaunt has Henry IV, this sausage, his only, ahem, legitimate male heir.'

'How can he have a king when there's already a king?'

'I always call him Henry IV to keep things clear. Whether or not he's king yet. He's got too many names: Earl of Derby, Henry Bolingbroke, Earl of Hereford and it can get confusing, so I always call him Henry IV.'

'I see,' said Clare, confused.

'Edmund next; he has a couple of sausages, but I'll use just one.'

'Right.'

'And so does Thomas, so I'll do the same.'

'Uh huh.'

'What do you see?' Clare knew better than to say 'a lot of sausages', so stared in their direction and waved her hands, wiggled her fingers, until Damian stepped in with the answer.

'You have a 10-year-old boy-king with four uncles who you'd expect to help him out, yes? But not so. Lionel is dead. John of Gaunt wants to carve out his own European empire and is off out of the kingdom for a lot of the time, Edmund will take what he's given provided he can get busy doing nothing, and then there's Thomas..., the youngest by a long way. Thomas is the politics. His brother John is better at everything. Thomas, duke of Gloucester, seethes with resentment.'

'So what? Let him seethe.' Damian's plodding outline had developed some drama and Clare's interest waxed anew.

'Now we're getting there. These facts are well known.

The observable universe, remember? A splash of Dolomiti perchance?' Damian topped her glass up. 'In 1388, seething Thomas gets a small mob of bigwigs together: the Earl of Arundel, Earl of Warwick, Thomas Mowbray the Earl of ..., umm, ... Nottingham, and Henry IV.'

'Henry IV?'

'Yes, well no, remember he's not king yet, anyway, his dad's left him behind in England and Henry wants to play with the big boys. The gang rides into town, captures Richard II, puts him in the tower, effectively deposing him for 3 days..., this is ten years before it happens again..., then Thomas lets him out but takes over the parliament, executing Richard's administrators and friends. Richard's wife....'

'Were they in love?'

'Very much so.'

'Ahhhh...,' and Clare took a wistful sip of wine. Damian smiled inwardly at the display of sentiment for long-dead people as revealed in her sigh.

'Richard's wife begs Thomas to spare the life of one of them. Simon Burley. She's on her knees for 3 hours, but he won't. Thomas kills as many of them as he can.'

'Bloody hell, that's raw!'

'It is raw.'

'Then what happens?'

'Richard's tormentors find that governing is harder than they thought, so they let Richard rule by himself, but they stay close to him.'

'Where's Big John of Gaunt?'

'Out of the country. Richard calls him back to bolster his position, which helps, but Thomas, Duke of Gloucester, stays part of the government in the royal council.'

'And then?'

'Now we come to the last part. As the story tells it, Richard II plots vengeance for his sufferings in 1388. His major crime is wanting to avenge his humiliation in 1388, so the story goes. In 1397 he's ready to make his move and captures Arundel and Thomas: Arundel is executed for his treason in 1388, Thomas is murdered in Calais, Warwick is exiled. Richard II, so vengeful!'

'What about Mowbray and Henry?'

'These two say they were corrupted by the others and are let off. It is Richard plotting and scheming to get his vengeance and having his uncle murdered which counts against him most. That's what Henry said, and that's what historians say. They're obsessed by it.'

'And that's the story?'

'Yes, but I don't think it's true.'

'So what do you think?' Damian knew he would be caught out at the end like this.

'I'm looking into it. I'm getting stuff from Behemoth, I mean Buynow. Can I come and work in a corner of the workroom? I won't disturb you, but it's lonely in the library all by myself. I'll be just making notes and reading. Not getting in the way.'

'That would be great. It can get a bit lonely in the studio too. Make yourself a little den in the far corner, and if you need to pop out, you can go the back way, otherwise you might trip over my stuff. What's for dessert?'

'Black Forest gateau.'

'Great. Can we have it in front of the telly?'

'Naturellement. You go through and I'll bring it in.'

17

They worked well separately together and the first day of
the new paradigm provided them a template for their future
routine: having coffee in the mid-morning lull, a scratch
lunch and then tea and a biscuit in the afternoon, just before
Damian would give in to fatigue, his head overstuffed, to pull
out of the workroom and pooter around in the kitchen or
library, whilst Clare kept going with her music blaring to perk
herself up a bit, and this first time she was playing an old tune
loudly:

Deww.....
    Deww.....
        Dewwww ... ... Da diddly da da ....
            Dewww.....

The lead guitarist was picking out the notes, seeming to
have some difficulty remembering which song they were
supposed to be playing; then, decision made, it was:

Chung
    Chung
        Chung – Thwack! :- three acoustic chord
thumps, drumbeat coming off the third and into the melody:
'As I was goin' over, the Cork and Kerry Mountains.........'
Damian had heard it a thousand times but had never been
able to make out what the first line of the refrain was. He
looked it up. 'You're kidding!' It made him laugh. It was often

hard to decipher lyrics but, in this one, the words were exactly as he'd heard them: 'Mush-a ring dumb-a do dumb-a da.' Amazing. They meant nothing. They were nonsense. He copied the lyrics into a document, inserted a picture of the band, and printed it off, ready to use later as a visual aid for some small talk with Clare in the evening. A verse near the end caught his eye.

> Now some men like the fishin',
>> And some men like the fowlin',
>>> And some men like ta hear
>>>> A cannon ball a roarin'.

The pleasures of the flesh were there, but, beyond that, there was the assertion that some men liked the pleasures of war. Sybaritic lotus-eating versus death, destruction, and gore. Some probably liked all three. Richard's deceitful cousin Edward of Norwich liked *fowlin'* certainly. He wrote a book on it, the authoritative textbook of the time, and *fishin'* probably too, if kings' cousins did that, or maybe it wasn't a 'thing' then, too menial. '*And some men liked to hear cannonballs a roarin'*'. Some people liked war. You could do things you weren't otherwise allowed to, despite the risks.

Elizabeth of Lancaster had been his first tomb effigy, the gateway to the rest, and she'd made it easy for him, sucking him in with her histrionics and sending him off to look up her old friends, and enemies. She'd had to remarry after her first husband, John Holland, chivalric knight extraordinaire par excellence, had been killed at Henry's command and she'd been forced to remarry a salty seadog of a Cornishman, a Henrician loyalist called Cornwall, John Cornwall. The story was that Henry gave her to him as a reward for beating somebody in a duel.

Yes, that was it, John Cornwall and their son John Cornwall Junior were besieging Meaux in France. The French fired a cannon ball which carried off John Jnr's head. He was standing next to his father when it happened. Damian looked up the date. 1422. John Senior vowed to never more make war on Christians, and, by all accounts, hadn't. An incident in the 100-years war. Not unimportant for those concerned, but now just a trivial detail in the bigger picture. Here's someone taking a belated moral stance against the war, their eyes opened to its immorality by a particular and very personal tragedy. The war the Cornwalls had been fighting was wrong. It was the wrong war. Father and son should have been fighting other people, not the Christian French. If his son had to be sacrificed, then it should have been in a better cause, a juster one.

'Well whack for my Daddy-o, whack for my Daddy-o, there is indeed whiskey in the jar-o!'

Repressed adrenalin tingled. That must be how it felt. That must be what it feels like to break through and make a discovery. He had found dark matter. An instrument buried a mile beneath the surface, shielded from anomalous interferences, had registered a hit and pinged. That's what the dark matter in the politics was. It was war, and not war. The politics of war and peace. And it might have something to do with the 'So what? as well. Damian got his small leather-bound jotter, which he'd not been able to resist acquiring from a medieval website, and used the pen, decorated with a brass-rubbing design, which he'd obtained from the same merchant, to write on its third page:

1) Henry.
2) Politics: War v Peace
3) So what? War v Peace?
4) What?

It didn't look as good written down as it'd sounded in his head, admittedly, but he knew what he meant, and this was a private dossier notebook, in red Moroccan leather, just for him, and it was a start.

18

Eight days later, not counting the weekend, and Clare's ducks were all lined up in a row. Damian was good to go as well, with the long-awaited full-on and no-holds-barred Dolmetscher meeting scheduled for the next day.

Organisational wisdom had come to him the hard way and this time he'd been sure to be more methodical. His attention to the preserving of references, weblinks and page numbers to forestall any enforced doomaky downtime had been meticulous. It was all up on the key.

Harry-Dan had phoned-in the rendezvous for 07.00 hours and was going to pick him up and take him he didn't know where for a pow-wow. It was, intriguingly, going to be an overnighter, and Damian would have to make his own way back, taxi fares and train tickets provided. Damian was looking forward to impressing his mentor with his new-found methodical ways of working.

Yes, he'd been scientific, and yes, he'd been objective. The law of gravity posited the exisitence of dark matter. It couldn't allow for it not to be there, so its presence, its existence, was a matter of logical deduction from first principles. If history was a collection of facts, to make an argument, a story, an explanation, then, by definition, and according to natural law, whether by accident or design, some facts, of greater or lesser importance, had to have been left out. And he'd found interesting and important facts. Which had been left out.

Dolmetscher's almost indecipherable beer-mat scrawlings

had given a distilled list of sources, mostly chronicles, and he'd got them all: taking notes, adding exclamation marks in margins after underlining, and using yellow highlighting felt-tip to append fluorescent lines, squares and circles, wherever needed. Chronicles. Chronicles. It was a word even crunchier than necromancy and he'd ranked them in order of their relevance to the historical action, under eight alphabetical headings:

A) Jean Creton, French: his was a rhyming song, or maybe a poem. First-person testimony from someone who had been with Richard II as one of his few companions at the end, been captured with him, then expelled from the country. It was vivid, emotional, heartfelt. Damian had felt ripped-off when charged £20 for a digital version by Cambridge University Press.

B) Adam of Usk, Welsh: he'd been involved on Henry's side at a high level, then crossed someone and gone into exile, returning to a somewhat diminished status some 10 years later. Nice old book. Extremely interesting testimony.

These two had been directly involved. Top class witnesses.

C) The Monk of St Denis. French. Written early, before 1412. 'Chronique de la Traïson et Mort de Richart II.' Print-on-demand. Reasonable cost. Surprisingly good production values for a one-off.

D) and E) Thomas Walsingham chronicle and the Chronicle of St Albans. Both were English and from the same place, maybe versions of each other. The Thomas Walsingham one might be the work of many hands. There was some confusion here; D) might be a summary of E), but they both came from the Benedictine abbey at St Albans in any case. One was a glossy modern edition with commentary and the other was a digital copy of an old one.

F) Sir Jean Froissart, French: Book 4 of his gargantuan record of European history from 1326 to 1400. This was going to be the most important. It was so obviously a masterpiece. Dolmetscher had signposted a version in French by Alberto Varvaro but clever Damian had found a version in English from an earlier translator which was more or less the same and this translation by Thomas Johnes was a lovely two-book set, though old and fragile. The Alberto Varvaro one was downloaded for a mere 4 Euros, a snip.

Then came some oddities:

G) John Hardyng's chronicle. English and only interesting for a later insertion and:

H) Two long songs, or poems: 'Richard the Redeless', about what a bad king Richard was, and 'Mumm the Soothsegger' about the virtues of speaking truth to power, both glossy and pricey, and as it turned out, of little use. But they added colour to the quest.

Damian hadn't needed to use his insightful breakthrough or his dark-matter detector machine as the missing politics were obvious. Before coming across the full English translation of Froissart's Book 4, he had mis-purchased several other Froissart editions, and there had been plenty to choose from. None was as good as the Penguin Classics version, but that version was itself rubbish. Damian had used a section of unused storage racking in the workroom to make a little library of his own. He had the Penguin Froissart edition stood between the two-volumes of Thomas Johnes' translation. Even the most cursory scrutiny could not fail to find the fault because you only had to look at the books as they stood side-by-side. The Penguin was 3 inches shorter, 2 inches less deep and some 4 inches less wide. Put your white lab-coat on Damian and make a calculation.

Volume of Johnes: cm (17x25x11.2) = 4760cm^3.
Volume of Penguin: cm (11x18x1.7)   = 336cm^3.

Some deft calculation. We can say that one two-book Johnes is equal to 13 Penguins and not quibble about it. The Penguin was also less dense in terms of word count; it had 12-13 words per line with 38 lines on a whole page. Let's say 500 words a page. Johnes had 17 words a line: 50 lines per page, giving 850 words per page in total.

Assuming a correlation between the respective word densities and their number of pages then, even allowing them the same number of words per page, which they don't have, there is a significant difference in word-mass between the two. Damian compared the pages in the Penguin which were directly concerned only with the doings of Richard II and Henry IV, to those first in Alberto, then to Johnes. The Penguin exhibited two classes of inadequacy: gaps and summaries.

The conclusion? For the period under examination, and that period further confined to matters pertaining only to England, the Penguin Classics was missing at least 30,000 words of the original Froissart. This was historical forensics at its most visceral. There was no need to even read the books to see that English History had based its verdict on a truncated evidence base. The Johnes-Varvaro version of Froissart was unabridged, was little known, and told a different story.

He wouldn't bother Clare with his preliminary findings. Clare's project had taken a noisy turn as she made wooden shapes, frames and forms, all of which needed sawing, cutting, nailing and cursing. This wasn't her favourite part, and Damian had been obliged to bale out of the studio in the morning, landing on the kitchen table. She'd been delighted to hear he was off on a jolly with Dolmetscher and asked him to ask about Bloch. He'd wait for a calmer time when she was less busy.

19

Three-quarters of an hour into their journey and Dolmetscher was still pointing out passing features of interest accompanied by a constant descriptive monologue whilst Damian, obedient to the instruction not to distract him by talking, moved his head this way and that to pick out the designated landmarks – involuntary 'uhs', 'ahs and 'ohs' slipping unbidden from his lips at irregular intervals.

It wasn't disagreeable to have an on-board tour guide, but Damian would rather have listened to the radio and taken in the constantly unscrolling landscape as a passive pleasure rather than play the ventriloquist's doll in the front passenger seat. He wondered if this was a conditioning protocol to soften him up for a mind-bending set-piece ahead.

'And that's where Tolkien got his idea for Saruman from,' Dolmetscher indicating Raglan castle's Yellow Tower of Gwent with a wave as they passed, 'somebody made infernal machines in there, or so they said. Mid-seventeenth century. Actually, he was only working with steam engines. Not making orcs. We've just come this way for me to show you. We'll turn around and go back up this road. There's a nicer way of getting there. It's the old road.'

Damian also delighted in finding old roads to travel along and looked forward to the diversion. It was tempting to ask where they were going but it didn't feel like quite the right moment, and Dolmetscher had been firm about not talking on the trip. He'd also seemed a bit on edge when he'd arrived to collect him, almost snappy when he'd told him to get his Phial with the Philtre, and it had been very much Damian's pleasure to pull it out from beneath his collar to show he had it with 'na na na-na na' unsaid, but heavily implied.

Harry-Dan's car was the old Volvo beloved of antique-dealers with homely green bodywork and a rather plush but understated interior. The colour-scheme didn't fit his aesthetic, Harry-Dan explained, especially that of the cockpit decor, called 'knäck' in Swedish, meaning butterscotch, but he'd got it for nothing some years ago and it was reliable. It was indeed completely knäckered throughout even though it never broke down, Damian thought, squirrelling the witticism away for a suitable future deployment. He'd tried a practical joke and flicked on the heater in Dolmetscher's seat to surprise him, but apparently it didn't work, although his own did, and wouldn't turn off.

The view from the old road was glorious. It ran along a ridgeway affording views to either side across many tree-scurfed miles. A 'Nearly there,' brought a 'Where?' from Damian, but no reply from the driver as he hunched over the wheel, brows furrowed, the tip of his tongue sticking out from the corner of his mouth and drove them through a small town and into a gravelly hotel carpark. Dolmetscher's triumphant: 'We're here!' brought no comment from Damian as he'd seen the town's name on a sign on the way in. It was Usk. This contrived destination had to be something about the chronicler Adam of Usk. 'We'll leave our bags in the car for now. We're on schedule. Let's go!'

Damian was hardly out of the door, having trouble closing it, a dodgy catch or something sticking in the lock mechanism, and Dolmetscher was already away at an unfeasibly fast pace. Damian managed to catch up but was always falling behind as they strode purposefully down the narrow pavements. The physical exercise progressively refreshed his lingering car-coma and, by the time they got to the church door, he was fully revived. Dolmetscher pushed open the heavy door and led the way into the Romanesque interior, steering Damian towards, then through, a gaudily-painted rood-screen to just past a dark open-work wooden partition carved into gothic arches and roundels, which didn't look that old, a nineteenth-century restoration perhaps?

'Here's Adam.' Damian looked around for an effigy, tomb or some kind of memorial but saw nothing.

'Where?'

'There.' Dolmetscher jabbed his short index-finger to point out a long and narrow golden metallic plaque covered in an inscribed rune-like script fixed at head height on the back of the partition.

'Vikings this far from the coast?' Damian felt the need to try and be clever.

'Damian, Damian, Damian. Not at all. Not at all.'

Dolmetscher had wound down and Damian sensed things were being set up. 'It's old Welsh, not the oldest, that would be the Cadfan stone of course, but very old nonetheless, and in brass. It's fifteenth century. 1430 or just after.'

'Not runes then?'

'No,' Damian was being typically slow on the uptake.

'In English?'

'I've just told you, it's Welsh, but the same alphabet, nearly. It's old Welsh, let me translate it for you: *There was fame, and now the tomb. Rest in peace, wise man and judge. Sleep here Adam of Usk. In a place of learning.'*

'That's nice.'

'Now, in case you are a scholar of old Welsh, I admit that I have slightly paraphrased what it really says, but you have to imagine that this is a high-culture invocation using lyrical tropes and figures from an ancient oral tradition, so to replicate it, I've had to bend it a bit, which is the art of true translation, I think.' Dolmetscher had applied Alberto Varvaro's oft quoted 'It's not one word for one word, it's one idea for one idea', commonly distilled as the maxim: 'Aye for Aye, not one for one', which could be expressed somewhat humorously as $i \ 4 \ i \neq I \ 4 \ I$, and thought he'd done it well.

'Well I have read his book in case you think I've been sitting on my hands.'

'You're not the dilatory sort. I'm glad you've been busy. Adam of Usk is the only English source worth talking to..., I mean Welsh of course.' Damian's face flushed. He hoped the subdued lighting would cover up the giveaway adrenal response. Did Dolmetscher know about his tomb effigies? Was he testing him?

'Yes, I enjoyed reading him.'

'Damian, I don't mean reading, I mean talking. Communicating. The words are just an interface, an interlanguage between two minds, two strangers.' Damian prayed he wouldn't hear an antique voice: 'Hello, I'm glad you've come. I've been waiting soooooo long for you.' Queasy wasn't the word.

'Damian!' Harry-Dan clicked his fingers, 'Back in the room!' and explained further. Adam of Usk had bequeathed his book to this church along with the inscribed metal bar, technically a tropar, and some other stuff, like a song book, and some clothes. It actually listed them in the chronicle itself. His chronicle had gone missing, probably pinched from the church in the Reformation, when this church had been a Benedictine priory for nuns, and been lost for more than 400 years, until it was rediscovered in the late nineteenth century hiding in the British Library.

His real name was Thomas Adams, or Thomas ap Adams, but he'd got his new name when studying at Oxford to differentiate him from others with the same name. Dolmetscher thought Adam's book the most interesting of the period because it was written for nobody. It was a secret journal for an unknown future audience. Like a time-capsule, or when they put a coin under a foundation stone. Or like his own silly prancings in Paris, which he didn't mention. It was superbly intimate.

'He must have been a very clever boy to get picked out for Oxford, a mind like a human computer. You had to know everything and get tested on it in disputations.'

'Sounds demanding, maybe he had a photographic memory?' Damian had come across a student who could memorise anything just by reading it once.'

'To get on in those days, through Oxford, you probably needed one. He was heading to be a bishop, but his Welshness, and his patron being the Earl of March, counted against him in the end.' Damian didn't need to ask why:

First count: a year after Henry IV took power, Owen Glendower raised his Welsh supporters in rebellion against him in a bitter 15-year fight. Glendower lost in the end, disappearing into the mountain mists, but outlived his enemy — being Welsh in the early 1400's made you very suspect.

Second count: Adam's patron, the third Earl of March provided royal descendants in a more senior line than Henry's, technically outranking him. Adam's career was blighted by a double whammy. Suspiciously Welsh and from a dodgy possibly disloyal background.

Harry-Dan continued his exposé. Modern historians seemed to look down their noses at Adam, and the other chroniclers. He was written off as 'unliterary', or disparaged as a 'Lancastrian apologist', which he certainly wasn't. He was another victim as much as anything. Professors tied themselves in knots over his book, analysing the chronicle into incomprehension, but it was really much easier than that. It was all there. But you had to play the game to understand it, and the game was….'

'Dark matter!' Dolmetscher was taken aback.

'Dark matter?'

'Yes, the space between the stars. That's where the universe really is. Where there's nothing. 97% of it all is nothing.'

Damian's pet theory was evidence of an uncharacteristic perception. Damian was a good student, dogged, persistent, but not given to perspicacious flashes like this. 'Dark matter'; the expression reminded him of something Varvaro sometimes said when he described the work of a historian, a word he used…, a French word…, it would come back.

'Yes, if you like. There are words on the page. We infer meanings from them, and what is meant lies between. Hidden meanings. It's a very medieval way of thinking. They were very comfortable with abstract notions, a bit like our modern physicists. Clever clogs who came later liked to look down on them as benighted, almost wilfully ignorant and blind to the empirical evidence offered by the world they lived in. They mocked them as scholastic dullards trying to calculate how many angels you could get on a pinhead. That was made up. They never did that. They would, however, debate as to whether two angels could occupy the same space, and that's an entirely higher level of speculation. They would have been able to understand Shrödinger's cat and all the rest of it quite easily.'

'That's very interesting. Like I said, I read it. I enjoyed it.'

'What I'd like for you to do is to really get to know him, and start talking to him, push him with your clever modern rhetoric and your sophisticated concepts. Can you do that for me?'

'Yes I can.'

'Do you think it's time for lunch?'

'Yes I do.'

20

After getting back to the car, putting their overnight luggage into their rooms and picking up a weighty kit-bag from the hotel reception, Damian Email followed his mentor, their picnic slung over his shoulder, through the small town's streets, to the gateway of Usk's crumbling castle, a matter of only a few minutes.

They walked up through the enchantingly gothic entrance and past the carefully chosen plantings of many years which had turned the former fortress into a delightful garden; swathes of late-flowering shrubs slashing through faded end-of-summer leftovers with strong blues, deep reds and yellowed ochres, dressing its ramparts in plaids of tartan. Had an eccentric garden designer calculated the precise aesthetic effect of these ill-disciplined herbaceous groupings and predicted their charm in the low-angled sunlight, tangled with cobwebs, buzzed by the last bees and perfumed in earthy vegetal musk, to create the acute multi-sensory impact of this very moment? Damian was numb with awe in this perfect place.

Dolmetscher headed for a particular spot in the grassy courtyard where he knew the sun would stay while dark shadows of broken towers, ruinous walls and slighted chambers moved around them, where the stones were dry and warming, where they could unpack, have lunch, and talk.

'This'll do us I think.' He took the bag from Damian and withdrew the contents: two foil-wrapped packages, flask, bottles, putting them down in the enclave at the base of a rounded outwork, and indicated they use the stones of the tumbledown masonry as impromptu benches. They sat down with a satisfied double – 'ahh', which Dolmetscher trumped with a jubilantly expressive: 'Ehhh my yay!', prompting Damian to echo him with:

'Yay!'

The word that had eluded Dolmetscher in the church had just fluttered past and he'd netted it. That could be a good place to start.

'Ehhh my yay. It's a word.'

'A. My. A. Three words, surely?'

'It's French.' He spelt it out for Damian – *Émailler* – 'I had a teacher who used it, Professor Varvaro. It's like your name. Means 'to enamel' in French.'

'This is a lovely place.'

'Yes it is…, it is…, I was thinking about your dark matter. Alberto meant the same thing, I think. *Émailler*, it's from the *cloisonné* enamelling technique.'

'Clare can do that. I think that's going to be her next thing once she's finished the glass job. What's special about it?' Damian thought he knew all there was to know about his last name. They'd already talked about it at their meeting in the pub when they'd first got to know each other. Dolmetscher had told him what his own meant as well: Dolmetscher – a sort of translator.

'Ummm…, I'm not exactly sure how you do it, but it's using gold wire to create patterns and the enamel powder goes in the gaps, gets fired in a kiln which melts it, and you get a nice pretty result.'

'I mean about my name.'

'It's..., it's..., it's about the picture being made of the gaps, where the enamel goes. In the gaps....The gaps is where the picture goes.... It's not about the gold. It's more than joining the dots. More than connecting. More like colouring in. Alberto said that was his job, to *émailler*.'

'I see what you mean, very interesting. Your motto used to be, 'Only connect!' so now it's 'Only colour in!' I suppose?'

'Connecting is fine for the first level, but there's a higher one.'

'Oh, I see. What's for lunch?'

'Ah well, we have the correct lunch for this place, have you heard of Belgian beer?'

'I have.'

'Do you know what goes best with it?'

'I do.'

'Both are at hand!' A sweep of the arm introduced the assembled refreshments. 'You did extremely well with your diatribe Damian. We're proud of you.'

'Thanks, I liked doing it, but now I want to move on.'

'Just what we like to hear. Have you any thoughts?' A quick division of the be-foiled chicken and tarragon rolls, the 'pschittt' of tops coming off, then chewing and thirsty draughts of strong beer taken straight from the bottle punctuated their conversation with sundry sound effects.

'I've got the main points. One, Henry: why was he exceptional? Two, politics, that's about peace and war. Three is the importance of it all, maybe how the carrying on of the war with France doomed them to civil war and what that meant for the monarchy up to Henry VII, or Henry VIII, maybe beyond, I'm not sure.' Damian had surprised himself. Number 3 seemed to have sorted itself out without him having to think about it.

'Well that certainly seems to be coming on really well. What's it going to be, a book?' Damian didn't like this idea at all. He could see pitfalls.

'Nah…, well maybe…, or something else.' Dolmetscher was up for the unconventional and blew on the embers.

'I like that. I like it a lot. Something else! Why not? Something arty? Something in glass with Clare?'

The idea appealed to Damian for a moment, but no, it was an unsuitable medium.

'Definitely not glass. Maybe pottery…, something in clay.' There was that ceramic artist on the telly who made sociological investigations and put his findings on his pots. He made carpets too, but that wasn't a discipline that interested Damian. And there'd been a stand-up comic who'd performed whilst sitting behind a potter's wheel making something. Maybe that could be the basis for a refreshed diatribe routine. He could maybe find a way of using enamel – 'Potting the Past with Damian Email's Enamellings?' But he and Clare were too intimate. Allowing her the space to collaborate with him would compromise his historical integrity which could turn out to be a problem.

'And not ceramics either, no, not glass or ceramics, something else. I'm working on it.'

That was enough for Dolmetscher. It was time to slow things down and enjoy the moment.

'Adam of Usk met some Indians from Kerala you know, when he was in Rome, devotees of St Thomas of India.'

'Hmm, wow…,' Damian had read that, but Harry-Dan giving it prominence by mentioning the anecdote out loud made it seem more interesting, 'Kerala in southern India?'

'Yes, doubting Thomas the apostle…, he went there, died there.' They were both a roll and a bottle in. Dolmetscher divvied out the same again, which they enjoyed more slowly. 'And he tells a funny story about the origin of the kilt you know.'

Dolmetscher retold the anecdote in infinite detail for 20 minutes with plentiful digressions, a summary being that the Scots were originally living in Egypt, but had been forced to leave when Moses brought the plagues, so they had to go to Spain where they did something naughty and the King punished them by cutting off the front half of their trousers, and then they did something else, and the king cut the back part of their trousers off, leaving them bare-legged.

Only two bottles down and it was still possible for them to safely explore the meandering paths and walkways which riddled the herby mountain of tottering red stones. They threaded their way along the uncertain tracks with Harry-Dan again providing a commentary. From one side an empty casement offered a panorama across the town and river to the South; the town had been ravaged and burnt to the ground by an army of Owen Glendower.

'You know, from up here, don't those headstones in St Mary's churchyard look like a socially distanced open-air-festival crowd?'

From another direction, from another vantage point, they looked across to another more pastoral battlefield where maybe the same fireraisers had come back for another fight but this time a superior force surprised them by pouring out of the castle and the would-be attackers were beaten. 300 of them were captured, then killed, right there, by that pond.

'I can't actually see it.'

'It's behind that big tree.' Dolmetscher led the way back to their lunch base to round things off. 'Anyway, there's no need to rush into things. Take your time and let me know what you decide will be the format for your new explorings. Right now it's time for…, do you remember?'

'Hypocras, surely?'

'Absolutely.' Harry-Dan poured from the flask into its two integral, detachable beakers and served the delectable cider and gin finisher. 'Any interest in Bloch?'

Damian had plenty to think about and Bloch was a hot potato. He'd end up messing it up and letting Clare down. And it was difficult. How did you start to communicate with the United Nations? Did they have MPs you could write to? He didn't think so. It would be a long slog.

'No.'

'Let's toast your new thing with the unbeatable Butts Bank hypocrastic digestif. Here's to Hubert Butt, its inventor!'

'To Hubert Butt!'

'All the way down!'

'All the way down!'

The deliciously unlikely cider and gin combination locked up their lunch perfectly and encouraged the most mellifluous sensations of contentment, despite its name.

'One more?'

'Absolutely!'

They chatted a bit, they smoked a bit, and then snoozed where they sat, resting their heads against the warm rocks, sunbathing, digesting, until Dolmetscher called 'Time' after twenty minutes and they dozily packed up their things and returned to the hotel; Dolmetscher to attend to some unspecified business, and Damian to occupy himself until they met up again in the early evening. Filling a couple of hours of enforced idleness with only a rural life museum, a couple of bookstores, some second-hand shops and a riverside café was as mother's milk to Damian, and he was back in his room watching television just a quarter of an hour before the allotted time. Going down early not to be late, he found his mentor reading at the bar in front of pretentious yet indifferent hotel coffee.

'Hello, have fun in Usk?'

'Yes thanks...,' Damian was intending to give Dolmetscher a bit of a run-through on some of the town's contributions to agriculture, especially the improvements to the sanitary conditions in milking parlours, and the consequent benefits to quality-control in the local cheese-making industry, but was interrupted.

'Now tonight you and I have business to attend to – a visitor will be joining us. A certain Mr Pinchman.' Damian had certainly heard of the famously opinionated historian beloved by ambitious TV producers for having a contrarian view on every subject within and outwith his field of expertise. He was also infamous as having been expelled from the Autodidactiiae society for unrepentant pedantry, to wit: his refusal to accept the mismatched masculine and feminine Latin plurals folded into the name of the society, the '*ii*' and the '*ae*' in *Autodidactiiae*. 'Expelled to the outer reaches' was the expression Harry-Dan had used when Damian had last heard Pinchman's name mentioned. What was he doing here?

21

'What's he coming here for?'

'There's a question of his readmittance. The two of us make a quorum. We can do it over dinner. Let's have a pint and decide.'

'Decide about what?'

'About having another one before he gets here.'

Harry-Dan expounded on the bothersome subject over the beers. Damian could see his point and went along with it; expulsion was not a word which sat well with the society's ethos of toleration in which redemption was always a possibility and all could be forgiven. There was just one caveat. The errant pedant had to say that they wished to re-join the Autodidactiiae; that is, the expellee had to pronounce the word 'Autodidactiiae' correctly, in full, with particular emphasis on the final three syllables: the 'ee…. ee…. aye. They also had to give a presentation and say 'I, autodidact' at the end of it to complete their candidature and be formally readmitted. Damian recalled the critical moment at the end of his diatribe. He'd nearly forgotten to say the closing words at his induction in all the excitement and Harry-Dan had had to remind him.

Something else was bothersome to Dolmetscher. Was his mentee more attached to Bloch than he let on? He would have to be utterly dissuaded from any lingering attachments to it, if there were any, and he couldn't take it for granted that there weren't. Damian was, he knew, over-familiar with the works of Tolkien, perhaps that could offer a helpful and indirect way of touching on the matter.

'And…, on top of the formalities, there's another thing. You know the Macguffin in The Lord of the Ring?' Damian's face betrayed no comprehension.

'The Macguffin?'

'The ring…, what it's all about, you know how it corrupts those who…, who have anything to do with it? Well…, I want Pinchman to be the ring-bearer.' Harry-Dan, the better to avoid misunderstanding, then clarified the parallel.

'Actually, I want him to be the Bloch-bearer and he's coming here tonight.' Damian looked stunned but was in fact extremely relieved. For an instant he had thought he was going to be designated as the chosen one.

'Does that make you Gandalf then?'

'Damian, your flippancy is unbecoming,' said the elder man with a comic sigh and an exaggerated and rueful shake of the head, happy that Damian's joke evinced no obvious further interest, and he went on sketching out his plan.

There was, in his opinion, only one person who had an ego sufficiently bloated to not only resist the dark power of the Bloch dossier, which had proved the ruin of more than one good person already, but who could even control it, take it forward, and that was Oliver Pinchman, the contrarian pedant and professional pain in the neck. He'd cleared it, in principle, with Clare, just this afternoon; the documents would be copied, Pinchman to receive facsimiles, originals to be returned.

The barman received a message from the young receptionist; their guest had arrived and was in the lobby, should he take him through? They would go to meet him. Damian later recalled how right he'd been to think he would be anxious in the physical presence of the demon. The memory of taking

the few steps from the bar to the lobby was indelible. It was
the last time when he could say, if asked, that no, he hadn't met
Pinchman, and it was to be a long-cherished memory.

The man himself was unprepossessing to the extreme and
proof positive that ascribing character to physical features was
no more than a much clichéd literary conceit. Could those lips
be described as sardonic? Were the eyes sarcastic? Were the
ears contemptuous?

No, no, and no.   But, but, and but....

'Mr Pinchman, this is Mr Email…,' they all shook hands, 'shall
we go through?' and their host led the way into a nearby
private room used for regular meetings of Rotarians and
other worthies, judging from the assorted lists of tenures and
achievements recorded in gold leaf on framed oak boards
which lined its dark faux-gothic panelling, and across the
handsomely patterned carpet to the corner in which their
table, laid formally with crisp starched linen and silver service,
awaited. A brief shuffling of seating positions, chairs and napkins
was brought to a close with Pinchman's first insult.

'So this is your new protégée Dolmetscher, your *'mannequin
de la maison'*. What's his background?'

This piqued Damian in fourteen different ways although
it was only the overture, almost kindly in retrospect, to a
relentless display of condescending disparagement usually, but
not always, disguised in the dissembling mock-bonhomie of
Oxbridge high-table dinner talk.

Pinchman's reputation for bumptious obnoxiousness was
well-deserved. He was the exemplarissimo of unpleasantness
and poured forth a cavalcade of sleights, provocations, and
rudeness's which marched past in a never-ending carnival

parade of affrontery the entire evening, Damian and Harry-Dan having to take their salutes as they went by. Damian wasn't the only subject of his scorn. The list was endless: the Autodidactiiae in general, Pinchman's colleagues, particularly the provost of his college, his many rivals throughout the world, the food when it came, how it was served, and, of course, the wine, which occupied his sneering for a considerable time. Nothing was said that wasn't a put down, sneer or gobbet of hurtful gossip.

Never had Damian's ability to achieve a waking state of suspended animation served him so well as it did now and he thanked God for giving thanatosis to the world, and to him. Despite having to field the rare enquiries that came directly his way, such as his reply to a question about his academic background, which brought the response that it was probably a good thing that those whose skills and abilities were less certain could get a worms-eye view before deciding whether they were cut out to face the challenges of uncertain progression, Damian managed to maintain his distance. Whatever it took to attenuate the torture, he would do; eating very slowly, taking extremely small sips of wine, examining every detail of the table, even occasionally holding his breath, knowing that he could do it for at least 45 seconds without giving himself away by turning red, and leave him 45 seconds nearer to the end.

Damian heard Dolmetscher saying: 'And now Mr Pinchman, the time has come,' at some point, but couldn't remember exactly when it had happened. Pinchman's lips had moved, and Harry-Dan had looked at Damian and given a slight nod which must have been to signal his own assent and check it with Damian. Damian was too inert to move, but he must have nodded back, as apparently Pinchman had got himself back in by saying 'Autodidactiiae', though he'd heard nothing.

Pinchman's presentation was the final agony. It must have lasted only an hour and a half, but it felt like five. Damian regretted being too bourgeois to hide under the table, tuck himself into a ball, clasp his knees in his arms, and count off the time remaining like a pendulum by moaning and rocking himself to and fro. It would have been the natural response. How had he managed to get through it without his heart slowing, then stopping, and seeing, consciousness fading, his own tortured soul tearing itself from his body in tattered ectoplasmic sheets to seek sanctuary elsewhere?

Every word of Pinchman's 'I, autodidact' discourse seemed cruelly and deliberately tedious as if the speaker had been trained by unfriendly 'black-op' agencies in how to humble western democracies by paralysing their intelligentsias with boredom and pedantry. The subject chosen was his college's world-famously ancient library with nothing left out; its construction, carpentry, the costs of repairs, names and biographies of successive librarians, infestations and classification systems: arcane, modern, and several in-between. At no point was an actual book mentioned.

There must have been an end to it. Pinchman must have said 'I, autodidact' sometime, and Dolmetscher must have nodded and looked to Damian for assent as before, and Damian must have nodded back. But like a boxer coming round after a prolonged and vigorous battering, the details of each punch were beyond recall, though he knew when it was definitely over as the pain had stopped. There was no hypocrastic ending to this meal. No jovial cider and gin Butts Bank toasts. Damian would have liked to baptise Pinchman into the society by throwing his drink at him, as he had been, but more forcefully, maybe several times, right in his pedantic face. But such baptism was not, it seemed, required if an errant historian had exercised free will and returned voluntarily to the bosom of the Autodidactiiae.

Eventually a taxi arrived to take Pinchman away. Damian imaginated an armoured car containing a Special Weapons And Tactics team – Pinchman's cover was blown and his arrest was imminent but the man was still slagging off to left and right as he fussed with his coat. Damian became over-helpful, trying not to appear eager in case Pinchman recognised it for what it was and stayed on out of spite, which he surely would have done. Then Pinchman left, back to his who knows what. The conversation had never got around to such small and common pleasantries as to finding out where he was staying. A rocky hole in a dripping cave probably. Who cared? He was gone.

Dolmetscher was Gandalf the Florid no longer but transmogrified by the epic encounter into Gandalf the Grey and looked exhausted. Damian worried that he'd been too passive. He'd let Harry-Dan bear the brunt. But Dolmetscher thanked Damian for going through it with him and apologised if it had been too much of an ordeal, which Damian assured him it hadn't.

Wordlessly, they made their way back through to the bar, back to 'the world' where carefree groups of unconcerned drinkers were happily enjoying themselves, oblivious, and through it to the stairs. Damian felt he ought to take some of the weight off Dolmetscher by putting his arm around him, but couldn't bring himself to do it, to guide his guide, and they mounted each step carefully and slowly, one-by-one, almost counting them off, Dolmetscher lagging behind and hanging on the banister all the way. They paused on the small landing where the stairs made a right-angled turn. Damian pictured Dolmetscher asking for a grenade, a revolver and some ammo; he would stay behind and make his last stand, there on the landing, against the possibility of Pinchman returning. Dolmetscher got his breath back and they made it to their adjoining rooms where they both fumbled with their cumbersomely-fobbed keys in the unfamiliar locks.

'Damo, thanks for being there.' His voice was low. He looked old, 'You've passed the final test. You don't need me anymore.'

'Is this goodbye?'

'Yes it is. It is…, until breakfast. Let's make it a late one, eh?

'Ok, see you then. G'night.'

'G'night.'

22

Bad dreams in lurid technicolour gave both men a sweating and fitful night's sleep as their respective subconsciousness's responded to the torments they'd endured. Neither intended to be terse or sullen but fatigue and their undermined morale banished all conviviality. They breakfasted together in near silence against a sound-track of percussive cutlery and the restrained hubbub coming from the other tables. Each took a cup of heavily sugared black coffee and a cigarette into the hotel garden when they'd finished. There, the kindly nurse of Time might change their dressings and maybe eventually discharge them. The reviving chill of the dank morning air was as a spoonful of brandy to an infantryman after a perilous and exhausting retreat. They began to regroup – new notions and possibilities began forming; they had survived after all.

Damian had the idea of enticing Clare onto the back of his scooter and obtained the keys to Dolmetscher's new headquarters, where it was garaged. Harry-Dan thought of changing his mind about the whole Pinchman thing and taking Damian straight back in his car, via his office to get the scooter if necessary, but no, he would carry on. Was he now the Pinchman-bearer? It would be too ironic. Their separate destinies awaited. The fellowship had to divide; Dolmetscher to the photocopy shop to collect his Bloch-Dunny facsimiles; they could be dropped off chez Pinchman with a covering note, no need to meet him again, and Damian was going back to Clare's by taxi, train and taxi. No, taxi, train and scooter.

His train was modern in that the seats were cramped and set too close to the one in front. Long-distance train journeys had been real adventures when he'd been a student, like a crowded troop ship carrying motley characters through the dark. It felt special. There'd been a gangway corridor connecting the compartments, like you see in old films, and he'd often sat on his luggage there, or stood in the space where the carriages connected if there were no seats left in the cabins. Damian loved those old films, those old train journeys, but in this one all you could do was look at the purple swirls on the back of the seat in front or close your eyes.

Patchouli, he could smell patchouli. But it was faint. Not hippy and pungent, more a dusky blackcurrant. It was the bass note to…, a beigey vanilla enrobed in spicy sandalwood with…, trilling flutes and dancing violas, there was jasmine…, and bergamot! Chanel No 5, no question. Opposite him in the compartment were two well-dressed ladies, one asleep, her head resting on a folded coat against the window, the other reading a magazine. You were allowed to make pleasant small talk in such situations but weren't compelled to. He was tired but, as he didn't want to be watched whilst sleeping, he took out his red Moroccan-bound notebook to try and capture what he'd been through on paper, as a reminder when he saw Clare, and work up some ideas for his new thing.

'Are your ears made of cloth young man? I asked if you were a writer?' She'd been talking to him, not to her sleeping companion. He'd heard 'Are you alright dear?'

'Umm…, no…, no. I'm a historian.'

'Oh, that's wonderful! I'm so glad you're not a writer. They always want advice on how to get on. I wanted to be a historian but..., you know how it is..., one compromises, one has to work..., next thing I knew, I was a writer.' Her laugh at an in-joke known to only one of them was inviting and promised a classic conversation between strangers on trains, which are generally pleasant, if not always welcome.

'A writer?'

'Ooh yesss,' she was decidedly Scottish, 'I'm quite well known actually. I'm Elizabeth Mackintosh, how do you do?' Damian received her small hand and shook it. Her grip was resolute and not in keeping with her small frame, long face, strong nose, and purposeful dark Spanish eyes.

'I'm Damian Email, how do you do?' She obviously didn't get out much as she gushed like floodwater overspilling a weir. Elizabeth was on her annual trip to London with her agent, who'd been up to stay with her in her native Inverness. She was so excited to go to the capital and had been looking forward to it for months. It wasn't a new outfit, she would get new ones made for her there, and they'd last the year, until she came back for a new set next year. Damian could see she was thrilled to be going down to 'town', as she called it, and that she was relishing the chance to warm up for it by chatting to him.

Either she, or he, must be on the wrong train, but to point that out seemed an unnecessarily clumsy interruption. Maybe he'd mention it at the next stop, sort it out there. She offered him a cigarette from a small packet concealed in a brocade purse, took one herself and Damian lit both. Smoke rose up towards the ceiling in silver-grey arabesques which swirled and gathered in the electric light, her sleeping friend propping up her makeshift cushion on the window to barricade it against the fleeting ghosts of trees. Elizabeth Mackintosh had said all she wanted to about herself and became interested in him, asking what he was toying with in his notebook.

'It's something about Richard II and Henry IV.' She became instantly animated, and he feared she would reach over and pinch his cheek, with a 'Ma wee laddie!' thrown in.

'Richard the Second! Richard the second, you say! I wrote a play on the very same subject twenty years ago, but it feels like yesterday, what fun we had...,' and she went on to describe the thrill of getting her smash West End hit staged with a quality cast led by John Gielgud, followed by a full provincial tour, and then on to Broadway. There was nothing like theatre, she loved it and had loved seeing her name in lights under its title 'Richard of Bordeaux'. Damian had been taking a polite interest in their largely one-way dialogue but now he was properly attentive; that was the name of the show that Inspector Grant had claimed to have seen five times at the start of The Daughter of Time. Five times he'd seen it! It must have been good.

'Two Richards made my fortune. It's all going to the National Trust when I'm gone. Not too soon I hope.' This seemed very intimate. Damian didn't like talking about money. You either had it, or used a credit card, and he went back in:

'Two Richards?'

'Richard of Bordeaux, Richard II, and Richard III, two Richards, yes.' Confused, Damian had to probe:

'So you wrote...,'

'Yes, I'm the author of the new one on Richard the Third. I call it 'The Daughter of Time.' My publisher wanted a more obvious title like 'Not Too Late For Justice!' but I stuck to my guns. It's already out. I'm doing a signing spree in London first and then there's a couple of literary festivals after. I can extend my holiday and drop in on friends on the way back to Inverness.'

'You're Josephine Tey? I've read it. I liked it.'

'Heesh! That's just a pen name. Thank you. I'm also Gordon Daviot by the way. It depends on what I'm writing about.'

'Could you give me some tips on being a writer…, writing about history I mean?' Miss Mackintosh gave Damian a masterclass in how to write about history her way. It had to be set in the present. A historical wrong needs to be uncovered and righted, not unlike a conventional crime novel. The principal character has to have a genuine reason for doing it. She'd been lucky; she had an off-the shelf detective she could use. Her hero only needed to be in a position of enforced idleness, that's Act 1 when the main character doesn't know they're in a story, and then they're prompted to action by an inciting incident in Act 2.

This intrigued Damian and he asked about 'face reading'; the way Inspector Grant is put on the trail after seeing a painting of Richard III – the king's face is too kindly and surely not that of the murderer of the princes in the tower. Yes, that was technically a weakness, but a necessary one. Not everyone spots it. It was a joke. She'd laid crumbs to it at the end of another book of hers. In 'Miss Pym Disposes', Miss Pym, a famous psychologist returns to her old school for a short stay. There is some bad business and some of the schoolgirls are involved. Miss Pym misdiagnoses some of the girls' characters and thinks she'd have been better off looking for clues in their faces.

'Agatha Christie and the rest are always giving it away by face reading and I just wanted to get in on the act, but you know…, ironically, like an in-joke: I don't want characters to be what they look like. It makes them caricatures and people are much more complex than that.'

'Do you think you went a little bit too far getting Grant to despise Sir Thomas More's book on Richard III?'

'My dear boy, Omelettes? Eggs? It's about creating drama. He had to get angry otherwise we'd have no reason to get to the end of the story. There has to be an opponent. There can't be passion without jeopardy in a story, can there? Thomas More had to be set up as the baddie.'

'But Grant says Thomas More should be, and I quote: 'cancelled, deleted'.'

'Maybe I did go too far with that, but Grant had to get his dander up somehow, his sense of justice had to be outraged, and here's another tip…,' They spent the rest of the time talking about her wide-ranging historical interests, how some historians treated people in history as two-dimensional cut-outs or puppets, like those in bad fiction, and yes, in crime novels, to move their stories along to their trite conclusions, and how she liked writing plays best, until the train began its long slow-down to the approaching station. Was the little silver brooch she wore pinned to her well-cut tweed jacket one he recognised?

Damian opened his eyes to see passengers stirring and getting up in advance of their arrival. His self-imposed daydreaming was usually vividly entertaining, and this had been a cracker. Very refreshing indeed. He stretched his shoulder muscles and, adding a last wakening yawn as grace note and full stop, he pulled himself up and out of his seat, and headed for the door at the end of the carriage to be ready to get out when the time came.

23

Walking from the station, jaunty and purposeful, whistling 'Yes
Tonight Josephine' to a rockabilly tune, Damian made his way
past the city-centre's backstreet beige-cream buildings and
out, through its brick-red suburbs, towards the local history
society's new location over the river, some 3 miles away.

Meeting Miss Mackintosh had been most extremely gratifying,
and there'd been nary a tomb, grave or any other memorial
to imply his encounter with her had been anything but the
by-product of a dozing mind. Everything she'd said had been
known to him already. It was no more than a home-made
mental hologram, albeit with useful and illustrative results;
a vividly ruminative mind belch, and nothing more. Nothing
necromantic about it whatsoever. She'd written a play about
Richard II and that was worth thinking about.

Yes tonight,   Jo se   phine, yes tonight,
Yes tonight,   ev ry thing   will be alriii – ight.

Alright!   He was alright. He was a new Damian alright. The
effigy problem was cleared up. It wasn't supernatural. They'd
told him nothing that he couldn't have known or thought out
for himself. Not supernatural, just mental.

I'm alright, I'm alright, yes alright.
I'm alright, I'm alright, yes alriii ..ight!

Was that maybe his distinctive personal power? To imaginate?
Damian saw himself on a couch, maybe more of a day bed,

a divan. It was mid-afternoon. He was tired. There came a disembodied voice, a sonorous non-threatening comforting voice, more suggesting than commanding.

'Use the nap Damian. Let go Damian.'

Could he have a genetic mutation? That would explain why he'd sometimes felt at odds with society. He didn't fit in. Like the X-men. Society didn't understand his gifts because..., because he was…, Napman? The Napman? The Dozer? No! 'They call me Mr Napman.' That was it! This power of his, there had to be restrictions, boundaries. He couldn't do it at will, like right now. Would he have to be napping in some kind of formal sense, rather than dropping off somewhere, casually, like in front of the television or on a bus? You were allowed to nap on trains, and in the afternoon. Society tolerated that, actually condoned it in some sense, but normal sleeping wasn't napping – those four o'clock in the morning revelations didn't mark him out as special because lots of people shared the ability to wrangle with knotty problems in their sleep, but in a proper nap! That's where his power lay. That was different.

Most of his walking meta-revery on the subject of napping had been worked off by the time he got to Dolmetscher's place and it was plain Damian Email esquire who took a few minutes to work the lock on the door and gain access, hoping he didn't come over as a burglar to the workers in the light-industrial business park. The unit's small office-cum-reception area was only big enough to accommodate a handful of standing visitors and a seated employee behind its high counter which made it clear why Harry-Dan's collection of furniture had been put in the larger part of the building, which was, in comparison, cavernous.

Damian went through to inspect Dolmetscher's dispositions. It was all there: the imposing chair, the over-large architect's desk, the old-school telephone, tiered wire trays for correspondence, a carousel of various vintage ink-stamps and the ridiculously large ashtray in an oyster-shell of onyx and blue-layered glass, all hemmed in by several tall metal filing cabinets which half-surrounded the desk, spaced out like standing stones around an altar. Harry-Dan couldn't mind if he sat in his chair. Supremely well-designed in swanky padded leather and chrome, it offered excellent lumbar support and could move in three dimensions. Sitting himself into the high-status seat, he gently swivelled it from left to right.

Adam of Usk, Adam of Usk..., he didn't need to talk to him..., he'd just read his crunchy chronicle again ..., at a time and place..., of his own choosing...,

... the bosses had it easier..., they always got better stuff..., how often had his standing been defined by the chair he'd sat in? ..., the teacher's ones were especially bad..., they never got thrown away...,

... you could only upgrade..., if you had some jammy luck ..., and managed to swap yours ... for some other teacher's chair ..., when they left, before the replacement teacher was any the wiser..., like swapping an evil changeling-baby into an unwatched cradle.

This chair would be easy to wheel out for a full-on high speed 360-degree rotation..., but no, just sit back ..., and take it all in. Over there by the far wall was his beloved scooter. He was looking forward to riding it back to Clare's, maybe they'd go out on it straight away. She didn't have a helmet. Have to get one..., and over there was an unused flip chart on an easel in front of a semi-circle of plastic chairs, made cosier with a small carpet.

Ah yes! The carousel of twelve ink-stamps with the thirteenth, the beguiling 'Erledigt' stamp, in its centre. But it called to him no more. The spell was broken. It was just a relic of a more methodical era in office organisation when paper was paramount, and the progress of each sheet had to be marked with ink stamps to record dates, departments, initials and actions to be taken. 'Erledigt' was the last one. The one stamp to stamp them all. It meant 'completed' in German. A curio. Nice on the mantlepiece maybe. He picked it up to feel the solid varnished handle chased in brass, gripped it, and put it back. It held dominion over him no more. All power gone; it was now just a mute conversation piece to sit next to a stopped Victorian clock above a fireplace.

A thin film of grey dust laminated the black-lacquer desk-top and Damian wanted to write in it but 'Clean me' was too obvious. He drew a horizontal line in it with his finger and waited for a clever or funny idea to come. Light coming through a skylight spotlighted an infinite number of particles in its beam. The air must be full of it. He tilted the chair back with a silver lever and closed his eyes to experiment. Was the timing right? Did he have to say 'Damian use the nap' or would it just come?

He was piloting a fast fighter-bomber low over the North Sea, his navigator to his side and behind, other crack crews were vectoring into the target area from different directions. This was the easy part; a long pre-dawn skim towards the rising sun over wave crests creaming into webby suds on the heaving waters......At the end, there would be anti-aircraft defences, enemy planes might be on the alert and attack. Only a falling mountain could destroy the Nazi nuclear-water factory, and it could only be brought down by getting a bomb, released at exactly the right time as he pulled the nose up to clear the overhanging cliffs, to hit the critical faultline. There was no margin for error. They wouldn't all make it. His standing orders were clear to his comrades. All the cocoa was to be drunk on the way out because they weren't all coming home. Damian pulled back on the lever and the chair returned to the upright position. It had been easy. You didn't have to say the words. Had Mr Napman been at the wheel or was it just an everyday mock-heroic fantasy?

He wanted to get on and left the chair to attend to his scooter. Starting it after finding the key where he'd hidden it disguised in a rag under a half-sack of sand, it came to life noisily at the third attempt. No clichéd 'spluttering into life' here, it roared away and he switched it off. Damian dusted off the seat with the cloth, lifted it up and rummaged in the storage space underneath to find his Swiss army knife, went back with it to the desk and sat down again. There was a tiny magnifying glass amongst its many fold-away tools, and he opened it out to examine the dust on the table. It was mostly dark matter with large white breadcrumbs of dusty precipitate on a background of blackness when you looked closely.

Damian found his helmet, gloves and jacket stored in a bin bag and got ready to move off. The roller shutter looked hard to use so he pushed the scooter out through the door he'd come in by, which wasn't easy. About to lock up behind him, he stopped. He'd almost forgotten. He went back in and sat at the desk again. Using the line he'd drawn in the dust to represent the top of a wall, he fingered in an egg-headed man with a large nose and two little hands. He drew him as if the little man was lifting himself up to peer over the wall. Damian decided not to write 'Kilroy was here' because less was more.

The scoot back to Clare would be fun but he was more interested in seeing her again than the ride back. Hopefully she wasn't miffed because he hadn't called. Hopefully there hadn't been some kind of emergency he didn't know about. They'd have a nice meal together, if everything was normal. He wouldn't tell her all about Pinchman. He couldn't. He wasn't a 'he said, and she said, and he said,' kind of person, but he'd tell her something about it. Maybe he'd say:

'Oh, and we met Pinchman, it was tairsome,' and she'd say:

'Was it awfully tairsome?' He'd come back with:

'It was simply too tairsome.'

'Vair vair tairsome?'

'Terribly tairsome,' and she'd say:

'You poor dear!'

Then he wrote 'Kilroy was here' on the dust on the desk.

24

No 8 was not a smouldering ruin. Clare was unannoyed that he was a communications blackspot when it came to keeping in contact, and he'd been able to impart a lot of detail about his ordeal without having to resort to the tairsome cadences of 1930s anyone-for-tennis farce. Their end of day getting-together and reuniting had been a very happy one and they were not divided.

Standing outside, under the canopy over the back door the next day, he was enjoying chewing the cud over their breakfast's final dose of caffeine and waiting for Clare to call him through to take some photographs of her. It was, as she called it, the 'tipping point', when she would be ready to start the nibbling of assorted coloured glass into the shapes needed to complete the project. Damian felt well prepared too; no longer Damian the New, but New Damian Two, also known as Mister Napman, although Clare was way ahead.

Some elements of his thing still remained to be sorted out. It could be a play like Josephine had done. That came with its own off-the-peg structure. There had to be acts and scenes, and there were conventions to respect. Plus, although it would be all dialogue, there were stagey effects that you could use to move the action forward – but what was the action? It couldn't be the personal tragedy of a deposed king and the liquidation of his friends. Nobody cared about that. Some other theme then..., a better thesis was needed.

There was something momentous in the replacement of

Richard's peace policy by Henry's war policy. It was all in Froissart, and that would be easy to show on stage but..., so what? They would say that a namby-pamby king like him couldn't fight a war anyway, so he didn't have a choice. Modern audiences wouldn't go for it.

The 'So what?' had to be the consequence of this about-turn from Peace to War. Damian girded his mental loins and drum-beated Mars with his lips: buh buh buh, buh buh-buh-buh, buh buh buh, buh buh-buh-buh, duh, duh duh..., duh, dah dah.

Henry brought war with him in his knapsack when he landed at Ravenspurn with his band of merry men and he offered it to the only two earls who supported him, Northumberland and Westmoreland. In Henry's first parliament, Northumberland had to get him to clarify to parliament that immediate war on Scotland was the king's idea and not theirs. On the northern border, without war's money, they were nobodies. Peace had been a pain. War was a moneyspinner. Henry was not good at war. Fighting rebels didn't count. That was internal, and he wasn't popular enough to raise enough money for a proper one. He couldn't even fight off a Welsh-French army who'd pushed 40 miles into England and then encamped themselves for a week 10 miles from Worcester at the battle of Woodbury Hill in 1405.

The War Party had to wait until he was dead and his son, Henry the Fifth, could take over and get them back into the war they were supposed to have. His lucky victory at Agincourt fuelled their appetite. They wanted more glorious victories like that. The French were weak. France was ripe for the plucking. But he dies. His son, Henry the Sixth, is 9-years old and about the same age as Richard II was when he became king, and like him, he has to depend on his uncles. They know that they have to keep fighting or fingers will start to point at the new usurping dynasty, so it's march, march, march to Joan of Arc, and then it's pull back, retreat, and withdraw from then on. England loses everything in France and is a continental power no longer. Only Calais remains, the forlorn souvenir of a 100-year holiday abroad.

And so what? Buh buh buh, buh buh-buh-buh.

Everybody's disappointed. 'Do we have to put up with Henry the Sixth just because his grandad grabbed the crown? Let's find out!' and they put it to the question in the Wars of the Roses, but this time it gets really nasty. Chivalry no more! Monarchy's mystique has gone. Only brute force can support a claimant. Everybody who doesn't win a battle gets killed.

And so what? Buh buh buh, buh buh-buh-buh.

Henry the Seventh comes along. The mafia clans can't take it no more and need a top dog to lid the cauldron of boiling feuds: a *capo di tutti capi* who can chair sit-down meets in hotel backrooms without people getting their guns out. The old monarchy has to be restored. And respected. The gang bosses all agree. He makes the right moves and says the right things. He knows how to play the new game. And so what?

The monarchy is back forever. Henry the Eighth cements it in by liquidating all church lands not run directly by state-appointed bishops and sends new wealth cascading into greedy mouths. He's stuck in sea-locked England. He has no choice but to start a navy. And so what?

The crown is definitely here to stay. Everybody knows who has it, and who gets it next: Henry VIII's ultra-protestant son, great! His daughter Mary: ultra-catholic and a woman? Not a problem! Get her in! Elizabeth, his next daughter, is another woman! Problem gone, there's a precedent and she's very much a safe pair of hands – Elizabeth is very much ok, until she dies…, and No! It can't be! England's new king a foreigner? Their arch-enemy and the long-time ally of France, England's other archenemy, the king of Scotland? Surely not! But yes! Come on down James I because now legitimacy trumps all; nobody wants to take the risk of a disputed succession.

Hang on, is the magical thread broken? His son Charles I loses his crown but it still takes them two and a half years to get round to killing him after he's captured, dithering for fear of what might happen. Oliver Cromwell tries a constitutional experiment which works fine until the manufacturer's warranty expires with the death of its maker, so it's 'Bring back the king!' But he's dead. So it's his son Charles II. Then it's Charles II's brother James II, then James's daughter Mary, then his other daughter Anne. Uh oh, we've run out of legitimate successors! Or have we? The next one in which the magical blood-royal flows is – no Catholics allowed remember – is Annes's second-cousin, the great-grandson of James I, 'Just in from Germany, give a big hand to George I' and there it is, but so what?

Henry IV saved the crown for the 21st century by fatally weakening it in 1399. It took 70 years for his fatal delegitimising of the line-of-descent to play out until Henry VII came in to secure the English monarchy forever with a let's-all-be-friends-again finale. The Lancastrian overthrow of Richard II sabotaged the longed-for peace with France and brought an unnecessary war which condemned England to losing her status as a continental power, which in turn obliged her restless spirits to become first pirates, then naval officers, and find themselves a new role offshore. Hello British Empire!

Damian had trundled his way through the story arc and permitted himself a self-congratulating smile. Was he quite finished? Was the race over, or could he move the finishing tape back a bit and attempt a higher smugness by forcing himself onwards with discipline and resolve?

England had had two constitutional experiments: Henry IV's usurping Lancastrian project and the Cromwellian one. One had ended in largescale bloodshed and the other hadn't. Legitimacy had been the solution for both. There would never be another because..., because.... He hesitated, then pronounced his politically scientific verdict: disputing sovereignty brings civil war, inevitably. He breasted the tape fully chuffed with himself and beheld his achievement with a righteous and historical affection; a loving father cradling a new-born child in his arms. Where had Mr Napman been all that time? This had been his solo achievement. Yet it felt unwieldy. A top-rank Holywood scriptwriter would be needed to sharpen it up. Damian pursed his lips and made puffy blowing noises, accentuating them by drawing down his eyebrows. It wouldn't be easy. Maybe a nap this afternoon could sort it out?

'Damian, I'm ready for my close up,' shouted Clare offstage.

'Coming darling,' was his response, and he hoped his first-time use of the commonplace pet-name would cause no offence. You never knew.

Clare was endearingly flushed with girlish excitement and she was ready for her photograph to be taken, fully costumed for the ('no close-ups, just me in my studio!') cinematic set-piece in her nibbling kit: a home-dyed yellow-leather full-length apron over a sexy striped Breton sailor shirt with matching long-sleeved leather gauntlets, which made, all-in-all, a most appealing outfit, thought Damian whilst fiddling with the camera to make sure he'd identified the right button to press.

She pulled a starry-theatrical pose, grozing pliers in one hand, nibbling shears in the other, and Damian took the shot. And another. He was getting into the part. Flash! It was la Dolce Vita: Flash! Flash! This camera didn't need a flash, but even so… Flash!

'Gimme *angry*!' She gurned. 'Gimme *lost*!' She arranged her features appropriately. 'Ok baby, gimme *Top Model*!' she used the vacant hit-on-the head almost unconscious, but not cross-eyed, mouth half open look which was so popular in the magazines. 'That's good, that's real good. I think we got it baby.' But Clare wasn't finished and started twirling, posing, sometimes teasingly. Damian was having trouble concentrating and coming up with suitable lines, getting as flushed and excited as she was, until she relented with:

'Let's do the show right here!', on one knee, jazz hands fluttering, to mark the end of the shoot.

'Break a leg baby!'

Donning a transparent face-shield, she gave him a thumbs up, and he left her to get on with it. He'd got great pics and he'd enjoy going through them. Maybe cropping some, not to get close ups, but to get arty compositions by cutting out distracting details. He was going to get the answer he was looking for as well although it would come to him much later, after downloading the digital picture files and working on the images in a folder labelled 'Showtime'.

25

Musical theatre! Musical theatre! Not a play Josephine, but a musical! It was so now, so on-trend and fashion-forward! Audiences went wild for them. They were queuing up round the corner for the 'Hamilton' musical. That's what his 'What?' would be. That! If the dialogue got too heavy you could go into a song, or a dance. Or both. And you could emphasis tricky bits with music if you wanted to. He'd broken through. Thanks for nothing Mr Dozy, chalk one up to a certain Mr Damian Email esquire, fully awake and at your service ma'am, fanyaverrmuch!

He hadn't seen many musicals, but the rules about how you did one seemed flexible. There was no shortage of historical personalities to take the starring roles, and there were plenty of minor characters left over for the big routines, so it wasn't a problem if there had to be a lot of them out at the same time. How the big themes fitted on stage could be worked out, they were just technicalities really, stagecraft. There had to be an interval, and afterwards everything heads towards the 'dénouement', which should be easy. It just meant 'unknotting' in French. So, set up the whole thing for the interval, and then untangle it for the end. Then have a finale. This would take some serious napping. Welcome back Mr Napman, there's a part for you to play after all.

Damian ticked off the seconds as the appointed hour for a formal nap, two-thirty pm, approached, and looked for ways to mop up his excess anticipation. Would the effectiveness of the nap be a function of the quality of lunch? He was chary of going with the traditional chicken and tarragon. He had moved on. To absorb the time remaining he scooted out to get ingredients for a cottage pie, enough to do for several meals, and prepared it. Clare turned it down for lunch – mashed potato would have made her sleepy, she said – so he made her a salad. Perhaps looking back he should have done the same. He must have overdone the portion control and eaten too much. Something lighter might have made for a better start.

It had begun, most promisingly, at the pavilioned entrance to a tented out-of-town literary festival, admittance free to anyone who wanted to go in. Laid out in carpeted walkways around open grassy spaces for lounging readers and tired families, it resembled a series of arcaded roman villas made of flapping plasticised canvas fitted together in themed rectangular sequences.

Damian mooched his way around it until he found the History section. This area was like the others in that it offered timetabled lectures in a dedicated auditorium, new books for sale in a very large open-plan stand where signings were in progress, judging by the queues, second-hand ones sold in quainter spaces, and special-interest groups were offering their various historical services from smaller booths. The floor-plan in his brochure told him where to go and, after a general sniff around the festival, he presented himself at the front desk of a private enclosure marked 'Chronicles' for accredited chroniclers, their translators, and academics with an established interest in their work. Damian asked for Adam of Usk, more to please Dolmetscher than anything else, as Froissart was first on his list.

The agency hostess telephoned his request through. After

a short wait, a response came back. She handed him the old-fashioned receiver. He'd noted down some highlights from his book: when he was poisoned in Viterbo, Italy, and the Pope's Jewish doctor Helias had saved his life, his crossing the Alps on a cart, blindfolded to stop him seeing how precarious the path was, his boozy bouts with various notables, anecdotal little icebreakers to help strike up a relationship, and go from there. Damian was eager to impress but didn't.

'Hello Mr ap Adams, this is Damian Email, I'm....'

'It's not ap Adams, it's Adam of Usk.' A Welsh-accented Dylan-Thomasy voice, tinny and distorted by the antiquated technology, snapped back, throwing him off.

'Hello Mr Adam of Usk, I wonder if I....'

'What do you want?'

'I thought that we could....'

'No,' and the line went dead. He handed the phone back. 'Thank you.'

Damian looked at the hostess who had clearly understood from his fragmented interaction that he would be proceeding no further than the front of her desk. She feigned ignorance of his embarrassing situation. He said nothing. Less was more. A bold stroke might do it. He could shed his bourgeois inhibition and just stride purposefully past the lady, find Adam of Usk and win him over with a concentrated burst of well-controlled rhetoric. The flustered female flunkey would arrive hot-footed: 'I'm sorry Mr Usk, I couldn't…,' and Adam of Usk would wave her away with: 'It's alright. He's with me.' Another scenario presented. A chase, futile hidings, discovery, more chasing, a cake-trolley upset, burly goons pinning him to the ground, his face all creamy, followed by frogmarching and an ignominious ejection. He didn't want to have to pick himself off the ground, wipe his face, dust himself down, rearrange his dishevelled clothing and be tempted to a peevish retort like: 'I've been thrown out of better joints than this, ya two-bit cheapskates!' Best to keep his powder dry and come back again.

It hadn't been a total waste of time though. Adam had been in. He'd talked to him. He'd go back but prepare properly first. It wasn't the research. It was all there. All up on the key and ready to go. It must be about gaining Adam's confidence, but he obviously didn't feel the need to meet. Damian would have to blag his way back in with something that Adam couldn't resist. His book was full of medieval abstract thinking. They never liked putting things plainly. A spade was never a spade with them. Woah! Steady on cowboy. That was it! A spade never was a spade. Adam of Usk specified his own 'blazon', like a picture for a coat of arms. His translator had put it on the cover of his book. Adam had said that his sign would be 'a naked man delving'. Delving, digging. He had to dig for it in the book. Damian dug and turned up plenty, until one particular nugget lay gleaming on the spoil heap.

Clare, fresh from showering away the sweaty nibbling-out of coloured-glass shapes all day long, had come down to further decompress by playing the passive listener to Damian's breathy account of his day's activities over dinner; her first taste of his cottage pie, his second.

'This is nice Damian, what did you put in it?'

'Well, as you ask, there are some, may we say…,' a two-handed ten-finger twiddle and a strange but apt face-look serving to add emphasis, 'special ingredients.'

'Yeah?'

'Yes yeah! Worcester sauce a dash. A pop or two of tabasco, balsamic vinegar, and tarragon to bring it all together.'

'Umm, s'great…. It really…, works.' Damian told her that he was thinking of doing a musical. 'S'great idea…, I can play the oboe,' and he went on to describe the nature and scale of his ambition.

'Wow!'

'Yes wow!' He recounted the story of his daydreaming research visit to the literary festival. How he'd been cold-shouldered at the last step, and how he'd been getting ready for another try tomorrow. He wasn't ashamed any more and wanted her to know all about it. Damian went into his Adam of Usk delvings over cheese and, due to a crumbling cracker, an ungulent camembert and a slurp of Dolomiti wine, Clare misheard a key word as:

'Amice?'

'No, lice.'

'I thought you said 'amice'.

'It should be 'a mouse.'

'No, 'amice.'

'Is that even a word?'

'You heard it didn't you?'

'I heard a sound, or two words.'

'I'll show you smart arse.' She pushed back her chair and nipped off to the workroom, coming back shortly with a photocopy of a page probably cut from an eighteenth-century illustrated taxonomy, similar to the larger prints commonly used to decorate restaurants, such as those displaying 30 coloured drawings of different types of bread-making equipment, or types of wheel, or military uniforms. Clare's photocopy showed an array of ecclesiastical vestments. 'There!' She pointed to a picture with an I'm-showing-you-smart-arse face, 'None taken.'

'What?'

'Offence, dumbo.' Damian saw a very unprepossessing item of clothing with a number next to it at the end of her finger which he checked against the index at the bottom. The reference read 'amice'.

'You're so smart, I love you,' it slipped out unnoticed, almost. 'What's an amice then?'

'I had to get up close and personal with priest and bishop clothing for the St Dunstan panel. It's what you had to wear on your head after any holy oil was put on it to stop it running off over the rest of you. Those are two long tapes so you can tie it on. Later on it became symbolic and less of a hat, or cap, and more like a shawl.'

'Bloody hell!' For the second time in his life all the wheels on the one-armed bandit stopped at the right place and there was an instant and substantial cash pay-out. 'Bluh ... dee ... ell!'

'Steady on soldier, it's just an amice.'

'It's much more than that!'

26

Damian surfed his insight's cresting wave and regaled Clare
with his understanding of medieval literary jiggery-pokery,
and how lice and amice fitted in. Adam of Usk's chronicle
implied that he'd been standing close enough to Henry at his
coronation to see lice on his head. But he hadn't. It was an
allegory. There had never been any lice. It was the amice that
Usk was talking about. Damian whizzed to the library and came
back with Usk's book to show her the quotation which said
that Henry IV had died in 1413 of a:

> 'Rotting of the flesh, by a drying up of the eyes and by a rupture
> of the intestines......that same rotting did the anointing at
> his coronation portend; for there ensued such a growth of lice,
> especially on his head, that he neither grew hair, nor could have
> his head uncovered for many months.'

'He caught the lice from the coronation. It was a portent.'
'Yeuch!'
'Yes yeuch, Archbishop Arundel found a special oil just for
Henry's crowning; one never used before; the Virgin Mary had
given it to St Thomas a Becket. Henry of Lancaster, Henry IV's
great-grandfather had found it abroad somewhere.'
'That is special. Maybe it'd gone off?'
'If it had gone off then Henry was in trouble because it was
very carefully applied all over him. They shaved all his hair to
get maximum contact with his skin. He wore a special shirt
with special slits in for the oil to be put on him, and then a

special cap-bonnet-amice is put on and tied in place to keep the oil on his head. He didn't change out of his shirt and amice for a week.'

'Poisoned by his special oil, hmmm…, being crowned king killed him. So *lice* is a word-rebus, a soundalike for something else. Lice for amice.'

'Indeed so, it's not obvious, it's well-hidden but it's there. The original word for lice in the Latin text is *pediculorum*, the reader has to do a lot of work. There's probably more to it than that, I'll check it out.'

'So when are you going back? What are you looking for?' Damian's answer was again muffled in camembert. 'What do you mean cooperation? How does that work?'

'No, corroboration. Modern historians are very snobby about the chroniclers. They like to pick out the bits they like for their arguments but generally they think they're untrustworthy. Unreliable is the word they always use. They think they know better.'

'What else do they have to go on?'

'Basically nothing,' and he whizzed off again for another book to quote from:

'Chronicles are often inaccurate, and rarely offer any serious comment on the character or behaviour of individuals, even of the King. They are usually biased in favour of the established order, and do not seek to explain the causes or motives behind events.'

'Cor blimey gov, dismissive or what?'

'Yes dismissive, and it goes on: *'Historians have increasingly turned to records for their sources, believing that they will be, within their own rather narrow limits, accurate and unbiased'.* What about that?'

'Lucky him, he's found records that comment seriously on character and motivation and can explain the causes of events. He sounds like a right dullard.'

'I know, it's hard to believe. That's why I'm going back to corroborate what the chroniclers say against records and such.'

'Seems like a scheme…. I'm sorry Damian, but I've come over all tired, mind if I go up? I might manage a bit of reading, but I'm basically all-in and I've got the same to do again tomorrow.'

'Sure you don't mind if I stay up? I want to take it on the burst, if you know what I mean?' Damian saw Clare to the bottom of the stairs, kissed her goodnight, almost gave the seat of her denim dungarees an affectionate double-pat as she reached the second step, and went back to tidy up the kitchen before he went outside for a supplementary Dolomiti in the fresh night air. The floodlight's artificial glare was out of keeping with his multi-layering thoughts and he moved to a place where the infra-red sensor couldn't reach him, and the light eventually went off.

He wished he'd been able to give Clare another training session. Wine glasses this time perhaps.

The dining table is England. Richard's not on it. He's in Ireland with his army, so put his glass on the shelf for now.

Henry isn't on it either because he's living it up in Paris, so put his glass by the sink, and put two more glasses next to his for the two other exiles: one for master politician Archbishop Arundel, brother to the Earl of Arundel that was executed in 1397, and there's the traitor-earl's disinherited son. Maybe use different colour wines to show who's who.

Henry and the Arundels get to England. Put the three exiled glasses on the table. They meet up with the Earl of Northumberland and the Earl of Westmoreland. Maybe smaller shot glasses. Move them down. Let them meet up in the middle then: bang – bang – bang, he would tap the glasses around the table for effect – they defeat all opposition without much of a fight.

Richard comes back from Ireland to Wales – put his glass on the edge by Clare – but it's too late. England has been overrun. Does Richard have an army? Sadly not, he's just got 16 loyalists with him by the time he's captured heading for Rhuddlan Castle in North Wales. The Nazgul have captured the crown-bearer and he's in the bag now, so it's down to London with him to get him off the throne so Henry can start being the new king.

What a great idea! He could test her when she'd finished her project; make a special meal with tomatoes and sausages and wine and get her to go through what she'd remembered. He'd help her over any sticky bits. His eyes, better accustomed now to the dark, searched the perimeter of his vision, looking for the places where he could see no further. Standing still in the night stripped away pretensions. It was the-here-and-now but, here alone, if you calmed your mind down, it could be anytime. With the wind sounding in the trees and the lightest of airs on your face, it could be 50,000 years ago.

You'd want a big bonfire to banish the blackness. You could make your own sounds to keep the dark at bay. Tell of the deeds of ancestors. Everybody knew the story. It would be in song. Everyone would sing their part and put on masks to show what animal they were. Dogs would howl and join in. And they might all sing about tomorrow so everyone would know what to do.

At the end, someone might make them laugh with a song about their lost arrow. Damian wouldn't be able to wait for tomorrow. He wasn't going to lose his arrow. If he really was Mr Napman then maybe it was within his power to bring forward his return to the literary festival. What about a late-night research session, say to three-thirty in the morning? You could imagine getting sleepy and accidently nodding off over the strewn papers and books, say around two o'clock, that might count as a nap.

27

Damian made himself a late-night historian's den in the library and emailed Dolmetscher: Subject: 'What?', Content: 'It's a musical', then thoughtfully appended an exclamation mark to make it more showy. He easily cracked Adam's lice-amice code courtesy of the awesome power-capacity of linked computing engines and got on top of any other stuff he might conceivably need. New Damian Two could swallow his pride and pay to see the records of medieval parliaments, although not before vowing, with an acute and principled resentment, to make an issue of it later on.

Henry's first parliament in late September 1399 was not really an official one. It was more a gathering of like-minded souls who could be relied on to sack Richard, get Henry crowned and deal with his enemies. As an afterthought, Archbishop Arundel had added 31 charges against Richard to give the deposition some appearance of legality. Most of these whinged about Richard taking on his 1388 Merciless Parliament persecutors in the 1397 counter-attack which executed the Earl of Arundel and packed the Duke of Gloucester off to Calais where he died, naturally or unnaturally. Damian found a quotation, one of the charges made in parliament that he'd been looking for before which stood out as it referred to foreign policy. He'd try and get Froissart to comment on it:

'Also, the same king was accustomed almost continually to be so changeable and dissembling in his words and writings, and

*altogether contrary to himself, especially in writing to the pope
and to kings, and to other lords outside the realm, and within it,
and also to other subjects of his, that almost no living person who
knew what sort of person he was, could or wished to trust him,
Rather he was thought to be so untrustworthy and inconstant that
it became a disgrace, not only to his person, but also to his whole
realm, and especially among foreigners throughout the whole
world who learnt of it.'*

Stern criticism indeed. Damian's stamina gave out and the
silence of the otherwise sleeping house became oppressive. A
frisson of gothic anticipation got him thinking of ghost stories;
if he'd used candles to light the room, they might start going
out now, one by one, despite his desperate efforts to relight
them, until…, the last one…, went out….

'I don't think Mr Usk is available, I'm afraid.' The pleasantly
professional hostess had recognised him. Damian wasn't going
to try and bully his way in. There were formalities to respect,
but he could be firm. He handed her his business card on
which he'd previously written two words.

'Give him this please. I'll be in the café.'

The queue for coffee had been slow-moving, and he was
about to get served when she came to tell him that Mr Usk
would see him now, and escorted him back to the Chronicle
enclosure, past her desk, and through to a meeting area where
a tall powerful-looking man in a neat grey suit was sat at a
round plastic garden table. He rose to greet them at their
entry with:

'Mr Email!' The hostess presented the visitor to him, and the
host indicated that he should sit.

'Thank you,' to the host from Damian.

'Thank you,' from both to the hostess as she withdrew to exit and they both took their seats, followed by a polite pause and a dry command: 'Explain!' from Adam of Usk. The Mr Usk in front of Damian was by no means what he'd expected. Where was the pale and flabby bookworm cleric of his imagination? This guy looked more like a Turkish wrestler, albeit a Welsh one. Damian was unfazed, and he held forth in a matter-of-fact manner; he didn't need to give chapter and verse; Adam of Usk would know exactly what he was talking about.

'Lice and amice. Amice to 'amictus', the Latin for amice. Amictus can mean all outer garments generally. Sometimes it can stand for cloak. An amice is always an amictus. This takes us to the Bible: Jeremiah, chapter 43, verse 12: *'Et amicietur terra Aegypti sicut amicitur pastor pallio suo et egredietur inde in pace'*, which I render thus: 'As a shepherd picks lice from his cloak, so Nebuchadnezzar will pick the land of Egypt clean.' Ergo: Henry IV is Nebuchadnezzar, the greatest enemy of the Israelites, called by them the 'destroyer of nations'. When we add this to your more explicit comments about Henry the Fifth's war expedition to France, we can read your book as a warning.'

'That's quite correct. It is. You're the first. Well done. Would you like a coffee, or a tea?' Adam of Usk was gone, to return with a 'They'll bring us some,' as he resumed his place. 'And the last word of my book?'

'The last word is *remittuntur*. Your translator didn't actually say what it meant.'

'Sir Edward Maunde Thompson is such a gentleman. Too polite to offer his own interpretation. It's just like him to be that diffident. There are a lot like him here in the festival, back there.' Adam waved in the direction of the enclosure's inner sanctum, from whence a hubbub of noisy conversations could be heard coming through the plasticated ersatz-canvas walls. 'We'll go through in a bit, but first, why have you come here?'

'Can I do *remittuntur* first? I'm all ready.'

'As you wish.'

28

'You stop writing your chronicle in June 1421 when Henry the Fifth is preparing another French invasion army. I don't speak Latin....'

'Come on, it was all in Latin! It's just the last word that Sir Edward didn't translate into English. I make it very clear what I mean.'

'Yes, you do. You pray that Henry the Fifth would not feel the sword of the wrath of God. The word *remittuntur* is a reference to a passage in Gratian's Decretum. The Decretum is a long legal treatise in which he tries to replace barbaric customs with proper laws.'

'That's right my boy, barbaric customs like trial by battle. Who could still believe, in the fifteenth century mind you, that almighty God shows His will through bloodshed? You cannot seek to know the mind of God through battle. It's probably a blasphemy. In fact, I'm sure it is.'

'Uh yes…, the actual passage is *Remittuntur peccata per Dei verbum* etcetera, which I venture to offer as: Sins are forgiven by the word of God, of which the Levite is the interpreter and the executor', and you are the 'Levite', am I right?'

'It's not 'me' it's men of God, they're the Levites, the Church is the Levites. Matters should be sorted out by them, and not by the petty whims of barbarous men. I got quite angry....'

They were interrupted by the arrival of cardboard cups of thin brown liquid covered in suds that claimed a cappuccino heritage and small plastic packets of biscuits designed to be opened only by biting, on a tray borne by a 'Staff Team Associate from which they served themselves.

'Thanks,' from Adam.

'No worries,' from the waiter.

'I'm sorry?' from Adam confused.

'No problem,' from a confused waiter.

'Well…, thanks for the coffee,' from Adam, and the departing servant bid them adieu with:

'Awesome!'

Adam was utterly bemused. Had he missed something important? His unfamiliarity with such modern speech tropes had given him time to calm down. Damian carried on from where he'd left off.

'Yes, there's anger everywhere in your book.'

'I know…, I know…, Henry IV thought he was sent by God, but he did nothing for the church apart from suck money from it and set it up as a target for the avarice of the knights. How they did drool, but they didn't get their way until Henry VIII, did they? God sent him warnings, but he ignored them. Owen Glendower was sent to….'

'You call Owen the rod of God's wrath.'

'Yeah, the rod to beat Henry with. And God sent Henry his grisly disease. Anyway, I was so upset that I stopped writing because it had all come true, and I just waited for the end of days to come.'

'But that's Henry IV. Your book ends with Henry the Fifth.'

'Yes. Henry the Fifth died the year after I stopped writing. He'd already had to come back to England ill once already, but no, he had to get back to the war. He was so angry when his brother the Duke of Clarence was killed by a Scottish army in

France, that nothing could stop him. As if his brother dying was particularly unjust. Well, that's what happens in wars. People get killed. He didn't bother overmuch about the people of Rouen starving to death in the city ditches, right in front of him, did he?'

'They say good-old fighting Henry the Fifth was a better king than sensitive Henry the Sixth, or at least that he was more popular?'

'Better? You mean worse! Popular Shmopular! Look, it was all part of the same thing. Henry the usurper promised war when he took the crown but couldn't deliver it. Henry the Fifth was the king that the country had wanted Henry the Fourth to be. He was dashing, glorious, victorious, warlike, and not at all like his father. Many believed it would have been better if King Henry the Usurper had died at the battle of Shrewsbury in 1403 instead of Harry Hotspur, the very flower of chivalry.' Damian had noticed a warmness towards Hotspur in Usk's book, and indeed also in an unguarded reference in the Walsingham chronicle.

'Anyway, Henry V knew that the wobbly usurped crown could only be kept in place with a proper old-fashioned war like Edward I and Edward III had, but he blew it by dying himself and leaving a child behind. Henry the Fifth was a blood-crazed maniac who wanted to usurp France as his father had usurped England. You know he married the sister of Richard's infant queen Isabella. Isn't that a perversity? Richard II marries Isabella de Valois to get peace with France and Henry the Fifth marries her sister Catherine de Valois to make war on France. With such…, such….'

'Awesome?'

'Yes, awesome…, thanks, with such awesome hubris of the father, and then the son, all the rest was inevitable. Henry the Fifth left a child king prey to the controlling ambition of others, just like Richard II was.'

'I like your analysis. The crown is like wealth, which they say comes and goes in three generations. So, the war with France was on the cards from the start?'

'Yes, they had to fight abroad to keep England together, and keep their crown. But mission-creep sets in and 'fighting' Henry V just has to be king of France, hasn't he. Then his stupid son, I tell you….' Adam paused. Damian found the silence disconcerting. Adam broke it: 'How could that ever happen? Two crowns for one king! Could a French king ever be King of England after fifty years of war? No, never! And the same vice versa. And Henry the Fifth was the son of a usurper. How would France ever let him usurp their crown after what his father did to them?

'What did he do?'

'He broke every oath under the sun. Talk to Froissart, he'll tell you. How could the son of a man like that believe that political opportunism could win him the kingdom of France?'

'It worked for his father in England.'

'Yes, but it's stretching it a bit to usurp two crowns, isn't it? Henry IV played all his jokers and picked up all the winnings. Nobody in history won a crown as easily as he did. He didn't have to play politics to get crowned. Henry IV basically conquered England by letting anybody who wanted to pillage, pillage, and those who wanted to loot, loot. Whilst they were enjoying doing that, he crowned himself. Is fighting Henry the Fifth going to be able to pull that off in France? At the very start he has to ally himself with a French faction. This is ok while it lasts, but it can't last, can it? You know, I actually was…, was heartbroken….Yes, heartbroken when they started up the war again. It made the church look powerless. So much for Christendom; Europe's two greatest nations were at each other's throats with daggers drawn. It was an embarrassment, shameful.'

'The way you tell it, it's quite a ….'

'Rant, I know. I'm still angry, it seems. Anyway, I'm always pleased to share it with a willing ear. Why have you come here?'

'I want to talk to the chroniclers first-hand and see what they have to say about things. A bit like what you've just been saying, which was very interesting by the way. I'm hoping for more like that.'

'I'll be glad to help in any way I can.'

'Thanks Adam, umm…, one question, why are you all in this private chronicler enclosure and not out there with the public?'

'I've never really thought about it. It must be how we like it.'

'But out there you could have your own stand and sell your books direct to the public. It's a well-attended festival. You'd have lots of visitors I'm sure. You could have a special area to yourselves out there. I was lucky to get in here at all.'

'You weren't lucky. I let you in. Look, years ago we could have done that. There was no end of delvers ferreting around for old manuscripts. Thomas Johnes did a great Froissart translation and that started it all. Then they were off. Any number of churchmen or ex-this or ex-that with a passion, a pension and too much time on their hands were publishing our stuff at their own expense. Great days for us. The Camden Society paved the way in 1838. Its mission was to re-print these unearthed histories and many a family fortune was poured into the production of lovely volumes. I think it turned into the English Society of Antiquarians – are you by any chance a member?'

'Not as such.' Damian then thought that maybe he was. 'Actually, I'm...,' and he partly exposed the Phial with the Philtre from under his collar.

'Oh, that's very much the same thing, I think you'll find. Indeed so. Sir Edward is back there in the chronicler's lounge, I think. You'll be able to meet him and the others.'

'I was hoping I would.'

29

'Anyway, as I was saying, they were great days. The Historical Manuscripts Commission was set up in 1869 to license the old buffers' amateur trawlings of forgotten piles of parchment in locked-up storerooms. That's when they found my book, and Sir Edward saw to it that it got the recognition he thought it deserved. It was originally a very private thing, just for me, but towards the end I thought it could be interesting for people in the future, so I left it in the church with my other stuff.'

'I went there with a friend…'

'Tell me all about it in a minute. I need to finish this. I'm sorry, I must appear very medieval and linear. I've noticed how you modernists like to jump about. It's quite funny how you can change subjects and not start fighting each other in frustration. I will continue. Where was I?'

'Sir Edward published your book…, umm…, they were great days….'

'Yes, after the glory days, little by little, we were pushed out of the limelight. We weren't good enough, apparently. Sometimes what we wrote was wrong, so they said, or unreliable, or whatever. Modern historians didn't want to talk to us anymore. It made them…, I don't know…, it made them look naïve, over-trusting, too credulous, not clever enough. They're out there, aren't they?'

'Yes, loads of them. They're only allowed to do one king at a time. It's just kings and queens. Or something else like soap, or mackerel.'

'Well, we like our own company. We have a get-together here once a year and catch up. We let academics in if they apply in writing in advance but historians? Not so much. They can stay out there and leave us here in peace. They don't despise us, nor we they. But they do look down their noses in our direction, probably because we're one up.'

'How's that?'

'We were there, and they weren't.'

'Nicely put. Maybe they're jealous. Well I'm here to find out what you can tell me. What should I call you? Mr Usk?

'Call me Adam. Shall we go through Mr Email?'

'Please call me Damian.'

They rose to leave and Damian began small-talking about how he'd been to St Mary's church in Usk and seen Adam's metal tropar, and been into the castle and had a nice picnic lunch there. Such low-intensity pleasantry, though one-sided, was maintained whilst Adam, in a peculiarly medieval fashion, held Damian's jacket by the elbow and guided him out and down through the entrance hallway – 'I remember that when you were in Beaune you commented on how nice the wine was,' – to the threshold of the pavilion from which steps led down to the main area.

This temporary building was supported by a geometric web of metallic stays overlain with a heavy-duty technical textile. Originally designed for outdoor pop concerts, it had been re-purposed, and the only vestige of its primary function was the empty sound-engineer's gantry at the top of the stairs, from where they stopped to look down and across the busy chronicler floor.

'Behold!'

'Wow!' Damian had forgotten how many chroniclers there had been over time. A shanty town of plywood partitions intersected by busy walkways filled his view. Berobed figures were sitting or standing in roofless open huts. Some were reading, some were standing by themselves and trying not to look bored, but most were talking to the men and women who gathered about their stands and filled the alleys with a squabulating mass of human bodies dynamised to movement like blood cells fighting off a virus.

'Those must be the academics. I didn't think there could be so many!'

The multi-frequency humming of human interaction and concomitant decibel incursion on his hearing forced him to raise his voice. Adam had to shout his reply to be heard over the din, leaning in to get closer to Damian's ear.

'That's right. The serious academics use this as their base. They go off looking for other records and sources around the festival and then come back to check with the chroniclers. Some are working on one-offs and we don't see them again.' Damian hadn't caught every word but had the gist. Adam showed the way forward by pointing: 'We're over there, if we get separated, meet in the corner!'

'Where?'

'Corner!'

'Ok!'

30

Adam again took Damian by the elbow and led him down the steps to the carpeted sprung floor which must have acted as a sounding board as the overwhelming voice-noise was not so loud here and they s'cuseme-s'cusemeed their way in elegant waltzing zig-zags through the thronging grid-like maze of people.

Not all the berobed figures he'd seen from above were chroniclers. Chronicler's robes were long, like overcoats, and some looked hot in them. Others wore ordinary academic gowns which were shorter, lighter in weight and cheaper looking; they must be the translators. The academics who were hampering Damian and Adam's progress had their own dress code: chino-and-polo-shirted men and well-turned-out women, all with a leather satchel or computer bag.

'And here we are.'

Damian could have used his trade-fair expertise to find an easier route around the outside, but if Adam had wanted to impress him by pulling him all the way right through the middle of Chronicle-Central, he had. Fourteenth and fifteenth century chroniclers, relative to European history, and with special relevance to Anglo-French relations, had been allocated a quarter alley in the far corner, which was normally, as Damian understood it, a bit of a dead spot in a conventional trade fair, unless it was next to a refreshment concession. Maybe festivals were different, as it was nevertheless well attended.

'You go through and have a look. My spot is at the end. I'll see you there.'

'Ok, see you later.'

Damian let Adam have a head-start, waited until he'd shimmied out of view down the busy alley, and began his own walk-through. There were more chronicler stands here than he was prepared for but, he reasoned, this was the time to focus on pre-targeted opportunities and not to get side-tracked. Damian's personal force field was set to full power. If it looked like he was going to get waylaid by a huckster trying to make a sale, he could use his blank 'I'm-not-here' expression, say nothing, and move on. It wasn't rude and he wasn't going to make an easy mark for them to practise their patter on.

Moving into the throughfare, standing dead centre not to appear too interested, he checked out the first stand where a large notice on the table, next to a stack of used, well-bound books, announced its occupiers to be Jean Creton and the Reverend John Webb. He could start with a 'Bonjour Monsieur Creton' to the Frenchman talking to the three academics, or 'Good day Reverend' to the other man, but their conversations were animated and looked like they would last a while, the Frenchman over-earnest, almost pleading, and the reverend looking to be in a nodding trance.

'I was there, I'm telling you, I was actually there.'

Were the academics buying what the Frenchman was selling? It didn't look like it. 'Yes, I do regret doing it as a song now, but at the time that was what we did if you wanted to get it out there and find an audience.' Creton had some convincing to do. 'If you read it you'll see that I turn to prose when things get complicated – I make an explicit reference to the transition in my text, you can...,' Damian could come back later.

On the other side was John Hardyng, looking tough despite

his dress, along with, as Damian knew without having to get close enough to see the name card or read his badge, Sir Henry Ellis, the illustrious principal librarian of the British Museum. Both were similarly engaged with questing professors. This chronicle was a very late one, from around 1460, and also in rhyme like Creton's and Hardyng had wanted to use it to undermine the Lancastrians at the start of the Wars of the Roses. Hardyng also had a solution to losing the war in France which was to start a new one in Scotland but his idea hadn't been taken up.

Moving down to the next stand and it was Benjamin Williams, Fellow of the Society of Antiquaries and The Monk of St Denis, French chronicler, who were both busy fielding questions. Odd name that 'monk'; Royal Librarian and Clerical Civil Servant would have been more fitting. What were they talking about? Probably about whether the monk's 'Chronicle of the Treason and Death of Richard II' was a rip-off of Jean Creton. It was probably some kind of a compendium, but it was also one of the certifiably earliest versions of the story, dated to 1412 or maybe earlier.

The double-sized Walsingham chronicle stand was opposite, and Damian was gratified to see that there were several people in monkish garb on it. He'd known it was never the work of one hand and the gentleman bobbing amongst the Benedictines in the school-teachery academic gown and mortar-board hat must be a certain Henry Thomas Riley. Academics were all over the stand. It was by far the most popular one in this area and off-puttingly busy. Damian's affected nonchalance had worked too well and he'd arrived at Adam's stand having successfully avoided any interactions, but feeling ignored.

'Hi Adam.' Adam deftly apologised to the group he was talking to. He would just need a moment.

'That didn't take you long.'

'It was just a walk-through to get a feel. Where's Froissart?'

'Let me introduce you to Sir Edward.'

'How do you do?'

'How do you do?'

'Sir Edward, do you mind showing Damian here to Froissart's stand?'

'Do you think I'll be able to talk to him?'

'Not a chance. You've seen what it's like. He'll be fully committed until lunchtime.'

'When's lunch?'

'We chroniclers like our medieval routines, so we eat at noon.'

'But it's noon now.'

'Noon is the ninth hour, it's in the word 'noon'. And noon is 3pm if daybreak is 6 o'clock in the morning, which it always is, so we've still got three hours to go.'

'Three hours! I'm hungry now,' interjected Sir Edward, overhearing, and looking like he'd been out late the night before. The knot of academics around Adam's stand were getting restless. A couple of them voiced American-accented alternatives to hanging around here. Adam looked uncomfortably overwhelmed dealing with both he and them at the same time and Damian showed mercy by holding up his hand, fingers outstretched, to signal a five-minute time-out, so letting Adam get back to his business.

The prospect of hacking his way back through to Froissart and then standing around like a zombie didn't appeal. Damian needed to play an ace. You could entertain clients. Take them out for lunch. Froissart might go for that. Think big. Take them all out. Like a fringe meeting, or break-out session, call it what you like. Lay on some entertainment if necessary. Damian butted straight back in when the Americans seemed to be winding up.

'What about if I take you to lunch?'

'By all means. Fine and dandy. Let's show mercy on Sir Edward and make it two-thirty, shall we?'

'I mean all of you, chroniclers and translators.' Adam didn't seem to get it. There was too much going on at once. Damian hovered around until Adam concluded matters with the Americans, waved them off and left the stand to talk to him on the walkway, just as another set of researchers filled the recently vacated space to the obvious discomfort of Sir Edward.

'All of us?'

'Yes.'

'That's impossible I'm afraid.'

'Oh.'

'But possible tomorrow. It's the last day and we can finish early, by that I mean not come back after lunch. We always have a nice sit-down to finish the festival off. Are you going to pay for everything?'

'Yes, I thought so.'

'What's the budget?'

'The sky's your oyster. This is my big chance. I need them all together.'

'Sounds good. Word to the wise. You need to distract the translators. They like a good meal as much as anyone, but they can start yapping and waffling on, especially the nineteenth century ones.' Adam dropped his voice to a conspiratorial clerical whisper – 'Even Sir Edward..., after a few drinks we'll get summaries of his long-running correspondences, usually about heraldry, then come the bawdy student songs, if we live that long.' – then, returning to a normal tone, he added: 'Can you put on some entertainment for them to draw them away?'

'What like?'

'You need an after-dinner speaker. Chroniclers won't be interested. Can you pay?'

'As I said....'

'I've got some ideas. I'll spread the word.'

'No historians!'

'They wouldn't go. They eat early, and they have their own historian-publisher party on the last day anyway.' Adam was eyeing new arrivals on his stand and clearly wanted to take over from the red-faced and floundering Sir Edward. 'Sounds like a plan. See you tomorrow at the entrance. I'll say two-thirty for three. See you at a quarter past.'

'Great, see you there.'

31

Coming to the surface from his self-induced night-time nap, Damian opened an eye to verify the peripherals. His alter-ego had done a good job and produced a vivid experience, but Damian wasn't much the wiser. Either his natural tendency to defer gratification was impeding progress, or Mr Napman was being too ploddingly literal. Whichever it was, now was not the time to amble around festivals like some hapless amateur. The ball was on the tee. He'd had a couple of practise strokes and he could give it a good whack by succumbing to drowsy somnolence…, by giving in…, and getting back. The eye closed.

Dammit! He'd gone too far, and it looked like the chronicler's meal was over. He was sat at the head of a white-clothed table littered with the detritus of dessert. Conversations were rippling up down and between the two rows of guests as stewards cleared away for coffee. He'd missed it all. Even the introductory drinks and canapés where he could've worked the room and to which he'd been especially looking forward, bloody Mr Napman! What were you thinking? He'd have to make do and mend. Where was Adam? Oh…, there he was…, and that must be Froissart opposite him in the big hat.

No notice was taken when he rose as if to speak formally, and the etiquette of how to further proceed was unclear, but it was definitely a do-or-die situation so, a few taps on a glass with a spoon serving as a handbell, he quelled the chatter to address them, and his: 'Gentlemen…, gentlemen…, I give you…, Adam of Usk,' appended by his own over-enthusiastic handclapping brought a rowdy cheer, followed by rhythmic chanting: 'Adam ..Adam ..Adam,' in tandem with table-banging when the expected response seemed slow in coming.

Adam got to his feet and, though dazed by surprise and a surfeit of the Beaune wine he'd taken the liberty of ordering for the convivial company, the rich timbre of his powerful Welsh baritone soon banished inattention.

'Brother chroniclers, and our dear translators, without whom, I'm sure, we would be as forgotten tomes lying in mouldering heaps, it was 650 years ago to this very day when I first...,' frantic semaphoring from the host returned him to the script.

'Ah yes..., brothers and translators..., Mr Email is with us at last..., I would like to take this opportunity of thanking Mr Damian Email for kindly sponsoring our end of festival feast and especially for his generosity in laying on the wonderful wine with which we have been regaling ourselves. I give you..., Mr Email!'

'Mr Email!' came back in a lusty roar from the berobed diners with a raising of glasses, a gulping down of what was in them, an appreciative applause, and much refilling.

'Thank you all for coming,' Damian had managed to compose himself, 'and thank you Adam of Usk for all your work behind the scenes,' which brought a couple of 'hear, hears' and some quipping attempts at funny remarks about Adam.

'It gives me great pleasure...,' – Damian resisted adding 'and it has done for some time,' which he'd used before to comic effect in a similarly critical situation, although it was most tempting, – 'to invite the chroniclers to join me in a symposium after coffee, and I think that Adam has put on something for the translators?'

'Ah yes!' Adam, thinking himself safe, had sat down, and had to get back up. 'Yes indeed…, our dear friend Thomas Johnes of the famously picturesque Hafod Estate in Wales….'

An attendee in gentleman-farmer outfit, Mr Johnes himself, broke in with a good-natured shout-out: 'Open to the public! Reasonable rates!' which occasioned some laughter. Adam waded on: 'grand tourist, inventor, husband to animals, supreme autodidact, will tell us all.'

'Thank you Adam.' One stood as the other sat. 'It's animal husbandry, and not at all the same thing, I think you'll find.' After milking the audience's reaction and letting the ribaldry settle down, Thomas Johnes enticed the translators to a talk by his great friend and reviewer Sir Walter Scott, to be followed by an interview with him by Horace Walpole, all under the title 'History and Fiction: Where does it end?'

Damian appreciated the Walpole touch. He was the one who'd done the Richard III book that Josephine Tey had based 'The Daughter of Time' on. It was a good choice. Now things could be go ahead. 'Thank you Thomas, I think we've got…, yes, ten minutes before we break off and go our separate ways, so it's the last chance for coffee and tea.'

The restaurant staff had been hanging back during the speeches and now buzzed this way and that to serve and finish clearing up around the guests who had started moving around in a game of dinner-party musical chairs. Adam had left the table and gone round to speak with Thomas Johnes who was standing next to a man, Damian would later know as Lord Berners, who was seated towards the middle. Damian saw his chance to take the seat opposite Froissart before he too moved somewhere else and darted to it.

'Mr Froissart. I am so happy to meet you. And you Mr Varvaro.'

'Alberto. He knows your name.'

'Yes Mr Froissart, I've been studying your work.'

'Oh, young man, nobody can do that anymore. They chop it and they chop it. It is now a thing just for the children.'

'I know. It must be hard for you after all you put into it.'

'Oh, what do they want from me?' Alberto Varvaro covered the chronicler's hand with his own and squeezed it gently, to show he understood, and shared, the old man's disappointment. 'I did all my own work, found people to tell me things, made enquiries – it was my life – to record and write down and now I am disdained. Lord Berners over there, he was my first translator in 1525, a fine man, but Macaulay here…,' a man two seats away had blushed bright red and was making a determined effort to appear as if he was listening to someone further down and not at all able to overhear, 'Macaulay yes, this Macaulay, he killed me. He killed me.'

'Umm…, killed you?'

Alberto explained that Macaulay had brought out a single volume in 1895 which purported to be a translation by Lord Berners but was, in fact a one-volume opportunistic cut-and-shut for the mass market in which he'd summarised major episodes in Froissart's chronicle to the point of uselessness. Subsequent historians had based their analyses on the Macaulay version and the more faithful one by Thomas Johnes became overlooked, and eventually hard to get. Macaulay's chopping out and ignorant summarising had rendered Froissart a laughingstock, although he carried on selling well in the multiplicity of similarly reduced exploitations which claiming his authorship.

'I know. Berners was six volumes in his original and Macaulay made it into one. It's a phoney. And the ones since. They're phonies because they're mostly based on the Macaulay phoney.'

'So you know?'

'Yes, that's why I'm here.' The ancient chronicler's lined features shifted to betray some of the energy of his younger days. Mr Napman had surprised Damian already by producing characterisations which were not as he'd expected, especially with regard to faces, but Froissart's resemblance to ex-doyen of the French stage, Jean Rochefort was uncanny and comforting. Had Jean Rochefort ever played Froissart? He would find out.

'Alberto, we can talk with this Email.'

32

'Would all translators wishing to attend the Sir Walter Scott event please make their way to the Waverley stand in Hall 3,' came over the public-address system and Alberto made to go.

'Mr Varvaro, I thought you might stay with us? It would be an honour.'

'Mr Email, you've read my book, haven't you?'

'Yes, it's a masterpiece.'

'Thank you….'

'Alberto, go if you want to. I'll be fine.'

'Jean, if you don't need me here, I'll go. It's not every day you can get to hear Sir Walter, is it?' The Italian philologist was desperately keen to go, although it was more for the chance of meeting Horace Walpole, author of the first gothic tale: 'The Castle of Otranto', and also that iconic exemplar of avant-garde pre-surrealism, the 'Hieroglyphic Tales', that really stirred his soup. 'You don't mind Mr Email?'

'Not at all. Not at all.' The translators were being drawn towards Thomas Johnes as iron filings to a magnet and he in turn was choreographing their stage exit until the door closed behind the last one and they were gone. Adam came back to the table. 'Coo, isn't it quiet?' from one of the Benedictines was enough to exactly fill the bubble of quietness left behind by the translator's evacuation and further served the monks as their cue to get back to the interminable gossiping which seemed to amuse them so much. Damian took it as a signal to get busy working on the man who knew all about what the first 'What?'

was in his second wind thing.

'Mr Email.'

'Please, call me Damian.'

'Damian,' they shook hands across the table, 'I'm Jean…, you are interested in my work, yes? So, what is it going to be? Another bad summary? You will use my work to add, how you say, a splash of colour while you show off with your clever argument? I do hope not.' Froissart's French-accented English was so strong, it had to be put on.

'It's actually going to be a musical.'

'A musical! That's a lovely idea. I was known for my poetry. We used to sing them to music all the time: *Je me puis bien comparer a l'orloge car quant Amours, qui en mon coer se loge.*'

'That's a nice tune, but I don't know it.'

'It's my 'L'Orloge Amoureus'. It's the one I'm most proud of. It's about a clock and all the mechanisms are related to….'

'I have read your 'Le Paradis d'Amour' though.'

'Ah yes. That's the one I took to King Richard. He liked it very much, I think.'

'I know. They've still got it in the British Library.'

'That's nice of them to keep it looked after. A musical. How can I help you with that?'

'The bit that Macaulay left out, the bit that no one knows about, is the bit about France and England in the twelve years before he was deposed. I'd like to go through it with you. Slowly, bit by bit.'

'Certainly, it's my favourite bit, but how does it fit into a musical?'

'The musical is going to be about how Henry IV turned peace into war and what that meant for England.'

'Yes. Yes, he did. Peace is love. There was a chance for love, but the times turned to hate, and he did that. Yes, I like that you want to find peace. There was peace, or very nearly.' Froissart had maybe never had to speak English. At the top level they all spoke French. That was maybe why his accent was so thick, or perhaps he had deliberately kept it to retain his exotic charm.

'At the end of my life I felt that my love of the nobles, their glamour, their chivalric code, had been misplaced, was a deception. I had been young. I had admired their deeds. But my naïveté, it had blinded me to the truth. Their code was a mask. It was self-serving, venal. It didn't just become horrible at the end. My Alberto, he thinks your Henry IV brought the end of chivalry in your country. But it had been horrible everywhere all the way through. I only saw it at the end. I had been blind all the time. Yes, blind. Henry was perhaps just the worst of all of them. You know, at my death, I thanked Henry for drawing aside the veil and letting me see, so that I could leave this world with my eyes open.' The melancholic turn was perturbing but Damian knew just what the venerable journalist meant.

'Yes..., I know what you mean…, umm…, could we kick things off by maybe sketching out how you came by your information? You know, generally.'

'With pleasure Damian,' Froissart moistened his lips with a sip of water and dried them with a napkin, 'Well, for the first years I just went to the treaties and asked around, then I went to England to visit King Richard and give him my book at the end of May 1395. It was the start of the marriage negotiations. I was there at his court for three months and then I came back. Getting information afterwards was really no problem. I could get all the details I wanted from my sources in France and in

England. There were people going backwards and forwards all the time to arrange the wedding and I had many friends. At the end, with Henry IV, it was not so easy. Nobody knew what was going on. They sent people to say what happened and someone came from England especially to tell me. I was quite flattered actually. I know what you are going to say. You are going to say what he said was all wrong, that what I wrote was wrong, but it's what he said. What could I do?'

'Thanks Jean, no problem.' Froissart had been fed some inaccuracies it was true. They might even be somehow important. That was for later. 'Can we talk about before 1395, the French-English truce.' The Benedictine Walsingham St Albanites had been earwigging:

'Excuse me sir, we know all about it.' Damian knew they did and waved them in with:

'Hi St Albans, please feel free to join in. Jean, if you don't mind, I'll go back a bit with them just to, you know, bookend the period.'

'Like a datum?'

'Exactly, exactly that.'

33

Froissart shifted himself backwards in his seat to settle in and enjoy any show the fractious monks felt like putting on. Damian decided that a more modern, less deferential questioning style would do for them:

'Brother Walsinghams, you cover the Merciless Parliament in detail, would it be fair to say you were supporters of the anti-king faction that took over in 1388,' provoked multiple reactions: 'Too strong!' ... 'What did he say about us?' ... 'He's one of them!' A single voice, perhaps that of a higher status and more used to laying down the law, or maybe that of their union representative, detached itself to speak for all.

'Steady on! Putting it like that makes us sound biased. We just wrote down what we were given to write. We never judged! Well, I mean that we ourselves personally didn't judge. It's what we wrote that was judgemental. We never got out and about. Anyway, if what we said happened – and we never got out and about much to find out, like I said – so if it happened like we said it did, given what I said before, then Richard must have deserved it; that's how God's will is made manifest. He got what was coming to him. We simply recorded God's work. We were his secretaries if you like.'

Damian didn't like. 'Sectarians' would have been better, but his new watchword was 'objectivity' and he let their bolstering outcries of: 'Yes! Yes! ... Hear! Hear! ... Quite Right! ... Outrageous!' pass. He hadn't meant to goad them like that. It was all ancient history. Forgive and forget. But he did need to get on and, if he felt like it, or they deserved it, he could needle them some more at the end.

'Your many-handed chronicle is a bit one-sided, isn't it?' The St Albans story was pretty much the Official English Version of what Henry had done. The monks had used the word 'tyrannical' once about Richard and it had stuck. No historian could talk about Richard without using it. Should he point out that 'tyrant' really means 'usurper'? No, he would maintain his non-diffident and self-confident probing:

'Actually, isn't your chronicle totally one-sided? In the Merciless Parliament, you call the king's men, and I quote: *'traitors, whisperers, toadies, evil slanderers, drones.'* Simon Burley was, and I quote you again: an *'oppressor of the poor, a hater of the church, a fornicator and adulterer.'* One can't blame us for thinking it sounds very much that you are working for one side, can one? Did they deserve to die?'

'As I have said, it wasn't for us to judge. They had fair trials.' For sure they'd had trials, thought Damian, unlike Henry IV's opponents, but fair? No, certainly not. 'I thought you were interested in the French treaty?'

'Yes, that's right, I am. Very much. 1388 is just the datum. We've finished with all that 1388 stuff. So, the leader of the faction who took over the 1388 parliament was the Duke of Gloucester, with the Earl of Arundel at his right hand, followed by wimpy…,' (pejorative, unobjective, it had just slipped out, never mind), 'Earl of Warwick, with young and impressionable future Henry IV, known then as Derby, or Hereford, or Bolingbroke, or whatever, tagging along with his friend Thomas Mowbray, the Earl of Nottingham or Norfolk or whatever.'

'Yes, the king got his power back when John of Gaunt

returned to the country and stood behind him, but thankfully the Duke of Gloucester stayed in the government.'

'Gloucester wasn't defeated or in any way humbled. He stayed in the government?'

'Of course. That's what we've just said. He stayed in. He was in it right up to his arrest in 1397. It was his idea to have a truce and make a treaty with France as the costs of always being on a war-footing were crippling.' Another monk piped up with: 'I thought it must have been John of Gaunt's idea, because it did turn out to be a bad one and...,' the self-appointed spokesman was having none of that, however, and berated the would-be contributor for giving any kind of a role to Gaunt whatsoever: that detested arch-underminer of the faith, that dissembling supporter of courtly heresies, that Wycliffite-Lollardian and putative anti-Christ who should have died in the Peasant's Revolt. Time hadn't healed those wounds. The Benedictine hatred of heterodoxy within the aristocratic ranks still burned fiercely, against which their unabated loathing of such deviation amongst knights, yeomen and lower orders was as a candle to a searchlight. Damian made a mental note: monks still mad.

'And Gaunt was a fornicator..., and probably a traitor too, but it was Gloucester's idea first and Gaunt went with him to France to help set it up, probably to spy on him. They did it at Leulinghem.'

'Sorry, I didn't quite...'

'Leulinghem.'

'Maybe some water?'

'Leulinghem!'

'Oh yes..., indeed..., what was the feeling in the country

about making peace with the French, may I ask?'

'It wasn't actually a peace; it was a truce. They met each year to try and make a final peace but could never agree so they would put it off until the next year. Both countries wanted to end the fighting.'

'Why was that? Isn't that unpatriotic?'

'Well yes, I suppose so, but basically it cost so much.' Other monkish voices could not be stilled. Or maybe they had been stilled for too long.

'And because it wasn't a just and righteous cause!'

'And it gave work to savage and immoral people!'

'I'll give you a just and righteous cause to stick right up your….'

'He thinks he's so all that!'

'Yeah, so all that!'

'Give him some of that!'

'The scriptorium wouldn't miss him!'

'He'd be better off looking after the fishpond!'

'Maybe that's why they call him Eel-breath?!'

'It's Brother Albrecht to you sunshine, and if you want some of this you can have it!'

John Hardyng was on the point of concretising his own anti-clericalism by knocking some sense into tonsured heads and shutting them up, but Adam mouthed a timely 'No' to him, made calming hand gestures to all, and Hardyng moved over to the St Albans contingent with mollification his only intent. He'd seen it all before and many times. Damian sympathised with their cloistered repressions but condemned their inarticulacy and hoped their bickering flare-up would soon blow over. Froissart's eyes had begun to evidence a lacklustre postprandial sheen. Damian needed to wrap it up before he nodded off.

'Thank you St Albans. That's excellent information. Let me sum up a bit before we move on, can I? We have our datum: 1388. Gloucester, Arundel, Henry etcetera defeat a royal army at Radcot Bridge, capture Richard, depose him for 3 days or so, then bring him back as a puppet while they take over, and execute Richard's loyalists for good measure, hence: 'Merciless' parliament.

Big John of Gaunt comes back, his mere presence in the land reinforces the enfeebled king's position and Gaunt works with his brother Gloucester to regain stability, particularly in the finances and, to that end, England seeks a peace treaty with the old enemy France.'

The monks' squabbling had alerted all to what promised to be at best a heated disputation, or at the very least an informative diversion and, if it didn't need them to personally pile on to the monks, and hopefully it wouldn't, then they could enjoy it collectively, and participate individually, according to how it went.

34

'Now it is for me, yes?' Froissart's accent had in the meantime become thicker. 'The datum, it is over?'

'Thanks for your patience, yes, now it's over to you.'

'There has been that treaty and we have had, I think, five years of truce. There is no fighting, so I want to go back to England. I had travelled all over her, and Wales and Scotland when I was there before, and I want to go back for a last time, but many of my old friends they are gone. I was there for three months in 1395, after the king, he is come back from Ireland in May. I was at the court with Sir Richard Sturry....'

'Lollard!', 'Enemy of the church!', 'Wycliffian heterodox!'

'Monks! Thank you! Can we let Mr Froissart speak please? Sorry Jean, do go on.'

'No problem Damian. The monks they are the same everywhere. Disputatious, no? No, not you my dear friend Monk of St Denis. Yes, I came back, and I took a book to give to the king and met some old friends, your Mr Chaucer for example: we first met 27 years before in Italy, with Petrarch, do you know him?'

'Sorry, I have to leave literature to another day Jean. Right now it's more about the politics.'

'Politics? What is that?'

'What powerful people did..., do.... How they get on with other powerful people.'

'You are meaning the Duke of Gloucester? Ah what a natural force that man had. So strong willed. Everyone in Richard's court was afraid of him. He had many friends in the country, all the ones that didn't like John of Gaunt and all the ones that didn't like the Wycliffe way of thinking.' Lowering his voice to a whisper, Froissart made a lightening aside: 'The Benedictines you have seen!', resuming seamlessly with: 'He was so irritable, shouting, shouting all the time. He thought he was the most important. You know, when I was there, I saw how he acted. He always must be right and for the king to do what he said. One day, it is funny, but he was like that, he shouted what he wanted to happen in the Royal Council with the king and all the lords and then left to have lunch all by himself. Was he excused by the king? Did he ask permission to leave the royal presence? No, no. Your Henry IV left the Council a little bit later to have his lunch with him also, and when the king at last he came to have his lunch with all the rest, you know, the Duke of Gloucester he said we have finished so goodbye, and he went home. Nobody else could do that I think.'

'That's great Jean,' manners maketh man, thought Damian, what a tell-tale sign, 'that's real politics, anything else?'

'Well, I was there when that happened.'

'Ok, I got that.'

'They said a lot about him. They told me he was cunning and malicious. They said he took money for his royal jobs but didn't do any work. He was not liked at all, they were afraid of him, and they all said that he had a lot of people behind him.'

'Great! Good background, what about the marriage?'

'Well yes, it was what they were all talking about. Richard, his poor queen Anne, he loved her so much, but she had died in 1394 and somebody said he should marry again, but a French one, and first, the French, they offer three royal cousins....'

'One at a time I hope!'

'You English, too much always the joking isn't it!' There was an unmistakeable irritation with Damian's light-hearted banter. 'Then it is a princess and it is incredible, no? The English, they say yes!'

'Why did that happen? She was far too young, surely?'

'So she was. Far, far too young. But this was a marriage not for love, no, maybe you are married Damian?' Damian couldn't keep the colour from his cheeks.

'No, not at the moment. What kind of a marriage was it?'

'Not love, no, no, no,' Damian appreciated the neat little finger-wagging hand gesture that Froissart used to underscore his negation of love as the prime mover in this instance: 'No, no…, not love,' and Froissart wagged again, 'it was your word…, policy.'

'Politics.'

'Yes that. This was very special. If the king of France is the father-in-law, then Richard, he can meet him, as you say, face-to-face, and they can talk about the treaty, and make a final peace between them.'

'So it's a political marriage….'

'But yes, of course!'

'Which will break the deadlock with the treaty?'

'It is exact. I was there when first they talk about it. Then I go home.'

'But you kept your finger on the pulse.'

'I did. I did. That is so poetic. Maybe you are a little bit the poet my friend Damian? I kept my finger on it. It was easy. There was much going and coming back. Ambassadors, heralds, much arrangement and negotiation.'

'Wasn't it about this time that you say Robert the Hermit was sent over?'

'Yes, he came over with the Count of St Pol, the ambassador. There were those in England and France who said this war between Christians must end.' Damian recalled the divisions in the monkish ranks. 'It is time to join together and take back control of the Holy Land. Robert was not really a hermit. He had been many years a soldier and was a knight of Philippe de Mézières' Order of the Passion of Christ.'

'Jean, your chapter all about Robert is not in any of the Froissart books we have, just in Alberto's and Thomas Johnes'. This soldier-hermit gave King Richard a book. It's in the British Library.'

'Yes, it was a kind of book. It was Philippe's letter to Richard. His vision for the future. France and England together leading a united Christendom. Robert, he stayed first with the king, then he went to see the Duke of Gloucester.'

'How did that go?'

'The duke, he was most polite, very courteous. Robert made a strong case for peace. The duke didn't think the king should join with his enemies and give away any future advantage that England might have by keeping up her claim on France. As Robert said war, it just makes more war. Those who are against peace in this life will be punished in the next. It was time to forgive, which is what Jesus would have done, he said. In the end, the duke, he washed his hands. He said that even if he agreed, the nation might disagree and anyway it was a matter for his two other brothers, York and Gaunt.'

Damian was two-fold smug: one, that he had found the book in the British Library which proved Robert's visit, and its purpose, and two, that he'd found that Henry IV, in his first so-called parliament, had enacted a ban on some kind of contaminating threat from abroad which proved that something 'over there' worried him: '*In the lands overseas a new sect has arisen, of certain people dressed in white clothing, and pretending to great sanctity; and because the people in the realm of England could easily allow themselves to be corrupted by such a sect and novelty…. to the great peril of the souls of his said people, and perhaps the overthrow of the same realm.*' Were these Philippe's religious knights, clad in crusader white?

'Do you know how many knights Philippe recruited for his order?'

'He wanted 2000. He spent his life on it. I think he managed 89 in the end.' Henry might have been fearful enough to get his ban into the order of business for his first parliament, but it didn't seem much of a threat. Philippe's order of chivalry was a flop.

'I was glad to be able to corroborate the Robert the Hermit episode from your book. How popular was peace?'

'There were many for peace. And many against. On both sides.'

'And the Duke of Gloucester was definitely for war?'

'I give him a dialogue with one of his knights, Lackinghay, and he sets out his real feelings.'

'Historians don't like it. You weren't there so how could you know what he said?'

'What he said was heard many times and reported. I dramatised it. Was I the first, do you think? The first to dramatise, like Sir Walter Scott?'

'It does have a modern feel. Maybe you should be given the

credit for breaking new ground. That knight, Laquingay in your
original, Lackinghay in English translations, was John Lakenheath,
the Duke's right-hand-man. He deputised for Gloucester at
the court of chivalry in 1389. He is the right person to have
talking to the Duke. Gloucester tells him that this isn't the
time for peace, something like: 'the people want war, they can't
live decently without it' and 'if I live a couple of years longer in
good health, the war will be renewed,' and I remember this bit:
'the king is too fat in the arse and only interested in eating and
drinking.'

'I wanted to show his way of speaking.'

'You did a good job. They should've given you more credit. It's
fresh, you make it come alive.'

'Thank you. I wrote it with a lot of care.' Froissart's eyes
watered and he gave a series of dry coughs. 'You know .. uhhu
.., Gloucester at the wedding .. uhhu .., he was not happy ..
uhhu .., Richard had to pay him to be happy .. uhhu ..,' and the
chronicler broke off to refresh his old throat with water.

Damian took this chance to reflect on the critical timings and
keep things in order. From May 1396 there is a determination
in England and France to make a lasting peace and Richard II
and Isabella de Valois, nearly seven years old, marry on 31st
October 1396.

Richard meets the King of France at the wedding near Calais
and it's really the peace treaty on the agenda, not the marriage.
But there are politics. Not all the English want peace and
Gloucester is the head of those that don't. This is where the
crisis starts and where Richard's end begins.

35

']ean, are you ok to carry on?'

'I'll be fine, it is my throat, it has a frog. I'm fine, really. It is now time to talk of the plots, yes?'

'It certainly is. This is the part of your work that the historians ignore.'

'How much do they leave out?'

'All of it. It's 30,000 words or thereabouts, probably more.'

'Trente mille! Sacré bleu! It is the most important!'

'I know, I know. Let's set a new datum; the January 1397 parliament, after Richard II has married Isabella at the end of October 1396 and she's been crowned.

Is there a sense that the conspirators are withdrawing from the court? That's a classic indication of troublemaking. Historians are a bit vague. Archbishop Arundel was certainly replaced as chancellor by the bishop of Exeter on 26th November and it seems that Gloucester and the Earl of Arundel may not have attended the January 1397 parliament at all. Or very partially. Or selectively.

The parliamentary roll records that some in the commons asked for absent lords to be called. Maybe they meant Gloucester, Arundel and Warwick? None of them attended the investiture of John of Gaunt's son as Duke of Somerset on 10th February. Quite rude. You talk of a plot to depose Richard and replace him with Roger Mortimer, the Earl of March. Is that at this time?'

'The timings precisely I do not know but yes, the Earl of

March is the next in line to the throne after Richard. Maybe this plot was just talk, but Mortimer he will not do it, and he goes back to Ireland. And Gloucester? He is not satisfied. Maybe he can make trouble for Richard in this parliament. Did he?'

Damian had a sinking feeling that he was going to have to change his mind about something. Old Damian's effigy quest had taken him to the Isle of Axholme where the Haxey hood game has been played on every feast of the Epiphany, 6th January, since maybe 1400, or something like that. He'd been convinced, at the time, that Elizabeth Fitzalan had been guiding him from beyond the grave and, in some way, shape or form, had led him there.

The folkloric revels were based on the legend of a fine lady whose silky cape had blown off and been recovered by some yokels. Damian had connected the woman of legend with Elizabeth Fitzalan, his 'lady in red' and 'Romana Clay'. There was, however, another connection, another 'Haxey' incident, from about the same time, and it seemed to be stretching it a bit far to say that these two Haxeys were not related in some way, the word 'Haxey' being somewhat unusual. It was disappointing to be obliged to re-evaluate his exciting discovery, but the new one was more important and he was now a historian.

'Good question Jean. If the Duke of Gloucester was meddling in parliament then that would corroborate your account, that is that the Duke of Gloucester was fomenting discontent, and I do think we may have something.'

'Oooo corroboration!' Froissart clapped his hands together in boyish glee. 'Maybe now they will take me more at serious, no?'

'Well..., in the second week of the January 1397 parliament they are talking about something serious, but we don't know what. Then Sir Thomas Haxey hands over a petition. There are four headings to it. The first three, no problem, but the fourth! Haxey says there are too many bishops and ladies living in the royal household and it costs too much. Richard II goes ballistic. He accuses Haxey of treason and condemns him to death.'

'To death! Is that usual in your country?'

'No, that's why it's so significant. What Haxey did was clearly more than usually impertinent. Maybe it was known that extra-parliamentary interests were behind it.'

'And they chop off his head?'

'No, they didn't. This is also interesting. Archbishop Arundel stands up and says there's no need to execute him, just give him to the church and we'll lock him up in St Albans for you, and the king goes for the merciful option.'

'And Sir Haxey, who is he?'

'He had been a clerk, basically a high-ranking civil servant during the Merciless Parliament, and done well out of supporting the faction that took over. He is recognised as being close to Archbishop Arundel.'

'So this Haxey, he is their man. He belongs to them!'

'Yes. So that's January. Now we can move closer to the big one in July 1397.'

'Ah yes, this one is fantastic, hardly to be believed!'

'We know that something happened in July, but the historians present it as Richard making his move to get vengeance for 1388. You tell it differently.'

'Yes, I had it from the Count of St Pol himself, after. Gloucester and the Earl of Arundel, they were encouraging rumours: the king was going to sell Calais to France. He will take the arms of France off the royal standard. Fighting people will have no work. The king, he is ridiculous. He is betraying England to the French. It was your famous John Holland, the Earl of Huntingdon, who was finding out it all, that they want to start the war again. The king's uncles, John of Gaunt and the Duke of York, they say 'Don't worry, our brother Gloucester would never do that', but they do nothing, and the king, he is afraid. And all his friends are afraid. They say: 'Look what is happened in 1388! They will take over again, and we will all be killed.' This is how they are thinking before July.'

'Was there a real plot?'

'You know that there was. They had done it before in 1388, and they had already tried again. Oh, if only the Earl of March, he would have gone with them, then it would have been no problem. He was next in line to the throne. It would be then so easy to replace Richard. You know, they thought the Earl of March was their man, their puppet? His father was dead. His uncle, Thomas Mortimer, was his father figure. This Thomas Mortimer was the man who killed the royal captain Molyneux at Radcot bridge in 1387. The Earl of March, when he was a little boy with no father, you know who was his guardian? It was the Earl of Arundel himself. They really thought they owned him. Yes, it would have been so easy. But…, he would with them not make the rebel, so they needed another plan.'

'It's the new plan I'd like to talk about.'

'Yes, this one was the more strong. They will divide England between the uncles: Gloucester will get London and the South, Arundel will get the West and Wales, the Duke of Lancaster and Duke of York, they will get the Midlands and North.'

'Who was going to be king?'

'I don't know. Without the Earl of March, they have no one. Or maybe it is to be Henry? Maybe they will kill his father John of Gaunt? I don't know.'

'Was this the plot that sparked it off?'

'Certainly, this one, or a similar.'

'It was this one!' piped up the Monk of St Denis from the French contingent. 'At last, I have been waiting. This was the one. Mowbray found out about it and told Richard that Gloucester had written to Warwick and Henry IV saying meet me at Arundel castle. It was to be the start of their rebellion! I had it from John Holland, the Earl of Huntingdon, almost his very lips, and he...'

'Thank you. It's good information but..., I'm sorry, we can't use it. You say this happened eight days before August 1396, and we're talking about 1397.'

'But maybe they made a writing mistake like...'

'I'm really sorry, there's so few facts left after so many years of covering up, that only rock-solid ones can be used..., sorry about that.'

Damian had what he came for and just needed to point up some details in his head. It was all in the missing Froissart anyway. There had been paranoia in Richard's court. It was believed that forces would strike against them. Forces who had already proved the seriousness of their threat by doing it before in 1388. A critical point was arrived at where Richard and his supporters believed that inaction would bring about their imminent downfall.

That seemed to be July 11th, 1397, at a meeting of the royal council in Nottingham. The arrest of Gloucester, Arundel and

Warwick is ordered that day. But the king is not well prepared, and he sends to Cheshire for armed men the same day, or the day after. He wants 2000 but gets 768. A tidy force nonetheless. On 13th July he made a proclamation. This could be checked with the Walsingham monks of St Albans:

'Yes, that's quite right: Richard was afraid of an outcry; he said in the proclamation that is wasn't for their old crimes, but for recent transgressions, and they would go over them at the next parliament.' Another stuck their oar in: – 'I wrote about it as well: in 1394, when John of Gaunt and the Earl of Arundel are fighting in parliament, and are forced to be friends, I say, ahem, I say: 'so for the time being a great storm abated'. Is this the storm?'

Froissart's professional storytelling seemed to have lulled the monks somewhat and, taken by surprise, they'd blurted it out. There, in the heart of the pro-Henry camp, was a very strong hint that King Richard was forced into heading off another 1388-style insurrection. It felt like a wrap, but there was one last thing, as they were all together.

36

'Froissart, you and the company of chroniclers here assembled have been most accommodating. You were all there, either actually, or like our esteemed Froissart, not actually, but with a passion for....'

'Yes good, a passion, I had a passion!'

'...finding out what was happening.' Damian glanced amiably at Froissart, who was much flattered, and continued with his address. 'So, what do you think Henry IV really wanted? What did he say he wanted?' Jean Creton jumped to his feet. He didn't have his arm in the air, fluttering his hand, saying 'Pick me! Pick me!' but he might as well have had.

'He said everything! He promised a war on Scotland to the Earl of Northumberland...,' this wasn't news to Damian; Henry had confirmed this in an announcement to his first parliament, 'and he told Norhumberland to tell King Richard that he was just there to be made Duke of Lancaster, help him with a parliament – 'I will help you govern better' – those were his exact words, but five people would have to be killed!' Creton was well away.

'And you know what else? Archbishop Arundel proclaimed to everybody that Henry, he had the Pope's blessing, that it was a kind of crusade. And Henry writes 150 letters to people, and he says Richard wants to rule from Ireland, he will arrest everyone and wants to take their money, and he will sell off all English territory in France. And Henry, he will kill you if you don't join him.' Adam of Usk joined his own experience to

Creton's passion with:

'That's quite right. When he was going round with his army, if he met anyone, he would say: if we fight, then you will die or surrender. Either way you will be stripped naked. Or you can join my army. Or words to that effect.'

'So, he said everything to everyone. What did he say he had come to England for at his coronation?' This was very much a leading question as Damian knew the answer. 'Sarky Steve', popular history teacher, had made them learn it off by heart for a sadistic Christmas homework. It was the first use of English recorded in parliament, Sarky Steve had said. It was written on the parliamentary roll and seemed to embarrass historians. 'Adam, this is one for you, I think.'

'Just so, thank you. I worked for Archbishop Arundel and was at Westminster for Henry's first parliament, if it can be called that, and at his coronation. I was given the job, along with a panel of other learned doctors of the church, to find corroboration for a claim Henry made. Henry sincerely believed that he was the real king of England, and that Richard was the imposter, and knew it. Our job was to find the proof.'

'Hot stuff Adam!'

'I know. I was appalled at the time. That's when I realised Henry was a charlatan. A jackanapes.'

'Please go on.'

'With pleasure. We were asked to go back 117 years and confirm that Edward I was not the rightful king. That his younger brother, Edmund Crouchback, was the first-born son, not Edward.

If this was true, then Henry IV – son of Blanche of Lancaster, the daughter of Henry of Grosmont, first Duke of Lancaster,

who was the son of Henry, 3rd Earl of Lancaster, who was
the younger son of Edmund Crouchback, his elder brother
Thomas having been executed by Edward II for rebelling – was
therefore, by right of direct blood descent from Henry III,
England's true king. This would have made Edward I, Edward II,
Edward III and Richard II illegitimate monarchs. It wasn't true of
course. It was nonsense, but it is what Henry himself believed.
It's all in my book.'

'Thank you Adam, very clear. Good points well made. Perhaps
I can recall the exact translation? Ahem…,' and Damian gave
his impressive and apparently off-the-cuff rendition of the
not-very-well-known declaration in Henry IV's own words,
confident that any spelling mistakes, circled in red by Sarky
Steve, earning him 3/20, which still rankled given how much
of the precious Christmas holiday he'd had to devote to its
memorisation, that and the Christmas Sums from the maths
teacher, whose actual nickname was 'Sadist', would pass
unnoticed, taking care to pronounce the 'y's as 'th's.

'In the name of Fadir, Sone, and Holy Gost, I, Henry of Lancastr
chalenge yis rewme of Yngland, and ye corone with alle ye
membres and ye appurtenances, als I yt am disendit be right
lyne of the blode comyng fro the gude lorde Kyng Henry therde,
and thorghe yat ryght yat God of his grace hathe sent me, with
helpe of my kyn and of my frendes to recover it; the whiche
rewme was in poynt to be undone for defaut of governance and
undoyng of the gode lawes.'

The which earned him well-deserved plaudits from all the
chroniclers. The which he accepted gracefully, and with a slight
bow. Henry had come to 'recover' the kingdom; the which had

been lost to England's true kings since the death of Henry III
by the deceitful substitution of Edmund the Nothing by Edward
the First. Completely nutty. No wonder Archbishop Arundel
made sure there was a pretence at a formal deposition in case
Henry's claim proved hard to swallow. Corroboration?

'Walsinghams, did he say that?'

'Aye, he did.'

'Not only did he say that…,' butted in John Hardyng, 'but it
was the accepted reason at the time, forget about the pretence
of a deposition. I put a note about it into my chronicle about
60 years after. I heard him say it myself, at the coronation. I had
to put a footnote in because they were still saying that Henry's
claim to be king came from Henry III. It was annoying because
the insertion looked clumsy, which I think spoiled the overall
effect a bit, as it was supposed to be a poem. Here's my bit:

> *'Many men have been misled and are still greatly confused upon*
> *the following point, they claim that Edmund, Duke of Lancaster*
> *was the elder son of Henry III.'*

I go on to say that it was John of Gaunt who made it up. But
it was me that made that bit up because I was working for the
Yorkists by that time and long-dead John of Gaunt was still
their bogeyman. Also, it was nonsense because no documents
were ever found. They even debated it in parliament in 1459
– or was it 1460? One of those two anyway, when Richard
of York was applying to be king. I rest my case and I'll fight
anybody who says different!'

Damian was surprised by Hardyng's belligerent parting shot
but it was obvious really; if Henry IV was England's true king
because Edward I'st brother was actually the first born, then

it worked for Henry V and Henry VI – they weren't a usurping dynasty at all. Adam of Usk, the Walsinghams, Hardyng, in fact all the English chroniclers agreed that Henry IV had made this insane claim. And abroad, what did they think there?

37

'Monsieur Froissart? Did the Henry III origin myth get over the channel?'

'Mister Damian Email, this is indeed most interesting. As I told you before, there are three parts to my story about the end of Richard. There was first my visit in 1395, then there was the contact of diplomats for the marriage and after, and, for the last part, a herald from Henry, he came to tell me the rest. In his story, there is no mention of Henry III. From him, it was given that Henry got England by conquest, because he was the heir, just that 'heir' no more, and that Richard had given it to him of his own free will.'

'Perhaps the message is being massaged?'

'Certainly it seems so, and there is more massage. He gave me more about how Henry thought he was the real king.' Damian had been hoping Froissart would open up on this.

'Please go on.'

'This herald from Bruges…,' an interruption from Adam cut him short.

'Was it John Lancaster? I met him in Bruges, or was it Paris, 1408? Could it be the same? I was in exile. I hoped he would fix my papers to get me back…' Damian didn't want to cut him off, but it was a tad embarrassing as Froissart had died two years before. Froissart brushed it aside.

'No, no, this was a certain Richard…, anyway, this herald had the whole story worked out for me…,' and altered, thought Damian, there's no mention of the northern earl's help in the first weeks of the invasion. In fact, according to Froissart, Henry doesn't even land in the North. He comes ashore at Plymouth with a small force from Brittany, and it's all 'Henry and the Londoners' from then on. This is what historians called an inaccuracy. Was this emphasis on 'Londoners' actually a code for a faction: the supporters of the Duke of Gloucester?

'Damian, do you like in my book when I talk about Henry in exile in Paris?'

'Yes, I do. Again, you very nicely dramatise the account of his stay. Sir Walter Scott couldn't have done it better: Henry paces around, looks out of windows thoughtfully, he's in two minds, shall he stay or shall he go, what about his reputation? It's all very well done. Maybe you were the first?'

'I know, I like it too. Maybe it's not exactly what happened there, but good drama, no?'

'It's great drama, Froissart, and there is truth in drama. Something did happen there. You understand, you engage, and you try and explain, I like it.'

'Yes, and in this drama, I have to explain Henry's motivation, yes? The herald, he gives me details, and I paint in the rest with colour. He was staying in a house of the Duke of Orleans. They were very close. They made a love-pact between them in writing. And he was arranging for Henry to marry Mary of Berry, but King Richard, he says 'no'. But Henry is thinking about England. Shall he go back? The archbishop has come over. Henry has some supporters with him. They say: 'Yes, go back, after all, you are descended in a direct line from St Edward the Confessor! That is a code, yes?'

'Absolument, the important word is here, I think, the word 'direct'. St Edward didn't have any children. It's a reference to royal descent in the direct line; king to son, king to son and so on. Henry was never in the direct line. It was massaged. The herald made it more palatable through vagueness, but it shows that it was Henry's lineage that was thought to count the most. And that it was somehow direct. And that, in your version Henry got the idea from his supporters. You are the only one who tries to explain it. Even though it can't be true.'

'As you say Damian.' It may or may not have been true but from a dramatic point of view, it was faultless.

They had reached the part of a meeting where the speaker asks if there are any questions, and the attendees hope to God there aren't any. A certain listlessness was evident: Froissart looked decidedly heavy-lidded, Adam was toying with a coffee cup, Hardyng was sat by the monks chin on breast-bone, and some of them had their cowls pulled down to cover their eyes, their hands knitted on their chests; Creton and the Monk of St Denis were murmuring to each other at the end of the table, continuing a conversation that had been going on throughout.

Damian had planned to go out with a bang. It would have been impolite to ask them to cheer him, so he'd planned to say: 'What did the people say when they were asked if they would accept Henry as their king?', and they, enthused by, and grateful for, his coming, and the meal, would take the hint and shout with sincere joviality: 'Aye! Aye!', 'Yes! Yes!', and, authentically from the French. 'Oy! Oy!', rendered textually in old French, he knew, as *Oil! Oil!*, but he could tell they probably wouldn't all play along and it risked falling flat. He would slip out with no fanfare.

'Thank you all again. Could I offer the collected chroniclers a hypocras to show my appreciation? My personal recommendation is the Butts Bank cider and gin cocktail,' to which the assembled medievalists immediately responded: 'Ugh, cider, what's that?', 'Did he say engine?', 'What are we having?' Adam of Usk threw them all a lifeline:

'My dear Damian, what a nice idea! Wine and comfits! They keep some special hypocras for us called 'Glühwein', it's nice and spicy, and they've got some artisan fruit pastilles, which we like. That would be a fine gesture, and a much appreciated one.'

'Ok. I'll get them to send it through. I'm off now…, don't worry Adam, I'll see myself out…, thanks everybody, goodbye!' A jollier send-off would have been better, but he did get a couple of nice face-looks and hand-waves as he was leaving. He could have gone straight back, but there was the question of the bill for the meal, Sir Walter Scott's and Horace Walpoles' fees, if there were any, and the last round of drinks. It would have been easy to just leave it behind but what might be the consequences? The ramifications? His name would be mud, a shunned pariah at any future festival.

The hostess at the front desk was very helpful and took him through the bill. It was astronomic. The bill for the Beaune wine itself was more than the food!

'Thank you. How would you like me to pay for it all? Credit card ok?'

'I'm sorry, we don't take credit cards.'

'Oh.'

'But it's all taken care of Mr Email. A lady from the Autodidactiiae has paid it. She left her card.'

Damian took the card which bore the familiar Autodidactiiae logo. A confident hand had added the initials 'E' and 'F'. Elizabeth Fitzalan? Get off! It couldn't be her! Not here! A set up? A hoax? A merry prankster pranking their merriment to get him…, to make him… But such a turn up could not be entirely unexpected in this context.

He looked again at the card. It was no 'F', 'twas an 'M'. 'E.M.' Elizabeth Mackintosh aka Josephine Tey, aka Gordon Daviot. That made sense and, service having been included, he could leave free of any obligation.

'Thank you.'

'Thank you Mr Email.'

'And if she comes back, thank her from me, would you?'

'I will. I'll be sure to do that.'

'Thanks. Cheerio.'

'Goodbye Mr Email.'

38

Mister Napman brought me a dream
Made it the best that I've ever seen.

The rhyme was: 'dream' with 'seen'. This was an imperfect
rhyme and thus held to be a cleverer one. Writing a musical,
how hard could it be? Words. Tunes. Ta-ta-ta, da-da-da, la-di-dah.
It couldn't be that difficult. You didn't have to use many words
and there was a restricted number of notes to choose from.

His night's work had come to an end and much later than
anticipated. Rather than expanding his historical mind as Mr
Napman, he must have been really asleep by the time he came
to, because it was just before dawn when he'd infiltrated
himself into bed without waking Clare. His mind working
overtime wouldn't let him lie and he got up to get shaved,
showered and dressed, before heading downstairs to explore
his songwriting skills in a low-risk kitchen context.

Clare had been up, and down unusually early too, wanting
to push on. She'd been happy to try his new cooked-breakfast
serving suggestion, wolfed it and, eager to press on to finish
nibbling out her glass pieces, was hard at it in the studio, leaving
Damian alone in the kitchen.

It had been his signature dish: boiled eggs, almost hard,
chopped bacon, all knifed-up together in a cup, salt, grey pepper,
plenty of butter, pinch of tarragon, all on toast. 'Egg' was hard
to rhyme.

Tap, tap, tap on the computer.

In German 'egg' was 'Ei', pronounced 'aye'. In medieval English it was…, tap, tap, tap: 'ey', also pronounced 'aye' and 'eyren', for eggs. *Egg* and *eggs* were themselves Norse words that had come south from northern England in the fifteenth century and taken over. 'Egg' had usurped 'ey' and no one knew why.

The original version was preserved in the word 'cockeney', meaning a small first egg from an inexperienced hen which – tap, tap, tap – was still called a 'cock's egg'. Such an egg, if incubated, could hatch out as a malevolent beastly hen-dragon, so it was best not to try it.

Tap, tap, tap.

The 'guh' sound in 'egg' was only evident in English, Norwegian and – tap, tap, tap – and Greek! The translator site could say any word out loud. The Greek for egg sounded like 'avgo'. The word had left Greece, become 'aye-go' somewhere, then dropped the 'Oh' at the end: 'aye-guh', to give 'egg', and it had replaced the good-old Anglo-Saxon 'ey' around 1400. Who'd have thought it?

Damian would have to develop some expertise if he was to turn out decent lyrics. What about song titles? What about a catchy name for his egg and bacon mini cooked-breakfast which didn't have one? 'Chopped eggs with bacon' was as far as it had ever got. Very pedestrian. He'd have to do better than that. 'Eggs Henry' was too dull. What about 'Eggs Bolingbroke'? Henry IV was known as Bolingbroke before he became king. Eggs, you boiled them. It almost rhymed. Perfect.

Jumbling words and phrases fought with each other as food-crusted crockery and cutlery clattered into the automatic dishwasher's cubicles.

By the time he turned it on, he had the first line of Henry's song which would be:

'Eys became eggs when I became Rex'.

The title could be 'Call me King!' But it was harder than he thought. Maybe the egg theme had been too restrictive? Could the cream first or jam first scone controversy provide material that could be turned into a smash hit West-End show tune?

'Butter is the relish, then jam if you want, never the other way round. Cream plays the buttery role, and the confiture stands proud.'

That was good. His experimentation was really working. But it felt forced. It needed to be snappier, more rappy. Hamilton had a lot of rap in it. Maybe it should be more like:

'It used to be ey, now its egg, but to me on my throne they said Aye! Get cream on the scone before jam and make it the right way or die!'

That had something. It worked however you pronounced 'scone'; whether you rhymed it with 'gone' or 'own'. The rhyme with 'own' was the more obvious one, so to make it cleverer it would have to be with 'gone', because it was imperfect, and imperfect was catchier, and better. The title couldn't be 'Fusty Buns', which he liked, as there was no way of fitting staleness in without over-working the metaphor and using 'buns' for 'scones' would put too much onto the audience.

Clare and Dolmetscher were going to ask him about the songs. He needed to get some answers. Another possible song title for Henry could be:

'I didn't need to be egged on.' or *'Egg me on! (They didn't need to)'.*

Damian found it easy getting words strung together, but then they set themselves to any and every tune he'd ever heard before. The tunes would have to be original as well. What about a Latin-American feel to bring attention to Henry's megalomaniacal narcissism? A catchy rumba feel?

Aye!

> aye-aye-aye…,
>> aye-aye-aye…,
>>> aye-aye
>>>> Aye! Aye! Aye! Aye!

That looked fun. He'd keep it in mind. The kitchen try-out hadn't been especially successful, but it didn't feel that he'd need 10,000 hours to write some decent lyrics. His new historical thing just needed to be well organised in his mind, and then the words would come easily. The music was more of a problem. That might have to be sub-contracted out. It was time to think about the story. Sitting and talking with Froissart would prove to be his second-best-ever historical dream contact. The tomb effigy conversations he'd had as Old Damian were, in comparison, pale shadows. It was all much clearer now.

Point one: Henry. No one around him had understood what was going on in his head. When Elizabeth of Lancaster's effigy in Burford church had confessed to giving Henry a king-complex by dressing him up as a little prince when he was a toddler, Damian had thought her self-denunciation and grief at the tragic consequences of her playfulness very overdone, but she'd been right. Henry IV couldn't conceive of a world in which he wasn't king. When he came from exile to claim his inheritance, it wasn't to be just the Duke of Lancaster. That wasn't the inheritance he had in mind. It was the whole kingdom. They'd stolen the crown from his ancestors, and he was going to get it back.

Point two: the politics. England was split between those who wanted peace, and those who wanted war. Lies are half-way round the world before Truth has got its boots on and many were ready to believe carefully spread rumours that painted Richard II as an effeminate peacenik ready to sell out to France. Henry offered an immediate war against Scotland to the two northern barons whose support in the first days gave him success in his usurping blitzkrieg.

This got his feet under the royal table, and Richard under lock and key in London, despite his lack of support within the rest of the aristocracy. Any opposition was fully neutered in an orgy of retribution known as The Epiphany Rising, three months after he made himself king of England. When Henry gets his first parliament together at the start of October 1399, after a usurping campaign of only 12 weeks, he's completely in charge because anybody who doesn't agree with him is dead or, within another 12 weeks, will die.

But…, but…, but….

The war party is disappointed. Henry is plagued with rebellions. He gets ill. He doesn't seem blessed and can't conjure up enough money to fight properly in Wales, and in England, let alone France. They have to wait for Henry the Fifth, whose star has always shone more brightly than his father's, to come and give them what they want, and it's worth waiting for: Agincourt! From there it's glory, glory, hallelujah all the way down! But the war is lost by 1435 when the Burgundians, the allies of the English, reconcile themselves with the French king.

Now it's just a 20-year French mopping up operation until the final Battle of Castillon blasts away their last hopes in a murderous barrage of cannonballs from a storm-cloud of gun smoke in 1453.

Point 4 was taken care of. The 'What?' would be a musical, but…, niggle, niggle, niggle…, Point 3? Point 3: 'So what?' So what? It was still up in the air. There wasn't enough for a musical. The themes were unresolved. He'd have to go in further. Explore the deeper waters with sensitive Henry the Sixth and the Wars of the Roses. He'd been in before, many times, but had always come out dripping wet and none the wiser. Now was probably a good time to leave the distracting kitchen and find how it all had to end in the library, no nap required, just by thinking it through.

39

Damian settled himself into the library sofa. He was nervous; an under-practised concert pianist about to perform. The bloody Wars of the Roses! Next thing he knew he would be having to deal with Henry VIII. Jeez!

The Wars of the Roses were like the dead marshes in Tolkein – it was hard to find your way through the mirey tussock-strewn pools. With a slight yet theatrical shake of his head, as if to rid himself of a bad memory, Damian vowed to ignore all the confusing details and happenings. They would never make sense on their own. Royalty is a family affair. The crown is the power. It's only about the family.

Fighting Henry the Fifth's reign ends vaingloriously because he throws it all away, after nine wonderfully warlike years, by dying and leaving all the dynastic hopes to nine-month-old Henry the Sixth, his only child.

Little sensitive Henry the Sixth needs uncles to run things for him until he comes of age 16 years later, but he's already lost his uncle Thomas, killed before he was born at the battle of Baugé in 1421. There's just two left: fighting uncle John, Duke of Bedford – the war won't stop while he's around but he dies leaving no heirs in 1435 – and clever uncle Humphrey, Duke of Clarence.

Humphrey is there to keep things steady and he does, because he loves war too, but he dies childless in 1447 and that's it; all the legitimate descendants of usurping Henry IV are dead, except 26-year old and sensitive Henry the Sixth himself.

He's the last of the line.

He must have felt vulnerable. By the time armchair warmongerer Humphrey exits stage left, the war in France is nearly lost.

Can the hopeless situation be stabilised? Would a marriage to feisty, French and beautiful Margaret of Anjou in 1445 help? It might, but Henry and Margaret won't have their first child until ten years later, at which point all the English territories in France have been lost forever, except Calais.

What would usurping Henry IV, let alone fighting Henry the Fifth, have thought of that? Adam of Usk would have said 'I told you so,' if called to comment from beyond the grave. Richard II wanted peace for its own sake. Now England faces an ignominious peace forced on her by total defeat and 400 years of England-in-France is no more. They've stayed at the card table too long:

> *You've got to know when to hold 'em*
> *Know when to fold 'em*
> *Know when to walk away*
> *And know when to run.*

Richard, 3rd Duke of York, is such a gambler, but only knows when to hold 'em.

This Richard, who is he? He's the grandson of slippery Edward, second Duke of York, betrayer of Richard II, according to Jean Creton, and betrayer of the Epiphany Rising, according to everyone, and grandson of Edmund, Duke of York, the fourth little piggy son of Edward III, who famously handed over England on a plate to Henry IV when he asked for it at Berkeley castle in 1399.

Having Edmund for a grandfather makes him a royal great-

great-grandson of Edward III. But, oh the consanguinity! He's even more royal than that! He is also the great-great-great grandson of the same king by his mother, and this lineage…, this has some of Lionel's blood, from the second little piggy, the next brother down from the eldest piggy, the Black Prince.

Could this Richard 3rd Duke of York feel that he is more senior in descent, that he outranks, and is ultimately more royal than sensitive Henry the Sixth, the mere grandson of usurping Henry IV?

Yes, and what's more he's got a chip on his shoulder because Henry the Fifth chopped his father's head off at Southampton, just before taking the English army over to stomp around France, and it was Lionel's blood, contaminated by royalty, that his own father shed at his execution. Proof positive, if Richard needed any, that he was the special one.

When the last uncle, Humphrey, dies in 1447, it's sensitive Henry the Sixth, all alone and heirless, against his worst enemy in royal terms; somebody who can legitimately replace him, Richard, 3rd Duke of York.

However and however, this Richard gets killed at Wakefield right at the end of 1460, with one of his two sons.

But, and it's definitely how he would have wanted it, his surviving son becomes Edward IV six weeks afterwards.

Edward IV has a glorious 22-year reign, with a short six-month interruption which requires only the death of imprisoned sensitive Henry VI to sort out. Then he dies and it's over to his 12-year-old son in 1483.

Oh no it's not! All his sons have gone missing. Enter Richard III, his brother.

Time to rewind. Henry the Sixth. Apart from sparky,

pugnaciously vivacious and good-looking Margaret of Anjou at his side as his queen, who else does sensitive Henry the Sixth have around him that he can depend on?

If there is someone that Richard 3rd Duke of York detests more than Henry the Sixth, it has to be the Beaufort family, especially Edmund and John.

40

Who are the Beauforts? John of Gaunt is Henry IV's dad and the third little piggy. Big John of Gaunt has a second family with long-time lover Katherine Swynford and she gives usurping Henry IV some step-siblings who carry the name 'Beaufort', and not 'Lancaster'.

There is first: John, dead in 1410, but father of John and Edmund who are both detested by Richard, 3rd Duke of York.

John Junior is a soldier but goes a bit bonkers trying to win an unwinnable war and dies a disappointed lunatic in 1444.

He has only one child, Margaret, the mother of Henry VII.

The other son, Edmund, is a fighter but dies of natural causes in 1455. Not so his three sons who endure blunt and sharp force Yorkist trauma and are all off-stage by 1471, taking their bloodline with them.

Then there's Cardinal Henry, extremely capable but married to the church, and he's dead in 1447. And there was Thomas, a good soldier but he's gone in 1427. And there was fecund Joan who has 16 children, 14 of which are Nevilles, one of which was the mother of Edward IV and Richard III. But no Beauforts.

1455 marks the death of the last close relative of sensitive Henry the Sixth who is old enough to offer him useful support: fighting Edmund Beaufort.

By 1456, sensitive Henry VI must fight off any claimants to his throne all by his sensitive self, helped only by his redoubtable french queen. She rocks their child to sleep in his cradle. A child who will one day be king. Or will he? No. He will be executed at the battle of Tewkesbury in 1471 at the age of seventeen.

Henry the Sixth's guardians are all gone. His only remaining close family are the sons of Edmund but they are too young to make a difference at 19, 16 and 14 years of age in 1456. They try to help him later on but are all killed.

Around 1455, 1456, we can see that the Lancastrian project is over, or at the very least, in an extremely difficult position. A king with no family around to support him – a king from a tainted usurping dynasty – a king whose heir is an infant – a king who has lost the Hundred Years War, is not going to make it, even if he has a wife who doesn't mind rolling her sleeves up.

The House of Lancaster is on a knife edge and is going to fall, to be replaced by those claiming a more magical bloodline under the brand name 'House of York'.

But…, I don't know, what if…, just imagine it…, what if all the Yorkists who had the magic blood were…, I don't know…, somehow…, dead?

Who would be left?

Wait, what? It's the revenge of the Beauforts. Their delayed revenge on usurping Henry IV for barring them from inheriting the crown, one of his first actions as usurper, and they've never forgiven him for it.

Big John of Gaunt and his delectable paramour Katherine: their eldest child is John, who begets John, whose only begotten child is Margaret, the mother of Henry VII. Who does Margaret marry? She can marry Edmund Tudor. Who is he?

Fighting Henry V's widow, Catherine de Valois, marries Owen Tudor, the illustrious and rebellious ex-Glendowerist who is doomed to die in 1461.

Owen and Catherine beget Edmund and Jasper; they're half-brothers of sensitive Henry the Sixth. Jasper is a long-lived colourful character, but he dies in 1495 leaving no children.

It's all down to Edmund now, but he dies in 1456. There's that year of destiny again. Edmund dies naturally of bubonic plague but, had he recovered, he would probably have been executed, or imprisoned forever.

Edmund left behind a mournful widow: Margaret Beaufort. She's just 13-years-old and 7 months pregnant with Henry VII.

Damian screwed up his eyes, made his hands into fists and rubbed his temples with them. He was feeling anxious. Wade back in Damian, it's all about Margaret. Rewind, pull back a bit. Margaret Margaret Margaret Beaufort. John Beaufort One – John Beaufort Two – Margaret Beaufort, she can't have any more children after wee Henry VII – she's the last of the house of Lancaster and so is he. What a precious baby.

Wee Henry VII's wife, is born 10 years after him.

She is Yorkist Edward IV's first born child Elizabeth.

Is there anybody in the land who can criticise Henry VII's legitimate right to wear the crown for any reason. No. He's the only one left, and in any case, he's married into the enemy family, so their male children will have an absolutely unassailable right.

Hello Henry VIII, he's Beaufort/Lancaster (Tudor) York. Henry VIII is the special one, and knows it. It's all neatly tied up in Henry VIII, that's why he's so self-confident.

There it was. He hadn't needed a Gollumy guide to get through the Dead Marshes. He'd only needed to follow the waymarking signs in the births, deaths and marriages section in the Historical Times which pointed to the tiny mewling infant at the end of it all: Henry the Eighth.

Damian had broken through and vowed to make a set of flashcards to help memorise it all in case he was cross-examined.

1456 was the year Damian had chosen to mark the end of the Lancastrian project and the tiresome Wars of the Roses.

Tap, tap, tap.

It had officially started in 1455 according to Wikkipedia. He'd managed to avoid the wars altogether. It was about blood certainly, but not blood on the battlefield. The 'So what?' in his thing was now clear and he couldn't wait to tell Dolmetscher. All four headings were covered. It was just the songs now, and the tunes.

41

Skipping an afternoon doze because Mr Napman's post-midnight festival-themed production was still percolating through the digestive tracts of his historical consciousness, and having not been found wanting when put to the test by the Wars of the Roses, Damian was now free to spend the rest of his afternoon choosing his top motivational music tracks and burning them to the neglected 'best of' compilation-cd project.

The original title for it had been 'War Cry!' but now that felt discordant, too bellicose and 'Too Catchy!' was the new name scrawled on it in black marker-pen. Each of his favourite tunes begged needily for inclusion in his musical but Damian was adamant; he was ripping the songs to his cd, sure, but wasn't going to rip off the public by giving them a show based on knock-offs. They deserved better.

'Too Catchy!' was most welcome to offer inspirational support as and when required and if that was an issue, concern, or some kind of a problem, then he was prepared to walk away. That was the deal. Take it or leave it. Old Damian wouldn't have thought to engage firmly with a possible encroachment on his artistic integrity right at the outset, but then again, he probably wouldn't have got around to getting it made at all.

New Damian Two, the historian, was otherwise and he put together a compilation of self-confident 60s pounding mod/rhythm and blues vibes with jazzy overtones which ought to have offered Clare the ideal ambience for her to finish off the last leg of her nibbling. She declined it however, leaving Damian

to enjoy it twice through on his own in the kitchen as he made
a celebratory salmon and tarragon quiche from first principles
to celebrate the impending end of her ordeal.

He'd played quite the host with the chroniclers at the festival,
but Mr Napman had mis-cued his entry and he'd missed both
the pre-prandial welcome drinks and the actual meal. Damian
insisted on making amends to himself by ensuring Clare did
not suffer from any similar inattention to detail. He found a
posh crisp dishcloth to give their glasses, plates, and cutlery
an individual polish, put Dolomiti wine in to chill, and made
everything just so – all under 'Too Catchy!'s beaty aegis.

Tantalisingly visible in Clare's open handbag was her latest
book: 'The Girl Behind'. Damian didn't touch it. New Damian
Two reflected. He had indeed noticed it, so it must still hold
some significance for him, but he wasn't drawn to it, as he
would have been before.

The 'Girl' literary genre had lost its allure. Good. The best
thing about them were the titles anyway. Making them up could
be funny: 'Go-Go Girl!', no, too upbeat, 'The Girl with the
Face', that was better, both portentous and dull, he'd tell them
to Clare later for a laugh, 'Girl Akimbo!' maybe? The door to
the studio flew open and Clare lurched through, falling on her
knees to implore with outstretched, yellow-gloved arms in a
tremulous and gasping wail:

'Get them off me! Get them off me!'

Before Damian, paralysed by shock, could be blamed for not
responding to the immediate situation with the immediate and
commensurate promptness the situation required, Clare stood
up, pointed at him with an accusatory yellow-leathered finger
and denounced him with: 'Gotcha!'

What a woman! Gotcha Girl! She'd got him good. She ought
to have flung off her face-shield, whipped away her scrunchy
turban, shaken loose her mane of golden hair and tossed
back her head to stand in the doorway triumphantly akimbo.
Instead, she subtly modulated one imploring hand and gestured,
beckoning him towards her.

'Get them off me will you?'

Damian went to her and started tugging at the fingers of her
gauntlets, still too surprised to speak. 'That was fun. You didn't
mind? Wait! Stop! There might be glass in them.' Damian stood
back, again nonplussed. 'Go and get a bin bag from the studio.
We'll put it all in there.' Damian did as asked, and the personal
protective equipment: gloves, face-mask, and apron, were
disposed of in a black plastic sack. 'God that was hard work. I
didn't think I'd make it, but I got a second wind just at the end.'

'Can I get you something? Fancy a drink?'

'No way. I'm too sweaty. I need to have a shower, but I won't
be long. I have to keep going or I'll fall over.'

'Ok baby, I'll be right here, mind if I…?'

'Go ahead. I've read it. It's rubbish.'

Damian amused himself while Clare showered by playing 'Too
Catchy!' a third time and having a quick flick through 'The Girl
Behind'. It was 'plot-driven' according to one of the mentions in
the five pages of puff at the start and, several dips later, Damian
could confirm that it was, in fact, all stage directions leavened
by staccato bursts of over-pointed dialogue.

The story was described as walking 'a fine line between
harrowing and laugh-out-loud', a fine line if ever there was one,
and 'The Girl Behind doesn't disappoint!' could only be true if
you'd sinned badly and craved a suitably harsh but redeeming

penance. He gave up, put it back, and went out the back to sneak a cigarette and some Dolomiti outside.

When Clare reappeared 15 tracks in, he came in and turned the music off.

'I liked your impersonation of Rosie the Glass-Nibbler, it was very fetching.'

'Thanks Damo,' she'd used the diminutive for the first time, 'I couldn't resist the joke, your face was a picture.'

'Yeah, a stern one I hope. You broke the quarantine protocol. The whole ship could have been contaminated. I was just about to push you back in and shut the air-lock on you.'

'You wouldn't have?' Damian needed to change the subject. The fictional set-up risked leading to an absurd argument, despite her egregious contravention of star fleet standing orders.

'Of course not. Dolomiti time?' Clare and Damian sat at the table, chatting and drinking wine, whilst the quiche warmed gently in the oven. The second day had been a terrible time for her. Her muscles had been aching from the start and by lunchtime she'd been wondering if she was going to get through it. She'd had to redesign a whole panel because it hadn't looked right. She'd got a little nick on her forearm; a tiny piece of glass must have flown off and made its way into the gauntlet, but she'd made it to the end.

Damian listened to her war-stories and then filled her in on some of his own: his nocturnal activity and the fruits it had borne, though he spared her the microdetails in case it didn't come over as altogether quite normal, then about his work today, and then his cd.

'I would have liked to hear it but I couldn't listen to any new music when I was working. It would have been distracting. I know where I am with my own sounds, especially if I'm knackered.' The Dolomiti wine, normally pleasantly revitalising, was having a depressive and soporific effect, though not on Damian. 'I'm starving. What's for tea?' Damian withdrew the quiche from the oven, here used as chafing dish, and served out two portions, enlivening the process with an everyday chefy banter:

'Tonight, Rosie, we have a humble egg flan.'

'Ummmm…, sounds dreamy! Tell me more.'

'With salmon in it.' He dialled it up several notches more with: 'It is of my own, how you say, creation,' and finally went full-Froissart: 'She has the asparaguses enrobed in a simple sauce. The flavour, it is…'

'Any, how you say, simple 'erbs in the simple sauce?'

'There is one, I don't know it in your speaking, but for me it is always the estragon.'

'Froissart!'

'Froissart to you! Good appetite! The family phone rang, its strident call echoing in the hall.

'Goldarn it! Give me a moment…, sorry,' and she was gone. 'Gotcha Girl Gone.' That would be a great set-up for a novel exploring all the might-have-beens if a telephone hadn't rung at a particular moment. There were two sides to it: the eponymous Girl who was gone, and the one left to their own thoughts by cuisinus interruptus. Bloody doomak! What was he supposed to do? Read a paper? There was that book….

'That was Dolmetscher.'

'?'

'I wasn't too long, was I? He's going to drop off dad's

papers…, mmm…, this is great… I said stay for dinner…, really good Damian, you should have been a cook…, you and him can help me tomorrow…, mmmmm…, in the studio…, I need some helping hands…, it'll be easier with the two of you…, yummy, you don't mind? Clare had been unselfconsciously stuffing herself like a schoolgirl from a restrictive 1950's boarding-school out for Sunday lunch with an indulgent aunt.

'Umm…, no. Like some more?'

'No thanks. I'm done in. I might just keel over right here. I've got to go to bed.' Clare had burned through her reserves. Both engines were coughing and spluttering and she was losing altitude. She had to get upstairs before she conked out. Would she have the strength to get undressed? Probably not. But she'd try. There was one last thing she would do, she vowed, before kissing Damian goodnight and hauling herself upstairs, because Damian wouldn't be able to do it by himself. 'I'll put the beeswax documentary on. You'll just have to press 'Play'. It's the sideways arrow.'

42

'Mind your own beeswax', as a title for a serious documentary, was too clever by half, and Damian took the hint, preferring to research the phrase on the computer rather than watching the programme.

Tap, tap, tap.

There was some doubt as to the origin, of the phrase, but it was also obvious: 'business' became 'bee's knees', as in 'You're the bees knees', and a wag had extended it. You couldn't say 'mind your own bees knees' and be funny or cool.

Tap, tap, tap.

His wanderings took a numismatic turn. Interestingly, the founding-fathers of the American republic had made introversion state policy by inscribing 'Mind your Business' on a 1776 paper third-of-a-dollar token and used it on some coins for a few years. Until 1788 in fact…, coins were quite interesting…. It was too early for him to follow Clare upstairs, but he was still a bit tired…, maybe he'd perk up later. He could rewind it and pay greater attention in case Clare quizzed him in the morning, but it was droning on……….

Damian had arranged to meet Rick Asthal-Stains and Dave Natch at the theatre and he could see them waiting for him in the desultory rain at the front of the queue which snaked down the road to the corner. He instructed the driver not to drop him off at the front but to go round the block so that he could be driven past and see his show advertised on the giant hoardings festooned with myriads of glaring bulbs which steamed hotly across the building.

A previous downpour dazzled theatre-land light from every glistening surface and the beads of rain on the car window trapped the tiny ghosts of its reflected glamour in watery droplets as Damian went by. Getting out in the side street, Damian walked back to the front doors, hoping to do a 'boo' on Rick and Dave for old times' sake, but they'd seen him first.

'Damo!'

'Damo!'

'Rick…, Dave…, great to see you. Here's your tickets…, in case I get dragged away…, what's new?'

'We're not working.' Dave had to exert himself to be heard over the chattering of excited theatregoers.

'Oh, I'm sorry.'

'No, I mean we sold up.'

'Yes, we thought we were in the marketing business, you remember our Wellbeing-You! campaign?'

'Yes, it's still going, isn't it?'

'Yes, but not by us. We were actually in the sub-contracting business but didn't know it. We didn't notice until we did the accounts. We made a fortune!'

'Yeah, we'd been picking up Covid contracts willy-nilly when the government was panicking and handing them out and we knew the right people. We passed them on, but kept an interest, you know, a percentage.'

'It was mad. The numbers were phenomenal….'

'We're thinking of going into arts administration – need any investors?'

'Thanks guys, I'll call you…, anyway, they're expecting me inside, got to go!'

'Good to see you!'

'Yeah, let's catch up!'

'Great to see you both, sorry I can't hang around.'

'Ok, cheers! How far Damo?'

'How far Damo?'

The three did the elbow-bump dance, clumsily, and announced in unison: 'All the way down!' like in the old days. The commissionaire, dressed as a Gilbert and Sullivan major-general, had spied him from the foyer and was hovering behind the half-open doors from where he'd also been using his authoritative ex-Royal Artillery voice to reassure the impatient audience that they'd be inside soon.

'Pep pardon sir?' It was noisy, the doorman's hearing had been affected over the years by the sound of gunfire, and Damian had spoken too quickly. Damian tried again and exaggerated the mouth-lip framing of the words for lack of consonants.

'Where are The Willoughbys please?'

Only hard-core theatre people ever called it that. It was something to do with an in-joke about water-bottles and a butler called Weeble from a farce which ran for a season in 1928. The commissionaire was not such a person. He knew it as The Actors Bar.

'The…, ah yes. You know sir, I've never been in, but do you know where they say it got its name from?'

'Sorry no…, could you point me in the right direction?' The guardian of the foyer obliged and began opening the front-of-house doors to the crowds outside as Damian sprung up the plushly-carpeted stairs two-by-two. Less noise or more attentive listening might have helped him avoid a starkly individualised mini-tour of the theatre's cramped and creamy back-offices but, eventually led on by distant bar-babble via a hidden mezzanine, he found himself in The Willoughbys. Everyone there was more-or-less known to him, and his arrival was met with well-choreographed nods, smiles, waves and salutations, towards the loudest of which, emanating from the gaggle of writers, he headed.

'Here he is!'

'Damian! What are you having? It has just got to be champagne!'

'Shouldn't we wait to…, isn't it unlucky or something?'

'Damian. It's all up on the key! The press reviews have been done. You must have read them. We're sold out for 18 months. What more do you want? And this isn't any of your cheap rubbish, this….,' world-class songsmith Zilka Kuchenbecker, better known under the nom-de-chanson Natty Bumppo, grabbed a glass from a pile on the bar and began filling it, 'is Dumm Oligarch! You won't even feel it. Have some!'

Damian, Natty, and her team had spent six months putting the show together in a Denmark Street den off London's Soho. He'd had to work hard to get his ideas across in the first couple of weeks, but once they'd worked through the angles, 'seen it from the inside out', as writers would say, Natty took the ball and ran with it.

Damian had been able to take a back seat from week five and thereafter spent his time just hanging about to help out when it came to bouncing ideas around. By the time it came to casting, and the first interactions with the director, Damian had the clear impression that he was a spare part and that the professionals had it all under control.

'Sorry Zilka, I want him. Come here you!' Martina Azimuth had been putting shows on Broadway for her entire career, always waiting for 'the one', her very own 'one'. Talent-spotting in New England, she'd seen Louise Email's staging of her father's rough-hewn musical and flown over to England on the next plane to bag it before someone else did. Louise's musical arrangements were very much altered, but she'd been credited as a consultant and was going to be the 'musical coordinator' for the run in New York.

'Damian!' Mwa! Mwa!

43

Martina's socially distanced air kissing was as fruit knife to apple, Damian being sliced off the writers by the big cheese herself.

'Damian! Why didn't you come to the previews? We missed you.'

'I wanted to, but I got nervous and....'

'Never mind! They're done. They're ecstatic. I knew they would be. Happier about the new name?' Damian had believed that his 'A handful of Henrys' was the right name for this show as it perfectly described the Henry fourth, fifth, sixth, seventh and eighth story arc, and drew together some important themes. She'd let it be the working title until just before final rehearsals. It was the only thing they'd argued about, and it had got a bit unpleasant.

Martina was used to working with highly-strung artistic types and had been able to bring him round to her way of thinking. She'd explained that she wanted to better exploit the revolving part of the stage by using it for quick-changes between set-pieces, and that the one recurring dramatic trope in this production was the repeated coronation scenes.

There were five Henrys to start with, not to mention two Richards, and the important part, set in Paris, where sensitive Henry VI gets his French crown. The audience would be wowed by the machinery and the decor but a lot of coronations might get boring. It needed a shorthand reference that spectators would 'get', and which would help the show move on and an

'Aye! Aye! crowd acclamation at a coronation did just that, could end up standing in for it.

'Yes Martina, 'Aye! Aye!' is fine. I like it. You were right.'

'Damian, you poor darling! It's my job to be right. Come with me and we'll watch it together.' Where Ms Azimuth was, was where it was at, and her announcement, as overheard by the various members of the differing professional groups nearest to her, produced an immediate reflux of curtailed conversations and glasses swiftly emptied which rippled through the thronging bar.

Gliding out arm-in-arm with Martina, their comet trailing bar stragglers behind, they strode purposefully into the busy public areas and headed through the crowding ditherers to their box where she fussed Damian and her followers into place. Damian had never understood why seats in the stalls were held to be the better ones as he always preferred looking down to a stage from the dress circle, and the view from where he sat next to Martina was just as good.

'How's that for a good view then?'

'It's great.'

'Secret squirrel Damian, there's a property out there and I want to be first in. Bloch. Do you know anything about it? I think you know something, you clever man.' Damian's nerves had returned and now wasn't the time for this.

'Umm, no, not really.'

'Do you know anything?'

'Umm….'

'There's a man called Pinchman. Do you know him? Does he own it?'

'Umm…, Martina, I can't really….'

'You do know something! Is it Pinchman's?'

'No. I'll…, I'll…'

'Damian, I knew you'd come through for me. We'll talk later.'

Martina turned to her subordinates. She, being the nexus of the assorted colleagues, lieutenants, confederates and sidekicks, commenced discoursing with them in her trade-mark patois of non-sibilant, and therefore quasi-silent, whisperings, leaving Damian looking down on the auditorium, which hummed like a beehive.

There was plenty to see. Late-comers were getting entire rows to stand up as they edged their way apologetically to their premium centre-seats. A young couple were sorting out some kind of seat-number mix up with agreeable audience-members who were eager to appear polite, and it looked like, after some swapping around and compromise at every hand, all would be well. They reminded him of a story his parents had told him once about one of their first evenings out as newlyweds.

Bells rang, ratchetting up the expectant tension. The orchestra started taking their places as small knots of people, standing in aisles to rekindle acquaintances or greet old friends, began untangling themselves and heading for where they were supposed to be.

The leader of the orchestra strode in once his underlings had finished messing around with their water bottles and music sheets. Damian wondered if modern instruments really needed tuning. Was it perhaps a redundant relic? A dramatic ritual? It always sounded the same:

Nnnneeeeeyyuunnnnguuuuuyyyyyahhhhhhhhhhhh.

Staring down at the musicians felt intrusive, but what else could you do? It wasn't transgressive at all, to pry and peer from up there. The men were stiffly conformist in black suits but the woman had a freer hand. The entire effect was charmingly animated. Everyone knew their business and were settling into their roles for the night. The audience likewise. A medley of tunes was struck up with the intention of thickening chest humours in those susceptible to judge by the sporadic and desultory rattle of coughs and rasping throat-clearings it conjured up. When all expectoration had ceased, so began the show.

Damian had never understood the appeal of musical theatre, or any kind of theatre for that matter, as cinema-going was what he answered when asked about his leisure pursuits. Nothing could have outdone that film about King Arthur he'd seen at The Odeon, Leicester Square 40 years ago but this…, this! Four dimensions, five…, passion, energy, conviction in a movingly manipulative sound-scape, six, seven…. How many were there? The interval came too soon. The audience was too stunned to applaud and stayed nailed to their seats with only the most irresolute of dipsomaniacs being seen to get up and go out for their must-haves in the bars.

'We expected this Damian; we've shortened the interval and they probably won't make it back in.'

Damian nodded mutely, sorry for the thirsty ones. The second part had the power of the first, but more so, by a factor of four. The separate story helixes had wrapped around themselves like ivy spiralling up the tallest tree in the forest to explode across the canopy and revel in the long-sought-for sunlight.

When the curtain fell there was silence for four heartbeats before all rose as one to add their individual applause to the combined clapping roar of the crowd, some of whom were trying to climb on stage. Mercifully, the curtain opened again, and the cast came forward to acknowledge the adulation and share in the joy of triumph as if show-people and audience-people had done it all together and were as one.

'I've told them no more than ten curtain calls and two encores. Let's get out of here before it all goes to Lenny's head. He'll point us out and get the crowd to make us come down. I'm strictly back room. Let's go!'

Damian could hardly breathe but couldn't work out why. Leaving the box with Martina's entourage he realised he was laughing…, and crying. He begged some time to pull himself back together.

'We're in the other actor's bar. Where friends and family can go. I'll leave Gloria with you.'

Damian had to get out of the box and away from the curtain-calls before the encores started as he might otherwise not leave the theatre alive, his heart had nowhere else to go and it would seem very sensible if it stopped now and sent him straight to the combined Valhalla for historians and writers of musicals.

Gloria showed him to a washroom where cold water on his face and the shocking sight of it in the mirror recalibrated him enough to let him think of following her to join the rest. The theatre's corridors were still empty and the pounding waves of ecstatic approbation from the auditorium were reverberating through its walls. Gloria pushed open the bar's half-glazed door, took two glasses of champagne from the nearest table and glided him over to Martina, who was holding forth to her mobbing fans in the centre of the room. His glass was empty by the time he got to her.

'Damian, what are you playing at? This is your night! Don't be going around with an empty glass like that! Don't you know it's unlucky? It's like saying *'the Scottish play'* when you mean the Scottish play,' and she got a new one found for him.

Martina was great to be with; a larger-than-life personality who could really make things happen, and he started to feel part of the gang again. By now onto his third glass, and not privy to all the in-jokes, he began to notice first-off actors appearing through the door who were met with good-natured, sometimes risqué showbizzy comments from those in the know and already there.

The curtain was definitely down for the night and was staying down. The audience was going home. Most of them were hoarse from shouting and red-eyed with dried tears. Few made it home without letting themselves go in pubs, restaurants and night-clubs as they fought bitterly to extend the moment, unable to cope with the banality of tomorrow by trying to explain to puzzled strangers about how a musical had changed their lives and could change theirs.

Damian thought he saw Mr and Mrs Dunny come in and watched their backs disappear into the bar crowd as they tried to get served. He side-slipped from out of Martina's spotlight and moved towards the door to get a better view of the receding Dunnyalikes. Standing with his back to the wall, the door flapping open intermittently to partially screen him from half the room and admit actors, well-wishers and those otherwise connected to the performance, its piston-hinges mechanically closing it behind them, Damian wished Clare had been there.

He might go over to Josephine Tey standing by a pillar talking to some Chelsea-types…, she'd seen him and was beckoning. Her feedback would be interesting….

The heavy door swung fully open and folded him away. He saw his mother and father entering the room through its glass. They were coming in, their backs to him now. In the passing view he'd had of them as they came by, they'd been their younger selves. Not how he'd known them, but how he'd seen them in photographs. He grabbed the door to stop it closing.

They'd evidently had a great night and were laughing and talking together, both flushed with emotion and vitality. They stopped in the centre of the room, uncertain where to go, and Damian sensed they were scouring the faces in the crowd. They must be looking for him.

He wanted to go up to them. He could surprise them from behind. Tap them on the wrong shoulder. Tap them both on the wrong shoulder to make them turn round and pop up right in front of them…. Heat rose in his eyes…. He felt them thicken. He knew they could never see him.

He pivoted around the edge of the door to get out of the room, pulling on it as he went out to get it closing behind him, and stepped to the side to stay out of sight in the hallway.

He wanted to stand there, pressing his body against the wall, letting his eyes do what they wanted to do, letting him do what he wanted to do, but he couldn't. All he could do was leave.

44

Mr Napman had staged a magnificently detailed and utterly compelling show, but Damian resented the way it ended.

By what right had his alter ego done that? It was well beyond the scope of his remit. Dramatically speaking, it was thus a failure, ruined by a final discordant note, but you couldn't help admiring the ambition. In poetry, an imperfect rhyme was a better one. Maybe the ending was the better for its dissonance. Either way, good or bad, Damian didn't want to leave the last word to Mr Napman. He'd work through the issues himself.

After writing an email to his daughter Louise in which, after the usual niceties, he broached his notion, sketched out his ideas and asked if she would collaborate with him in working-up songs for his musical, under the working title: 'A Handful of Henrys – Aye! Aye!', he took a bottle of wine outside as a libation for his shaman.

The rain had stopped, which was a pity. The night's stillness mocked him for cowering by the door, daring him out. Damian went back in for an overcoat, found some old rags and strode purposefully up to the garden seat where he wiped off the wet with them and sat down to look back in the dark.

It was cold. He buttoned himself up to the chin and bemoaned his lack of scarf, and maybe a hat, as he helped himself to Dolomiti, and puffed away. It was all probably going to kill him: the booze, the cigarettes. He enjoyed them too much. Could Mr Napman help him with that? But he was there in the moment, the here and now. There was a succession of here-and-nows, like fire-doors dividing a long theatre corridor, and he could go down it, through them, to the end. The exterior light went off with a click, jack-o'lanterning the kitchen windows and flooding the garden with black.

They used to have ceremonies. You'd have to wear special clothes. You'd have to be prepared. Now you had to sit blinded and cold in the stink of wet grass and corrupted leaves. He was pathetic. Why didn't he just pitch himself forward and bury his face in the ground? You couldn't get more here-and-now than that. He'd be able to smell the mud in his nose, feel each blade of grass pushing into his face, claw his fingers into the earth and feel his body warmth being dragged out of him. He wasn't pathetic, that meant to be worthy of, or deserving of, pity. He was ridiculous. A musical! A bloody musical! More wine maestro. He was 'ridicule'. Reed … ick … cool. It sounded better in French. If you said someone was 'ridicule' it meant something, it was strong, hurtful. Said in English,' ridiculous', it only worked if someone had dressed as a clown for a wedding. He wasn't French. He was a clown.

His eyes were readjusting. What had been pitch dark was now less oppressive. Damian, an audience of one, pulled his collar up against the night and gazed at the house where the kitchen windows, a row of glowingly orange-yellow abstract paintings, framed in black, against a black background, absorbed his unquiet thoughts.

You could capture young wolf spirits and, if they were willing, they'd stay with you and help you hunt. You learnt their language. They learnt yours. And they wanted their place at the fire, as you did. Tree-language, river-language, animal-language, wind-language, we spoke them all once. Voice-masters of every sound, we beguiled speech from sticks and skins in beaten rhythms.

Where we were wordless, our bodies would show in dance to give meaning in movement. Fire-lit feastings were for the stories. The shaman could be bird-man, could be beast-man, could be any-man. We watched his story. Heard his story. And we became bird-man, beast-man, or any-man. Damian made a vow to finish the bottle. There wasn't going to be enough left to justify putting it back in the fridge. It was also unlucky. To do so presumed that there would be a tomorrow.

Musical theatre. Musical theatre. It would be musical theatre, or it would be nothing. Naaah Zing!

45

'Concentrate boys!' Do it just like I showed you.' Harry-Dan
Dolmetscher and Damian Email had received their instructions
from Clare and were ready to start helping her put the St Dunstan
stained-glass panels together. Dolmetscher had arrived just
after breakfast and, after divesting himself of the Bloch portfolio,
and bringing Clare up to speed on his version of the Pinchman
encounter, Damian and he had been put through Clare's training
module and were ready to start.

'What about fumes?'

'No need to worry Harry-Dan, there's not much, just whisps,
and I've opened the windows, but you should wear gloves. I'll get
you some.' Clare went to look after the last-minute health and
safety considerations and Dolmetcher made the move he'd been
practising in the car on the way over.

'Musical theatre Damian? What were you thinking? It's ridiculous!'

'You're wrong. It's perfect.' Damian's quiet authority rendered any
further attempt at using comedy-cruelty to exploit the situation
churlish. Only an instant cave-in could redeem.

'You're right, it's genius. I wish I'd thought of that years ago. I
could have had a lot of fun. So, you're writing the book.'

'It's a bloody musical!'

'No, 'the book'. That's what they call it. All the things that are in a
musical and aren't songs. That's what they call it, 'the book'.'

'Yes, ok then, I am writing .. the book.'

'Where did the idea come from?'

'It's been around for years. And there's 'Hamilton.'

'Need a hand with it?'

'All I can get.' Clare was back, front and centre, the day's work could begin. H-section lead profiles, confusingly known collectively as *'came'*, were stacked at the end of the worktable in six-foot lengths and grouped according to their characteristics. Clare knew exactly what to do and the two others only had to hold things steady as she fitted them around the glass and soldered the ends together. The two historians took their duties seriously but, six hours later, tired and a bit bored, the end in sight, they were getting demob happy and an easy-going historical banter punctuated their labours.

'Ok Damian, give me the elevator pitch!'

'Well, how tall is the building?'

'Empire State. Pitch me.'

'You've got to change lifts to get to the top, three times I think.'

'Ok, all the way up, and you can talk to me as we wait for the next one. Off you go.'

'Very well. Richard II's administration suffered a brutal take-over in 1388. The…, umm…, attackers? No, we'll call them *'The Faction'*. The faction found day-to-day administration not to their liking and let the king do it. Eventually, he felt strong enough to challenge them. The king was reinforced by the return of John of Gaunt from abroad because he was the most powerful aristocrat in England. The faction loathed him, for various reasons. The faction maintained their presence in all Richard's royal councils from 1388 until their overthrow in 1397. Richard's enemies stayed close to him.'

*   *   *

Hold that and don't let it move again.

*   *   *

'Overthrow? Is that the right word?'

'I don't know..., neutralisation? Anyway..., going up! All were agreed, after 1388, that England couldn't afford the military expenses of constant war with France. The faction leader, the Duke of Gloucester, began to look for a truce, and brought his brother Gaunt on board because Gaunt's reputation in France was good, but they, the faction, still hated him.'

'I like what I'm hearing. Pitch me more.'

'Gaunt became a political problem for the faction. Gaunt took on the Earl of Arundel, a leading *factionisti*, in the 1394 January parliament, and trounced him there. Anne of Bohemia, the king's wife, dies that year. Arundel is outrageous at her funeral. The king puts him in the Tower of London for a spell. Gaunt and Arundel are mortal enemies. It's a low point for the faction.'

* * *

It's too short. I'll cut another one. Don't let it slip out!

* * *

'Go on.'

'Gaunt makes things worse. He has the bright idea that the king should marry a French princess to facilitate peace with France. This is too real and completely not what the faction wants, especially as it's what Gaunt wants. They begin to agitate discontent. Froissart calls the fractious faction 'Londoners', but that's misleading.'

'Rumour-mongering?'

'Yes they are. Massively. Peace will mean the glorious good-old-days are definitely over.'

'Only long-haul crusades from then on? No more nipping

over to France for a quick biff and some looting?'

'Exactly. Giving up biffing and looting on a permanent basis is a big ask. An ask too far. They don't want that. Once the king is married to the French princess, the faction has no political option but to get rid of Richard – as they nearly succeeded in doing before. But you can't keep big conspiracies like that secret. Their first attempt with the Earl of March flows into the sand, so they think bigger. The country will be divided up between them. The king part can be sorted out later.'

'They haven't got a republic in mind?'

'I think not. The Duke of Lancaster is to have the North, but it's not John of Gaunt they've got in mind, more like his son Henry. Henry is still loyal to Richard at this point, but he used to be well in with the faction. Thick as thieves. Maybe he can be turned. Who knows?'

'I like that.'

*　*　*

We'll do these three the same way.

*　*　*

'Yes, Adam of Usk has an incident at the 1397 trial of the faction in parliament where Henry joins with his father in denouncing Arundel as a traitor. It's very telling. Henry is still loyal. I want to get back on track.'

'Ok. There's a plot, and it's all wound up ready to go. All up on the key.'

'Yes, word gets out. There's fear at court…, and paranoia. The king acts. Arrests the conspirators. The plotters are tried. Arundel is executed. Gloucester dies in Calais. He might have been murdered but that's the politics of the time. Wimpy Earl of Warwick admits all and is exiled to the Isle of man. Game over for them. They've lost.'

'That explains the Cheshire archers. They are always portrayed as the bully boys of a repressive tyrant.'

'That's another side show, but yes. Richard had made the mistake in 1387 of not having any force near enough to defend him when the faction brought their rebellious army into the field. They intercepted Richard's army, coming down to London from Cheshire, and destroyed it before it could rescue him.

That wasn't happening again. Richard had sound reasons for reinforcing his bodyguard. He mustered his entire army at Kingston-on-Thames on 20th August 1397. I think we can say for certain that there was a real crisis in England from at least mid-July 1397, and over the summer. When I say 'crisis', I mean that the king was definitely threatened. Richard certainly felt threatened.'

'Ok, pitch me more.'

'All is well until Henry stirs up trouble again some months later. His motives are unclear. Henry and Mowbray were both rebels in 1388. Now they're both well-in with Richard, Mowbray the more so. What nobody wants is old political rancour brought back to the surface, but Henry does just that and denounces Mowbray for harbouring treacherous thoughts.'

'Historians have got their knickers in a twist about Henry and Mowbray, haven't they?'

'For sure, but it doesn't matter who started it. They all want the whole thing to go away. It's not what anyone wants to hear. It's raking over the ashes. 'Move on. Move on,' they all say but Henry doesn't want to, and they both get exiled. They are destabilising the *status quo*.'

Harry-Dan hold these. Damian, get ready to push when I say.

'And Henry, peeved at being disinherited, plots revenge?'

'No, he's never actually disinherited. He receives a £2000 yearly annuity whilst he's away. In fact, Henry's agents pick up £1586 from the exchequer on 20th June 1399, just a couple of weeks before Henry comes back hot, bothered and angry on his usurping expedition.

No, the inheritance thing is a distraction. It doesn't matter because Henry has a different inheritance in mind. He is convinced he's the real king of England and that Richard is an imposter.

There's a lightening war. Henry is not well supported. Of the 20 men in England who were earls or above, 11 were committed to Richard, 3 were boys, 2 kept away, leaving 3 for him: Westmoreland, Northumberland and himself.

'Despite those odds he won!'

'God must have been on his side and wanted to rid England of foppish wastrel King Richard. Richard's forces were divided between Ireland and England. There was a failure of organisation and leadership. Richard was in Ireland when it went off. It took a month to land Richard's army when he went there. Clever Henry knew Richard would not be able to get his army back in time.

Richard got back to Wales on 24th July, but it was too late, his uncle, the Duke of York, surrendered the royal army to Henry on the 27th July and it was all over. Henry made no bones about by what right he was king.'

'I like the bit in Adam of Usk at his coronation banquet. There is a tradition that a champion rides in and challenges anyone who doesn't accept the king…'

* * *

More attention, less gabbing. I've got to get this right.

* * *

'Yes, I know. It shows Henry's contempt for feudal propriety. He dismisses the champion with: 'If need be Sir Thomas, I will in my own person ease thee of thy office!'

'It's a great line. I will in my own person ease thee of thy office. Henry is so macho. He disdains feudal niceties. He doesn't need a champion.'

'Yes, it is a great line.'

'Yes it ease!'

'Archbishop Arundel is embarrassed by Henry and his claims. There are naysayers, especially some bishops. He cobbles the articles of deposition together so that he can say: 'If you don't believe Henry is the right king, then here are some other reasons. It's all legal, so don't get talking too much about it because that would be sedition.'

'Sedition! Sedition! That's got to be a song for the show, surely.'

'Maybe. Henry now only has to kill the king and all his friends, and that's all arranged. He's in. But nobody likes him. Even his Walsingham friends seem sniffy. God seems to have withdrawn his favour. Nothing goes right. He gets nothing done in Scotland and it's worse in Wales. His bed tries to kill him…'

'Well, they find a prong in it.'

'Same thing. His tent tries to kill him. His stuff gets washed away in floods. He gets some kind of pox, and his son wants to take over, maybe depose him, and his archbishop pal hates him because Henry executed the Archbishop of York. He dies unmourned.'

'That's a bit of a blue note to end on.'

46

'It's not the end. There's 60 years to go.'

'But we must be nearly there Damian?'

'Harken unto me yetawhile, there's more. Henry's power-grab condemned his son to a war in France....'

'Didn't Adam of Usk say something about that, something like: in a great and solemn council on 16th August Henry said something like his adversaries of France and Scotland should be assailed in war?'

'If you say so, anyway, they got a war going in the end, which went well at first, but unfortunately it killed him.'

'Who?'

'Henry the Fifth, and his infant son was left holding the war in his pudgy little fingers until he was old enough to be crowned King of France, which turned his head.

The war gave work to marginal, unstable elements in society: farmers who didn't like farming, heirs waiting for people to die, younger sons, illegitimate sons, criminals who wanted pardons. When the war is lost, they come back angry and pointing their fingers. Old Father Time has scythed away sensitive Henry the Sixth's family and he's on his own against another faction who think their boss is more royal than he is. They win and sensitive Henry the Sixth goes the way of Richard II.'

'Finish your pitch, we're slowing down!'

'At the end there's just two left for a battle royal. God grants one victory. That one forges a new king on the anvil of Vulcan.'

'You mean by that: in his wife's womb?'

'Just checking you're paying attention. I'm thinking of the musical. Yes, emergent avatar for the new monarchy, it's baby Henry VIII.'

'All in a nutshell now. Pitch the pitch of pitches, we're nearly there!'

'Henry IV normalised rebellion. Not a problem when they were all distracted by war but losing the war brought Peace, which they didn't want. As they sowed, so did they reap; War wasn't finished with them, and it presided over a revolutionary tribunal to decide who was right, found them all guilty and executed mercilessly. That's the War of the Roses.

Henry VII smuggled little baby Henry VIII out of the smoking ruins to become England's first unchallenged king since…, since forever. Hence his power. Hence his nickname: Tyrannus Maximus, which is written on coins to this day.'

'You jest!'

'I jest! Hence his determination to get a male heir. Hence….'

'Ding! Observation platform, everybody out. Yeah ok…, you're wandering and it needs polishing but I like the depth of your perspective. It goes far beyond the dead-eyed golem of binate classifications.'

'Binate what?'

'That's what they call it now. Good king, bad king. Black and white; binate classifications – proper historian talk. It's got good depth, but it's got to be relevant to a modern audience. Is Henry IV like Donald Trump?'

'How so?'

'So far beyond the understanding of most people that he could almost be a different creature, another type of human?'

*   *   *

That's it. Thanks for your help boys. Help me tidy up

*   *   *

'That's interesting. In that Henry believed that he was the real king, he was delusional. But, as he became the real king, he was rational. Maybe the same with Trump. If his ego demanded that he take on his country's highest office, and he'd not achieved it, then again, he would have deluded himself. But he succeeded. It was rational. What supreme validation! What price does that kind of super-success exact on super-egos like his? Where can you go from there?'

'Yes, they're both very special people. I'd like to use them…, you know…, frighten ghosts with them. They wouldn't know how to react.'

'The ghosts?'

'Yes, you could send Trump into a haunted house and see demons and entities shooting out of the chimney.'

'That's right. The blood would jump out of the sink and go back up the tap.'

'The rocking chair would never move, even if you pushed it. It would never move again.'

'All the dolls would look cuddly.'

'Hands coming out of graves would wave goodbye.'

'Give a thumbs up. Nothing to see here.'

'Nothing would squeak.'

'No plumbing problems.'

'Or electrical.'

'No problem with TV reception.'

'OK, Henry could be Trump.'

'That was good. Funny…, but what do the public take away at the end? That's the big 'So what?' in the room. Is it about Brexit?'

'Umm, no…, it's…, it's that understanding anything, in this case old history, isn't about the story. It's about questioning the story, being free to question the story. Sometimes the story's got to change. And it's about consequences. It's about how what you think is normal can be the product of a process that started long ago, so long ago it doesn't look like it matters.

And it's about political demons and entities that get shut up in haunted houses, until something comes along, and they shoot out of the chimney.'

'Henry VIII is a ghostbuster?'

'Yes, wasn't it obvious? I'm kidding…, I'm still working it out.'

'And where are the songs?'

'I've got some ideas.'

'I did one. Maybe you can use it. It's got a cool rap title: Call me King, written with a 'K'.

'How else would you spell it?'

'The 'K's on 'call'. It makes it cool. Listen.'

'I did a 'Call me King' song too. Can't quite remember how it went.'

'Here's mine.':

Kall me King
You've called me Derby, Hereford, Bolingbroke
But that's not how I identify.
I'm standing above you, crown in my hand look
It's me who's the real one, no lie.
Call me king when you kneel, and king when you beg.

241

Call me king if you know what's right.
You'll call me king and you'll wait for my call
'Cos we're going to France for a fight!

'Harry-Dan, you're a legend. I didn't know you could write like that! Or sing!'
'Damian, I haven't always been a historian, you know.'

47

Glad that their shifts as stagehands for Clare's one-woman show was all but over, Damian and Harry-Dan demonstrated their close identification with her project's terminal phase by being seen to actively engage with the extended clearing up process.

Finally peeling off and binning their latex gloves, Arty-Crafty and the Two Stooges took a silent time-out to contemplate the experience and share the satisfaction of completion, which Harry-Dan broke thoughtlessly:

'I thought you were finishing today?'

'It is finished. It's too big to move if the panels are joined together. It's too heavy. It's dimensionally unstable. It's all done on site, bit by bit. It needs iron bars put in to hold it up. They're coming tomorrow to pack it, then crate it. I'm going to Bury St Edmunds next week to supervise the installation. Did you like my amice joke?'

'Uhhh…?'

'You two were blethering. Can't you multi-task? I pointed it out when I was doing it.'

'I like to do one thing properly,' from Damian fizzed like a firework about to go off, which Dolmetscher doused with a verbal bucket of water:

'Which was to help you. Maybe we overfocussed?'

'Yeah…, right! It's in that stack of panels. There's a little red corner piece. Six little hats all joined together with strings, next to a cat. It's a hat for mice. A mice hat.' Dolmetscher didn't understand why Damian found that so funny, so stepped in before Clare misunderstood whatever was going on and felt mocked in her moment of triumph.

'Thanks Clare, it was a pleasure to play a part in this endeavour which will stand as a testament through time to....' which Clare cut short with:

'Now let's celebrate!' Clare wanted out of there. 'I've got some champagne,' and she chivvied them out to the kitchen where they stood round the table to ritualise the end of the mission with high-status French wine. Dolmetscher would stay for Damian's cottage pie, but not later, or over, as he had an early flight to Italy in the morning, but he had something for them, and this was the time. Handing Clare a cardboard wallet, he explained that it was a dvd which he invited them to watch when he'd gone, and he'd prefer not to say anything more about it at this stage, or make any promises.

Intrigued, and disappointed that Dolmetscher wasn't staying longer, Clare and Damian moved from champagning to Dolomiti-ing over the scratch evening meal, Dolmetscher abstaining from further alcohol but not from praising Damian and offering assorted song ideas. His extraction, when it came, was anti-climactic, but they appreciated his parting shot on the threshold:

'See ya Clare. Damian, you've done a great job. Your musical is going to put historical long-division on the map,' – he'd rehearsed a slightly forced joke for his exit.

'How so?'

'It's maths. It's history. Truth into lie won't go! See ya!'

'See ya!'

Being one-man down was temporarily deflating but, high

on their respective achievements, and wine, they carried on without him and a feel-good double-act snuggled into the chintzy sofa and put on the dvd to see what Dolmetscher had brought.

'Dibattito Della Dolomiti', or 'D.D.D' as the studio décor announced, was an Italian late-night talk show for intellectuals and political heavyweights. Clare's Italian, hitherto described by her as 'conversational' could only have been that if you used the term to mean dazzling luminaries with sparkling wit at an ambassador-level cocktail party, and she was straightaway rapt.

Damian worked hard to follow it all. Longer Italian words were a bit like English: contradictions were 'contradizzione', and French helped: international relations were 'rapporti internazionale', and it made the meaning of 'la prima guerra mondiale' obvious.

The programme's host, Fausta Faustini, was introducing a montage item that had graphics, pieces to camera, sweeping panoramas and commanding voiceovers. The numbers were staggering: 'quattrocentosessantamille', 'soldati', 'morti', in the 'montagna'. That was just Italy. 7% of the Romanian population. 15% in the Ottoman Empire. And all the others. It was 'incredibile'.

The show's anchorwoman said some words to sum up what the viewers had seen and swivelled her chair round to face a panel of serious men and women whom she introduced individually, supported by pop-up animations which gave their names on the bottom of the picture as they nodded back in acknowledgment from the other side of a gigantesque desk.

There was Paolo Monte-something, Carla della Somewhere, three others and Oliver Pinchman. The hostess was mostly interested in him and kicked-off the discussion with a long question which he answered in perfect Italian.

'Look! That's me. I can't believe it. It's me. It's me and daddy!' Clare's voice was broken, her last syllables smothered by sobbing. A holiday snap had filled the screen. A blond-haired girl in a red cagoule screwed her face against the sun next to a man in canvas climbing gear wearing a bobble hat. The shadow of the photographer pointed towards them in the snow.

The video zoomed into the man's face. Clare pushed herself forward, framing her head in her hands as if wanting to shut out all distraction and turn herself into a camera. Damian didn't want to breathe. *Signore Dunny…Signore Dunny…Signore Dunny.* It was all about *Signore Dunny.*

Damian caught only snatches: *'Nazione Unite', 'Pace', 'Riconciliazione', 'Gratitudine',* they were speaking too quickly, but he understood. The other people on the panel joined in. Pinchman was in the middle of it all and was involved in every contribution.

They all agreed. Fausta Faustini, looking straight down the lens, summed up and handed over to another segment live from the United Nations council chamber in New York where a young journalist was getting reactions from delegates, too busy, or too aware of the ramifications, to say much apart from 'It's early days', and 'Yes, we'll see,' and who were returning from casting their vote in the council chamber.

'Oh Damian!' Clare was crying. 'Dolmetscher's done it! Pinchman's a hero. He's done it!'

Damian remembered some of the things he'd said about Pinchman. Clare might forget. Maybe it wouldn't matter. Clare's tears ebbed. She pulled her blouse sleeves over her hands and used them to wipe her eyes and turned to look at him, her face lit from inside by joy.

'Damian, Damian…,' she sniffed a couple of times, exhaled and inhaled twice, 'Damian. I've been thinking…, about us.'

'Froissart?'

'Don't you think the time is right?'

'Froissart?'

'Shall we get a puppy?'

'Froissart!'

*   *   *

Epilogue

The nine muses, lissom, fetching and becoming, dressed diaphanously as always, are holding hands and dancing in a circle, just like in the old days. Sometimes it goes round one way, sometimes the other. Then it stops. The muses break away and get out their clay tablets to gaze at. Urania steps up to her viewing platform, the better to scan the skies.

Calliope: 'Urania, you absolute legend, that was great, thanks.'
Urania gives no reply. She is already intent on seeing the stars and the space between them.
Polyhymnia: 'Yeah, that's Urania off for a while but yeah, she certainly pulled out a plum there.'
Kleio: 'Yes, thanks Urania…, have you got that review, I'd like another look.'
Calliope: 'It's on my tablet. I'll send it to you.'
Clio: 'Got it, thanks. I'll read it out if you don't mind.'
Calliope: 'Only if you use your special 'history' voice.
Clio: 'Okay, here we go, ahem….

Clio, singer of deeds, brings back the days of old. Melpomene proclaims sad acts in tragic groan. Thalia rejoices in comedy, for her speech is lusty. Euterpe besets the sweet-toned pipe with breath. Terpsichore moves, commands, and swells the feelings of the harp. Erato, holding her plectron, leaps and dances with foot, song, and face. Calliope gives unto books heroic songs. Urania follows the sky's movements and the stars. Polyhymnia suggests everything with her hands and speaks with gestures.'

Polyhynia: 'That says it all, good one Urania.'
Terpsichore: 'Time for volleyball? What say you muses? (Yeah, yes, I'm in, same, sure, me too, and me.) Urania?'

Curtain down

*　　*　　*

Curtain Calls

Jean Froissart 1337-1405

The greatest editor of his works is Alberto Varvaro 1934-2014. **'Chroniques de France et d'Angleterre'**, Livre Quatrième. Jean Froissart. Édition critique par **Alberto Varvaro**. Académie Royale des Sciences, des Lettres et des Beaux-Arts de Belgique. 2015. It's 25 Euros, or 4 Euros as a pdf. It's in cleaned-up medieval French. If you speak French then you can read it.

The problem with using the works of Jean Froissart as a source is that, although his works are exceptionally well-known, there has been no complete text commonly available.

To remedy the situation, Ceramicon has published: **'Froissart's Book IV: England 1388-1400.'** This is the most complete and up-to-date rendition of Froissart's Book IV in English. Find it at **www.iautodidact.co.uk.**

Apart from the above, what else is available is heavily reduced. I have used the most complete version: **'Froissart's Chronicles' Vol I and Vol II. George Routledge and Sons, 1884.**

This edition modernises the spelling of Thomas Johnes' 1806 translation but it's hard to find. The entire work is available online though: **https://quod.lib.umich.edu/cgi/t/text/text-idx?c=moa;idno=ACG8357**

via: The Making of America website – **https://quod.lib.umich.edu/m/moa/**

I offer an appendix, see below, cross-referencing the 1884 version above against the authoritative Varvaro edition and the commonly available, though useless, Penguin one.

If you want to find Froissart, then below is described some research pitfalls.

1) **Chronicles of Froissart. Thomas Johnes. 1806 translation**

   This translation was originally 4 volumes but was later produced as 12 volumes.

   You can find the 12 volumes offered as print-on-demand individual works. For the period in question volumes XI and XII are required, possibly X as well. These retain Thomas Johnes' anachronistic use of 'f' for 's' – he had his own printing press – so they are not easy to read. Make sure you don't get the wrong volumes. Each volume says 'From the reign of Edward II to .. Henry IV' but that's the name of the entire 12 volume set, not an indication of the book you might be looking at online.

   Online: https://babel.hathitrust.org/cgi/pt?id=inu.30000007256708&view=1up&seq=16

2) **'The Chronicles of Froissart' G.C. Macaulay. 1904**

   The Chronicles of Froissart, based on the 1904 translation by G.C. Macaulay, have important chapters missing and is useless. It's a reworking of Lord Berner's 1525 translation. This is the version commonly available as a complete 'Froissart'. But it's exceptionally incomplete.

   Of the 26 'canonical' (Varvaro) chapters in Froissart's Book IV of his chronicles, Macaulay summarises 18 of them. When we say 'summarise' we mean down to 50 words.

Macaulay seems more interested in events outside England and tends to leave them entire.

3) 'Froissart Chronicles'. Penguin. 1968.

Very common, but wholly useless.

4) And all the other ones, as above.

5) Froissart's poems: 'Le Paradis d'Amour':

- the one he gave to Richard II in 1395, and 'L'Horloge Amoureus', : Librairie Droz. 1986, introduction by P.F Dembowski.

Note from the author. In the text Damian Email states that the amount of original Froissart text, and by that I mean text that directly concerns events in England or Anglo-French relations, that is missing from the Penguin Classics edition – and by implication from other abridgements, amounts to 30,000 words. This is false. Appendix 1 will demonstrate that the missing words amount to 43,000, at least.

Froissart on the bookshelf.

Left to right: two volumes of the Thomas Johnes translation, Alberto Vavaro's edition of Book IV, Macaulay's edition of Lord Berner's book, another edition of Macaulay's version, Book X11 of Lord Berners' translation, the Joliffe abridgement and finally, ahem, the Penguin Classics version.

* * *

Adam of Usk 1352-1430

'Chronicon Adae de Usk, 1377-1421'. Edited by Sir Edward Maunde Thompson K.C.B Oxford University Press 1904. An excellent work.

Adam of Usk 1352 –1430

Sir Edward 1840-1929

Available second hand or read online https://archive.org/details/chroniconadaedeu00adamuoft.

Note the first half is the original Latin, the translation into English is the second half.

* * *

The Walsinghams

There is confusion as to what the chronicles of Thomas Wallsingham are.

'The Chronica Maiora of Thomas Walsingham (1376-14220'. The Boydell Press. David Preest. 2005. This is easy to find and a good read.

There are other Walsinghams.

Sometimes they are called 'Walsingham', sometimes not. Some say the 'canonical' Chronica Maiora above is a summary of the other versions. The other versions, whilst sometimes appearing in bibliographies and footnotes (eg 'Chronicles of the Revolution'. Given-Wilson) as 'Walsingham', are sometimes ascribed to other authors. In any case, these others are harder to find:

'**Annales Ricardo Secundo**' Henry Thomas Riley (1816-1878), may also be known as the '**St Albans Chronicles**'. Sometimes referenced as **Johannis de Trockelowe** and **Henrici de Blaneforde**. This is all in Latin, but the introduction picks out variations in the so-called 'Walsingham' sources.

Available from Cambridge University Press as a pdf at a stiff price – for completists only.

* * *

'**French Metrical History of the Deposition of King Richard II**'. **Jean Creton.** (1386-1420). This translation was read by the Revd John Webb in 1819 for a periodical called 'Archaeologia' in 1819. It makes excellent reading. Very vivid. Revd John Webb 1776-1869. It's available as a pdf from Cambridge University Press. Not given away, but a really good read.

* * *

'**Chronique de la Traison et Mort de Richart II**.' **The Monk of St Denis**. Translated by Benjamin Williams. 1846. Available from various sources. Original French and translation into English. A good read.

* * *

'**The Chronicle of John Hardyng.**' (1378-1465). Henry Ellis. 1812. Forgotten Books

Henry Ellis 1777-1869. Don't get the one edited by Simpson and Peverley as it's only about King Arthur.

* * *

An exceptional resource.

Parliament Rolls of Medieval England. British History Online. A superb work. Unfortunately, you have to pay £35 annual subscription. It is excellent, however. Sometimes known as 'Rotuli Parliamentorum' in references.

* * *

Outwith the chroniclers, I recommend the following:

Is War now Impossible? J.S. Bloch. Gregg revivals 1991.

A History of Parliament. Ronald Butt. Constable. 1989. (Ronald Butt 1920-2002)

Richard II. Nigel Saul. Yale University Press. 1997.

The Royal Household and the King's Affinity. Chris Given-Wilson. Yale University Press. 1986.

I've also used, for a quotation: **Henry IV of England, a biography.** John Lavan Kirby. Constable. 1970, p8.

* * *

Appendix 1

The tabulated information below shows:

   a) The Berners Macaulay version of Froissart is useless.

   b) The Penguin Classics version is excessively shortened by 44000 words.

   c) Two important chapters from the canonical and authoritative Varvaro edition of Froissart are either entirely missing chapter 44 on Robert the Hermit) or egregiously reduced (chapter 56 –Gloucester plots Richard's destruction.)

('Johnes' below refers, of course, to the Thomas Johnes 2 volume edition).

Varvaro Chapters / Chapter headings	Johnes Chapters	Page Nos	Penguin Summarised or missing		Berners Macaulay Summaries
			pages	words	
40 My visit to England	LXII	568	402	392	S
41 Duke of lancaster and the Gascons	LXVI, LXIV	571		3208	S
43 Ambassadors to England for marriage	LXV	582		1922	S
44 Robert the hermit	LXVI	584		4215	Omitted
50 Royal marriage arrangements				1098	S
51 The royal marriage				3489	Omitted
56 Gloucester plots Richard's destruction	LXXXVIII	635	422	3959	S
57 The Duke of Gloucester is captured			428	239	S
61 Death of Gloucester and Arundel.	XCII	655	430	1658	S
63 The Mowbray Henry affair	XCIV	661	432	3075	S
64 They are banished	XCV	666	439	341	S
65 Henry leaves England	XCVI	667		1300	S
66 Henry goes to Paris	XCVII	674		852	S
67 Henry in Paris				1234	S
68 John of Gaunt and Henry	CII, CIII	675		2008	S
69 Henry's marriage plans spoilt	CIV	678		2246	S

Varvaro Chapters / Chapter headings	Johnes Chapters	Page Nos	Penguin Summarised or missing pages	words	Berners Macaulay Summaries
70 Richard prepares to go to Ireland	CV	681	441	2020	S
71 Archbishop Arundel goes to France	CVII	684	442	930	S
72 Henry slips out of Paris for Brittany	CVIII	685		1351	S
73 Henry goes from Brittany to London	CIX	687	447	733	S
74 Richard hears the news				119	S
75 Richard gives himself up to Henry	CXII	690	453	228	S
76 Richard to the tower	CXIII	693	455	369	Yes
77 Richard resigns the crown	CXV	694	460	0	Yes
78 Henry is crowned	CXVI	698	466	582	Yes
79 News gets to France	CXVII	701		2977	Yes
80 Epiphany 'rising'.	CXIX	704	467	1691	Yes
81 King of France raises an army	CXX	707		647	S
82 Death of Richard and truces.	CXXI	708	468-471	930	S

= 43813

Appendix 2

Extract from the 'Philobiblon' (The Love of Books) by Richard de Bury (1281-1345).

https://en.wikisource.org/wiki/The_Love_of_Books:_the_Philobiblon_of_Richard_de_Bury/Chapter_17

You may happen to see some headstrong youth lazily lounging over his studies, and when the winter's frost is sharp, his nose running from the nipping cold drips down, nor does he think of wiping it with his pocket-handkerchief until he has bedewed the book before him with the ugly moisture. Would that he had before him no book, but a cobbler's apron!

His nails are stuffed with fetid filth as black as jet, with which he marks any passage that pleases him. He distributes a multitude of straws, which he inserts to stick out in different places, so that the halm may remind him of what his memory cannot retain. These straws, because the book has no stomach to digest them, and no one takes them out, first distend the book from its wonted closing, and at length, being carelessly abandoned to oblivion, go to decay. He does not fear to eat fruit or cheese over an open book, or carelessly to carry a cup to and from his mouth; and because he has no wallet at hand he drops into books the fragments that are left.

Continually chattering, he is never weary of disputing with his companions, and while he alleges a crowd of senseless arguments, he wets the book lying half open in his lap with sputtering showers. Aye, and then hastily folding his arms he leans forward on the book, and by a brief spell of study invites a prolonged nap; and then, by way of mending the wrinkles, he folds back the margin of the leaves, to the no small injury of the book.

Now the rain is over and gone, and the flowers have appeared in our land. Then the scholar we are speaking of, a neglecter rather than an inspecter of books, will stuff his volume with violets, and primroses, with roses and quatrefoil. Then he will use his wet and perspiring hands to turn over the volumes; then he will thump the white vellum with gloves covered with all kinds of dust, and with his finger clad in long-used leather will hunt line by line through the page; then at the sting of the biting flea the sacred book is flung aside, and is hardly shut for another month, until it is so full of the dust that has found its way within, that it resists the effort to close it.

But the handling of books is specially to be forbidden to those shameless youths, who as soon as they have learned to form the shapes of letters, straightway, if they have the opportunity, become unhappy commentators, and wherever they find an extra margin about the text, furnish it with monstrous alphabets, or if any other frivolity strikes their fancy, at once their pen begins to write it. There the Latinist and sophister and every unlearned writer tries the fitness of his pen, a practice that we have frequently seen injuring the usefulness and value of the most beautiful books.

Again, there is a class of thieves shamefully mutilating books, who cut away the margins from the sides to use as material for letters, leaving only the text, or employ the leaves from the ends, inserted for the protection of the book, for various uses and abuses—a kind of sacrilege which should be prohibited by the threat of anathema.

Again, it is part of the decency of scholars that whenever they return from meals to their study, washing should invariably precede reading, and that no grease-stained finger should unfasten the clasps, or turn the leaves of a book. Nor let a crying child admire the pictures in the capital letters, lest he soil the parchment with wet fingers; for a child instantly touches whatever he sees.

Moreover, the laity, who look at a book turned upside down just as if it were open in the right way, are utterly unworthy of any communion with books. Let the clerk take care also that the smutty scullion reeking from his stewpots does not touch the lily leaves of books, all unwashed, but he who walketh without blemish shall minister to the precious volumes. And, again, the cleanliness of decent hands would be of great benefit to books as well as scholars, if it were not that the itch and pimples are characteristic of the clergy.

Trans Ernest Chester Thomas 1903

References

Chapter 1: Appendix 2 Philobiblon

Chapter 6: Bloch, see bibliography.

Chapter 8: Lance corporal Brown.
http://news.bbc.co.uk/1/hi/england/essex/4182213.stm
https://www.loos1915.fr/en/john-young-brown-uk

Chapter 17: 'Whiskey in the Jar' as performed by Thin Lizzy.
Edward of Norwich, 2nd Duke of York, 'The Master of Game'.
Written 1406-1413.

Chapter 18: Froissart analysis, see Appendix 1

Chapter 19: Usk inscription and bequest – Brass monument Society
June 2014. PDF free download
https://www.mbs-brasses.co.uk/public/files/bullletin-126-
june-2014-1948122618.pdf
Y Cymmrodor the magazine of the Honourable Society of
Cymmrodorion (1900-1951). Free download from The national
Library of Wales

Chapter 20: Origin of kilts, Usk p280. Poisoning and cure by Helias,
Usk p277.

Chapter 22: Josephine Tey, Sir Thomas More 'cancelled, deleted': The
Daughter of Time, Josephine Tey, Arrow Books, p85.

Chapter 24: Henry says war on Scotland is his idea. British History
Online, Parliamentary Roll mention, Oct 1399, pt 1, 80.

Chapter 26: Adam of Usk: 'That same anointing did at his coronation
portend; for there ensued such a growth of lice, especially on his
head....', P298, Usk, Thompson 1904.
Monks from India, Usk, p267.

Holy oil
https://www.canterbury-cathedral.org/heritage/archives/

picture-this/ideological-associations-and-henry-ivs-tomb-the-
first-lancastrian-kings-connection-to-thomas-becket/. Mentioned
Chronica Maiora Walsingham p312

'Chronicles are often unreliable…' p8 Lavan Kirby. 'Historians have
increasingly turned to records.' P8 Lavan Kirby

Chapter 27: 'Also the same king was accustomed almost continually….'
British History Online. Parliamentary Roll, Oct 1399, pt 1, 42.

Chapter 28: 'Remittuntur….etc'

Decretum Gratiani – C. XLIX. Aliquando puniuntur peccata per
populos diuino iussu excitatos. (digitale-sammlungen.de).https://
geschichte.digitale-sammlungen.de/decretum-gratiani/kapitel/
dc_chapter_2_2817

Sympathy for Hotspur: Chronica Maiora, p326, 'And at the same
time Henry percy, the younger, to whom fortune up to that point
had always been kind, and in whom were placed the hopes of the
whole people…' Interesting: p327 'And indeed many felt affection
for King Richard.'

Chapter 30: Creton turns to prose, Creton, p151.

Chapter 32: L'Orloge Amoureus – see bibliography.

Chapter 33: Walsinghams – Chronica Maiora: Richard 'tyrannical'
p305. 'Traitors whisperers', p261. Burley oppressor of the poor, p262.
Gloucester looks for truce, p279. Richard deposed 1388, p260.

Chapter 34: Duke of Gloucester's lunchtime rudeness, Johnes p577,
Varvaro p375. Robert the Hermit, Varvaro chapter 44, see also
appendix 1, Johnes chapter LXVI. White-dressed foreigners, British
History Online, Parliamentary Roll, Oct 1399 pt 1, 82.

'Laquinghay' identified as Lackenheath: Armorial Urféhttp://www.
armorial.dk

'A preliminary edition of the English segment from Paris, BnF,
ms.fr.32753 by Steen Clemmensen Farum, Denmark, October
2007. Section 380 380 messire jehan laquingay, d argent a chievron
de sable,'

Chapter 35: Gloucester and Arundel missing from Jan 1397 parliament; British History Online, Parliamentary rolls, introduction to Jan 1397 parliament. https://www.british-history.ac.uk/no-series/parliament-rolls-medieval/january-1397

Gloucester stirs up trouble in parliament; Varvaro p501, 'Faites une requeste au roy....' Johnes LXXXVIII p638: *'the Duke of Gloucester whispered the citizens to petition the king to abolish all taxes and subsidies which had been imposed for the last twenty years as it was reasonable they should now cease, since a truce had been signed for so long a term, and they had been levied solely as a war tax, to pay men-at-arms and archers in support of the war.'*

Absent lords; British History Online, Jan 1397 parliament, 8.

Haxey and plots; Butt p427.

Haxey associated with Merciless Parliament appellants. 'Was Thomas Favent a Political Pamphleteer? Faction and Politics', Gwilym Dodd

https://nottingham-repository.worktribe.com/preview/2547333/Dodd%20-%20Thomas%20Favent.pdf

'Many of the clerks who helped the Appellants, like Scarle and Martin, had personal connections to the Lords Appellant or their supporters and were handsomely rewarded for their loyalty. Scarle counted amongst his many patrons the chancellor, Thomas Arundel and Henry Bolingbroke, Earl of Derby. John Burton, **Thomas Haxey**, *John Stacy, Edmund Stafford and Richard Ronhale also all had connections to Arundel.'*

Haxey pardoned 1399, Parliamentary Roll Sept 1399, pt 2, 90.

Duke of Gloucester seeks Richard's destruction, Earl of March plot, 4 duke's plot: Varvaro chapter 56, Johnes LXXXVIII, Penguin 421-422, – appendix 1, 4000 words of Varvaro are either missing or summarised in Penguin in this section alone.

Arundel Castle plot: Traison et Mort, p122, p124-5. Interesting aside: Usk states that Earl of Warwick implicated St Albans abbey at his trial either in reference to 1388, or 1397. Either way there is a connection. Usk p161.

Richard II's proclamation re: plot – Chronica Maiora, Walsingham p 299. Richard II, Saul. p375.

Chapter 36: Henry: 'I will help you govern better.' p168, Creton. Arundel's letters from Pope and 'crusade', p47, Creton. Henry's letters, Traison et Mort, p180.

Henry IV's claim to throne based on descent from Henry III. British History Online Parliamentary Roll, Oct 1399, pt 1, 53. Chronica Maiora, Walsingams p311. Annales Ricardi Secundi, quoted Given-Wilson chronicles p124. Hardyng p195.

Adam of Usk investigates the claim, Usk p182.

Henry's followers tell him he is descended directly from King Edward the Confessor. Johnes CVII, p685. Varvaro p604.

Hardyng on Henry's claim to royal descent and John of Gaunt's dispersal of fake proofs in abbeys, p353. Lancastrian descent from Edmund Crouchback and Richard of York; 'Henry VI', Bertram Wolfe, YUP, 1981, p324.

Chapter 37: Aye! Aye! – Traison et Mort p220: Yes Yes, Ouy Ouy. Creton: 'Yea!' p200, p201. Varvaro: 'Oil!', p633. Johnes: 'Ay!', CXVI, p700. Penguin: 'Yes!', p465 Berners: 'Yea!', p470.

Chapter 45: Muster, Saul, p375 – Richard II sends to sherrif of Chester for 2000 archers 0n 13th July 1397, general muster on 20th August. Money for Henry, The Kings Affinity Given Wilson p224. Number of loyal earls The King's Affinity, Given Wilson p224. Henry's response to Dymock's challenge, Usk, p188. Dangerous bed, Chronica Maiora p320 (1401). Dangerous tent, Chronica Maiora, p322. (1402 august 15th) and floods p339 (1405).

John of Gaunt and Earl of Arundel fall out in parliament. British History Online, January 1394. Butt, p419.

Chapter 46: Great and solemn council. August 1401. Henry IV declares to 'the peers from all parts of the realm that had been summoned there of his intention that his adversaries of France and Scotland should be assailed in war'. Usk, p237.

Epilogue quotation: Ausonius. Peiper 1924. Teubner p412

Clio gesta canens transactis tempora reddit. Melpomene tragico proclamat moesta boatu. Comica lascivo gaudet sermone Thalia. Dulciloquos calamos Euterpe flatibus urget. Terpsichore affectus citharis movet, imperat, auget. Plectra gerens Erato saltat pede, carmine, vultu. Carmina Calliope libris heroica mandat. Uraniae caeli motus scrutatur, & astra, Signat cuncta manu, loquitur Polyhimnia gestu.

* * *

Cover art

* * *

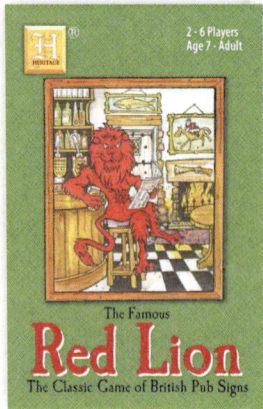

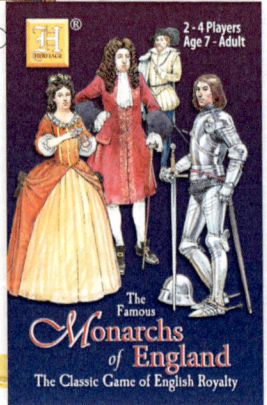

Bringing history to life!

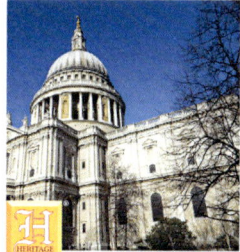